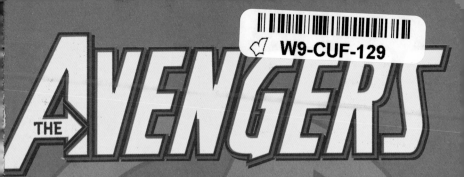

THE AVENGERS

THE NEW RECRUITS

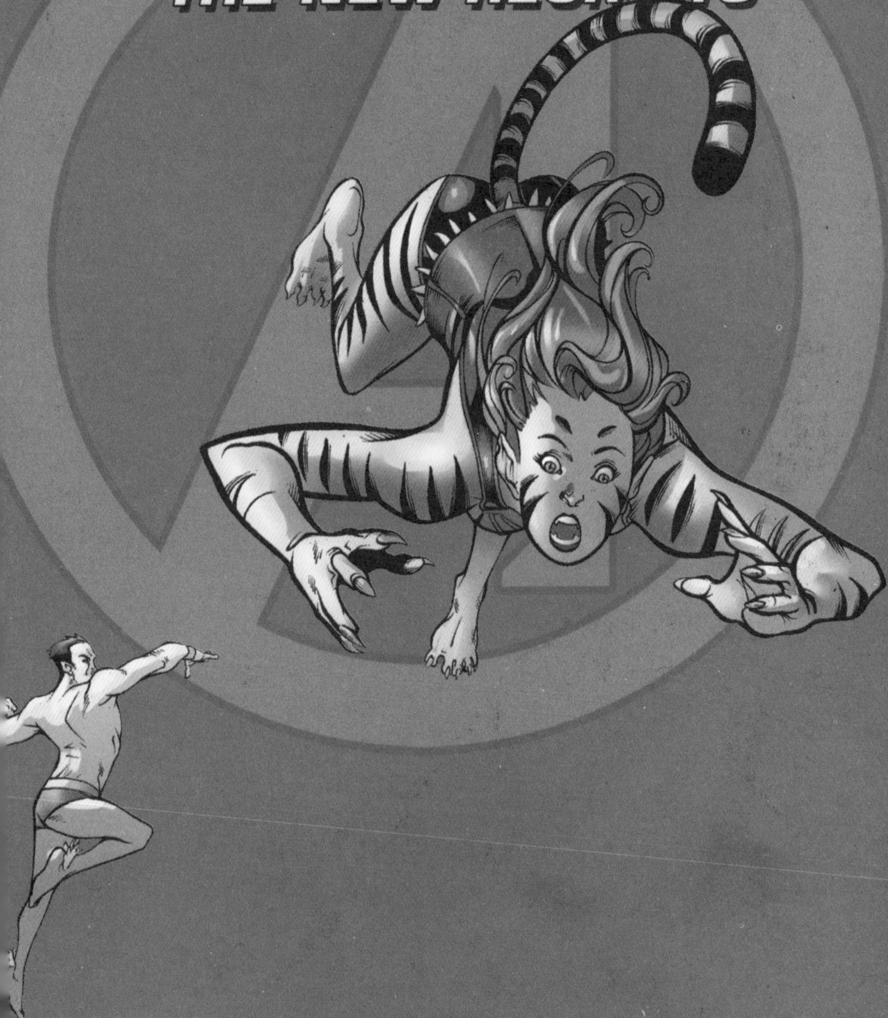

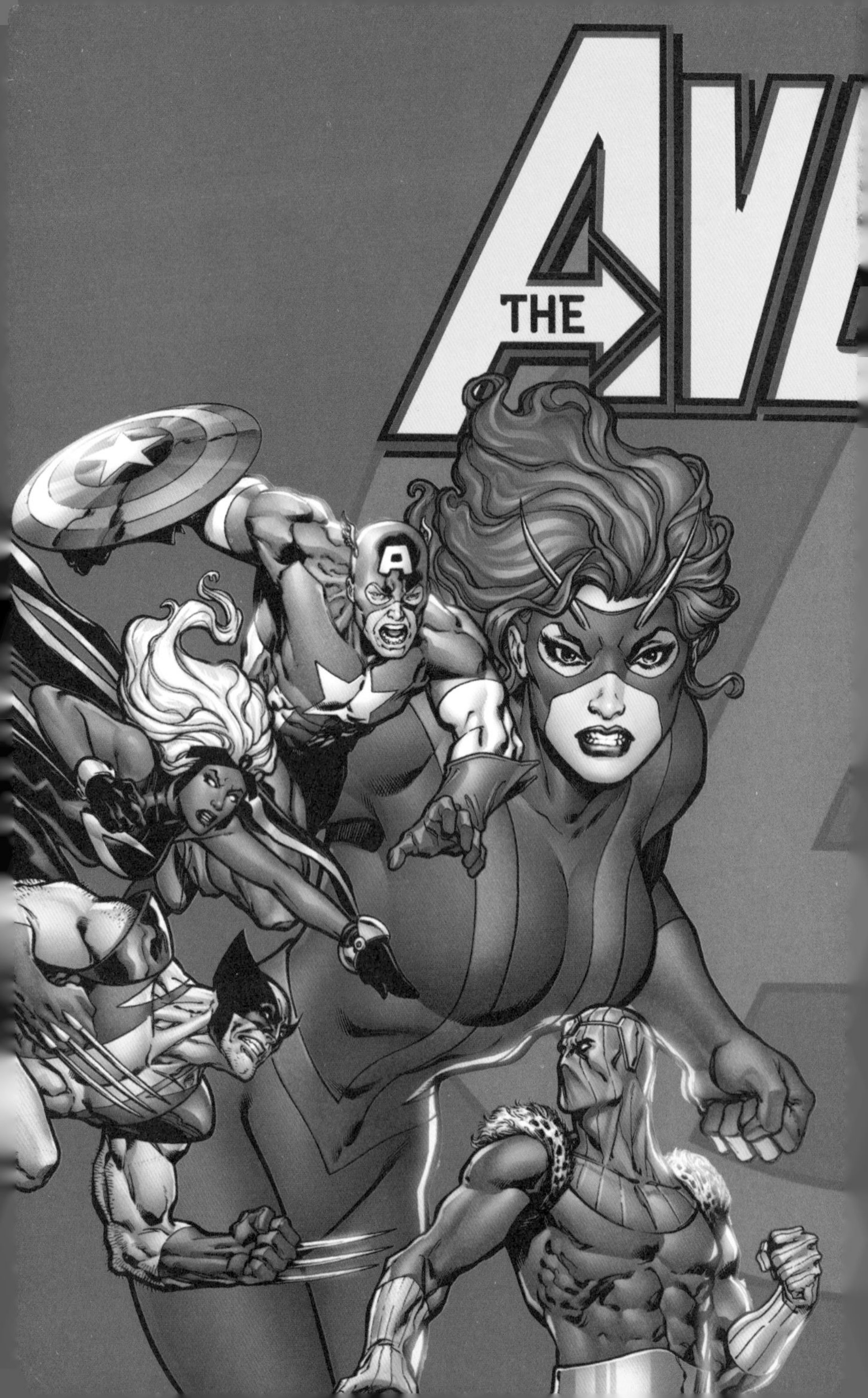
THE

NGERS

THE NEW RECRUITS

Writers: **Jeff Parker & Paul Tobin**
Pencils: **Rodney Buchemi, Ig Guara
& Matteo Lolli**
Inks: **Rodney Buchemi, Sandro Ribeiro
& Christian Dalla Vecchia**

Colors: **Ulises Arreola & Chris Sotomayor**
Letters: **Dave Sharpe**
Cover Art: **Leonard Kirk, Terry Pallot, Sean Murphy,
Graham Nolan, Salva Espin, Guru eFX, Ulises Arreola
& Wil Quintana**
Consulting Editors: **Mark Paniccia & Ralph Macchio**
Editor: **Nathan Cosby**

Captain America created by Joe Simon & Jack Kirby

Collection Editor: **Jennifer Grünwald**
Editorial Assistant: **Alex Starbuck**
Assistant Editors: **Cory Levine & John Denning**
Editor, Special Projects: **Mark D. Beazley**
Senior Editor, Special Projects: **Jeff Youngquist**
Senior Vice President of Sales: **David Gabriel**
Vice President of Creative: **Tom Marvelli**

Editor in Chief: **Joe Quesada**
Publisher: **Dan Buckley**

#28

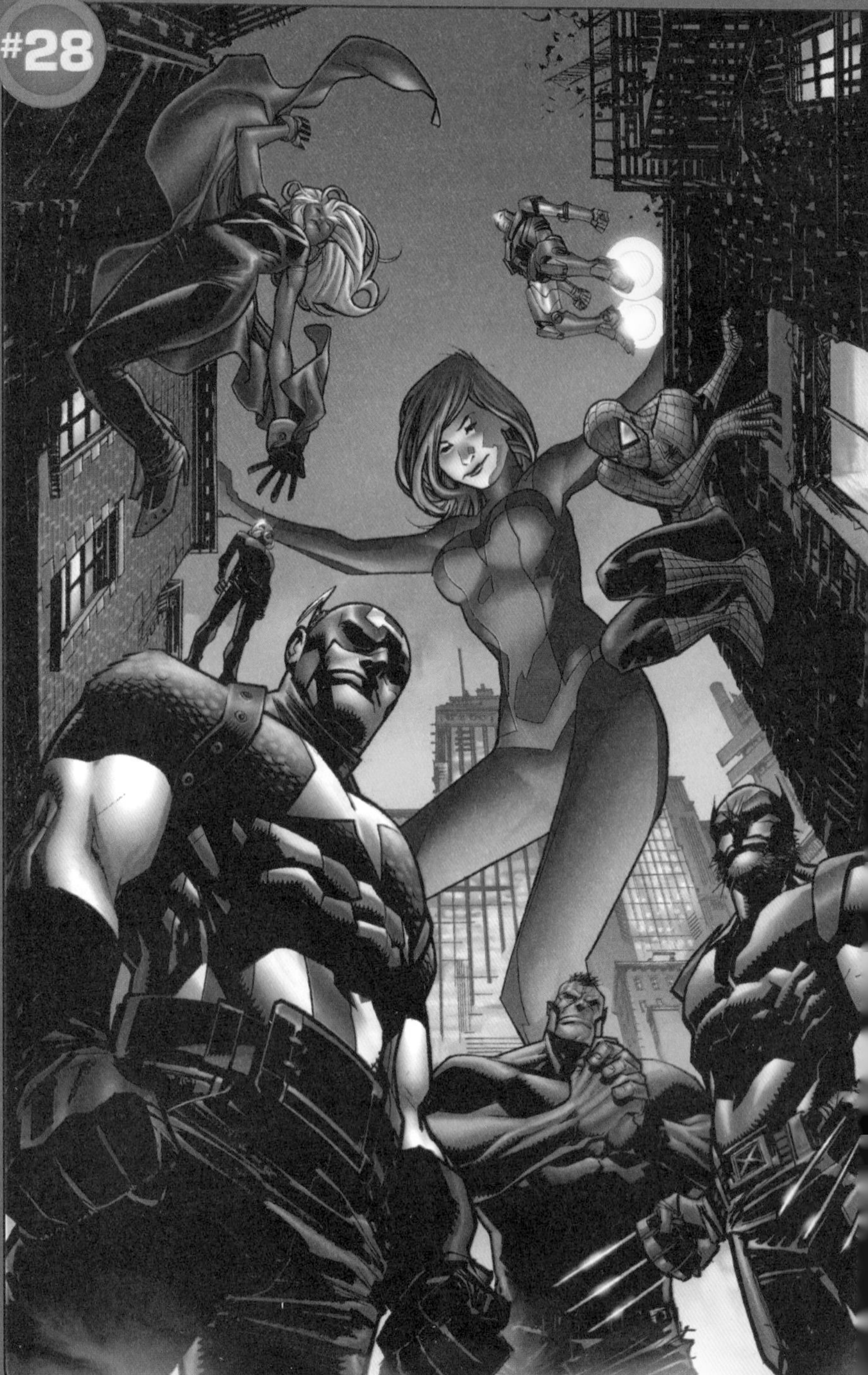

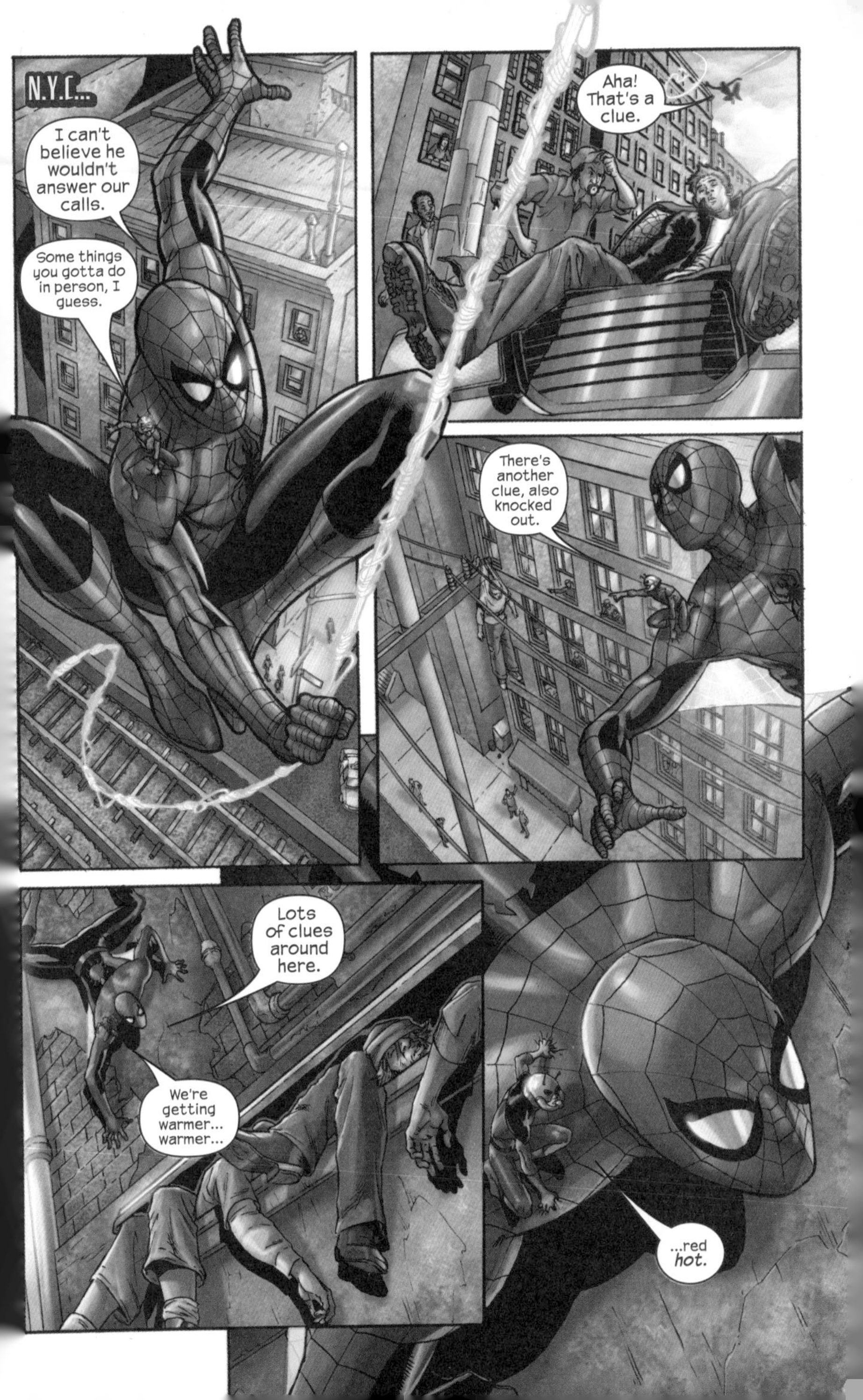
N.Y.C...
I can't believe he wouldn't answer our calls.
Some things you gotta do in person, I guess.
Aha! That's a clue.
There's another clue, also knocked out.
Lots of clues around here.
We're getting warmer... warmer...
...red hot.

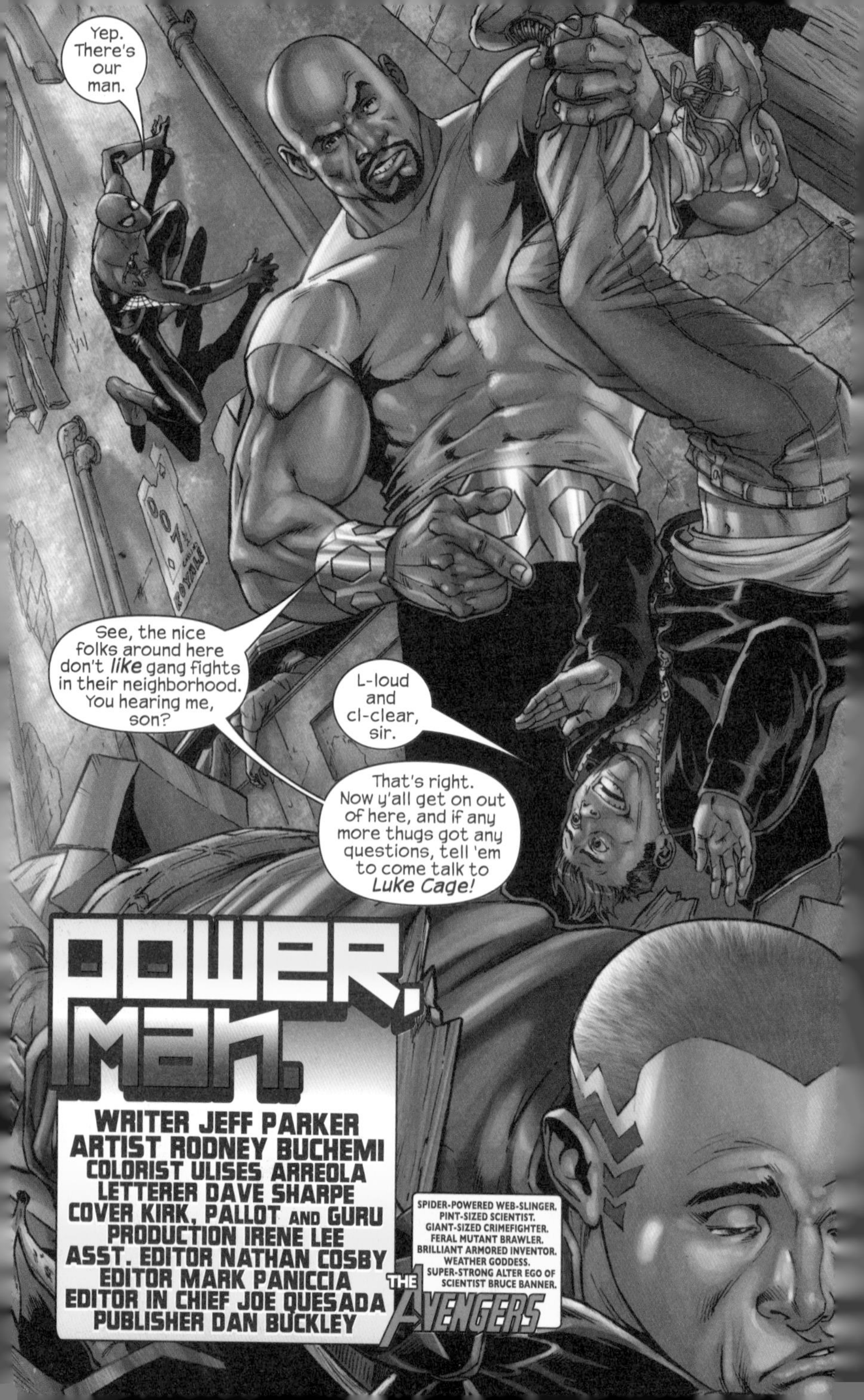

Yep. There's our man.
See, the nice folks around here don't *like* gang fights in their neighborhood. You hearing me, son?
L-loud and cl-clear, sir.
That's right. Now y'all get on out of here, and if any more thugs got any questions, tell 'em to come talk to *Luke Cage!*
POWER, MAN.
WRITER JEFF PARKER
ARTIST RODNEY BUCHEMI
COLORIST ULISES ARREOLA
LETTERER DAVE SHARPE
COVER KIRK, PALLOT AND GURU
PRODUCTION IRENE LEE
ASST. EDITOR NATHAN COSBY
EDITOR MARK PANICCIA
EDITOR IN CHIEF JOE QUESADA
PUBLISHER DAN BUCKLEY
SPIDER-POWERED WEB-SLINGER. PINT-SIZED SCIENTIST. GIANT-SIZED CRIMEFIGHTER. FERAL MUTANT BRAWLER. BRILLIANT ARMORED INVENTOR. WEATHER GODDESS. SUPER-STRONG ALTER EGO OF SCIENTIST BRUCE BANNER.
THE AVENGERS

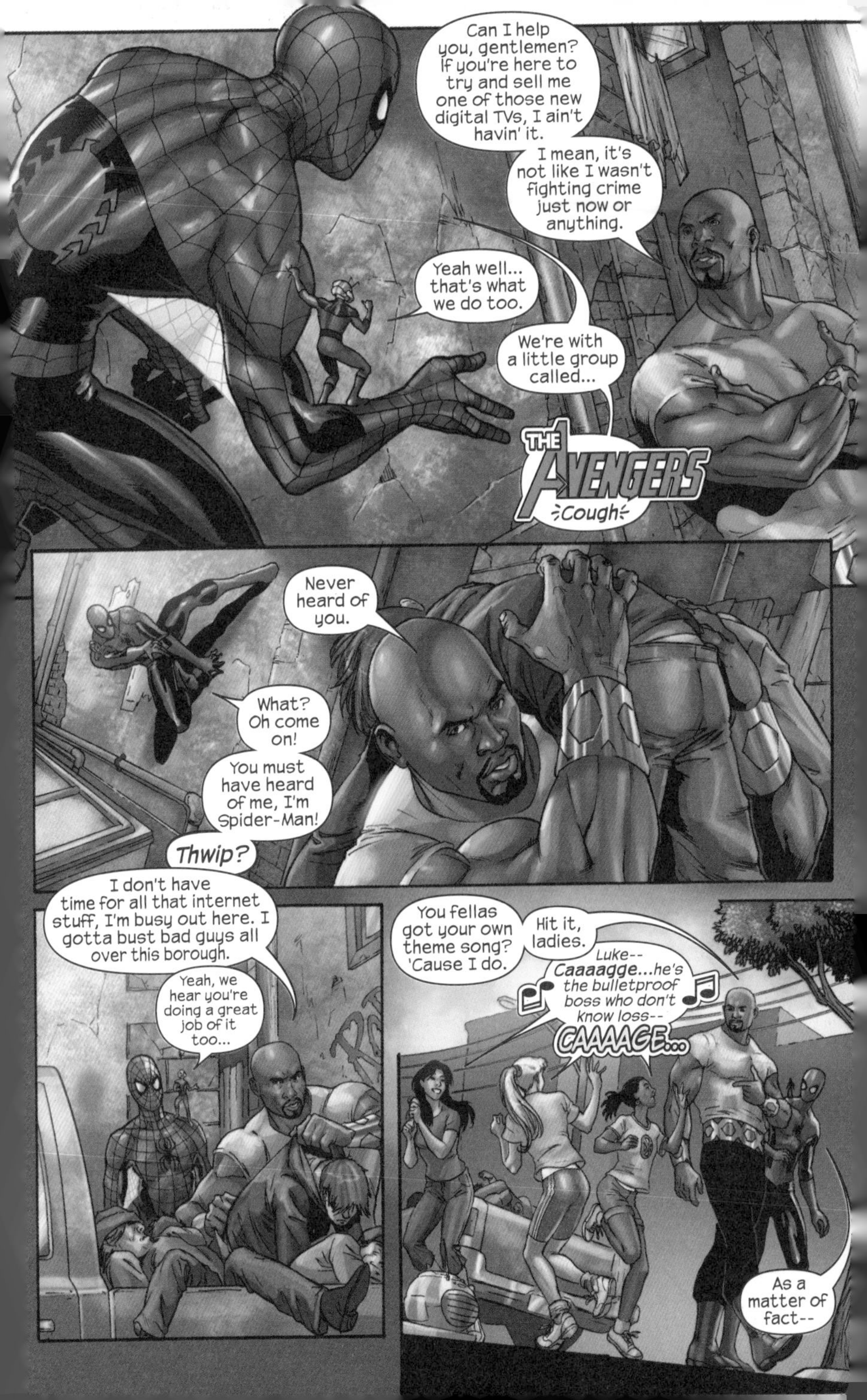
Can I help you, gentlemen? If you're here to try and sell me one of those new digital TVs, I ain't havin' it.
I mean, it's not like I wasn't fighting crime just now or anything.
Yeah well... that's what we do too.
We're with a little group called...
THE AVENGERS
Cough
Never heard of you.
What? Oh come on!
You must have heard of me, I'm Spider-Man!
Thwip?
I don't have time for all that internet stuff, I'm busy out here. I gotta bust bad guys all over this borough.
Yeah, we hear you're doing a great job of it too...
You fellas got your own theme song? 'Cause I do.
Hit it, ladies.
Luke--
Caaaagge...he's the bulletproof boss who don't know loss--
CAAAAGE...
As a matter of fact--

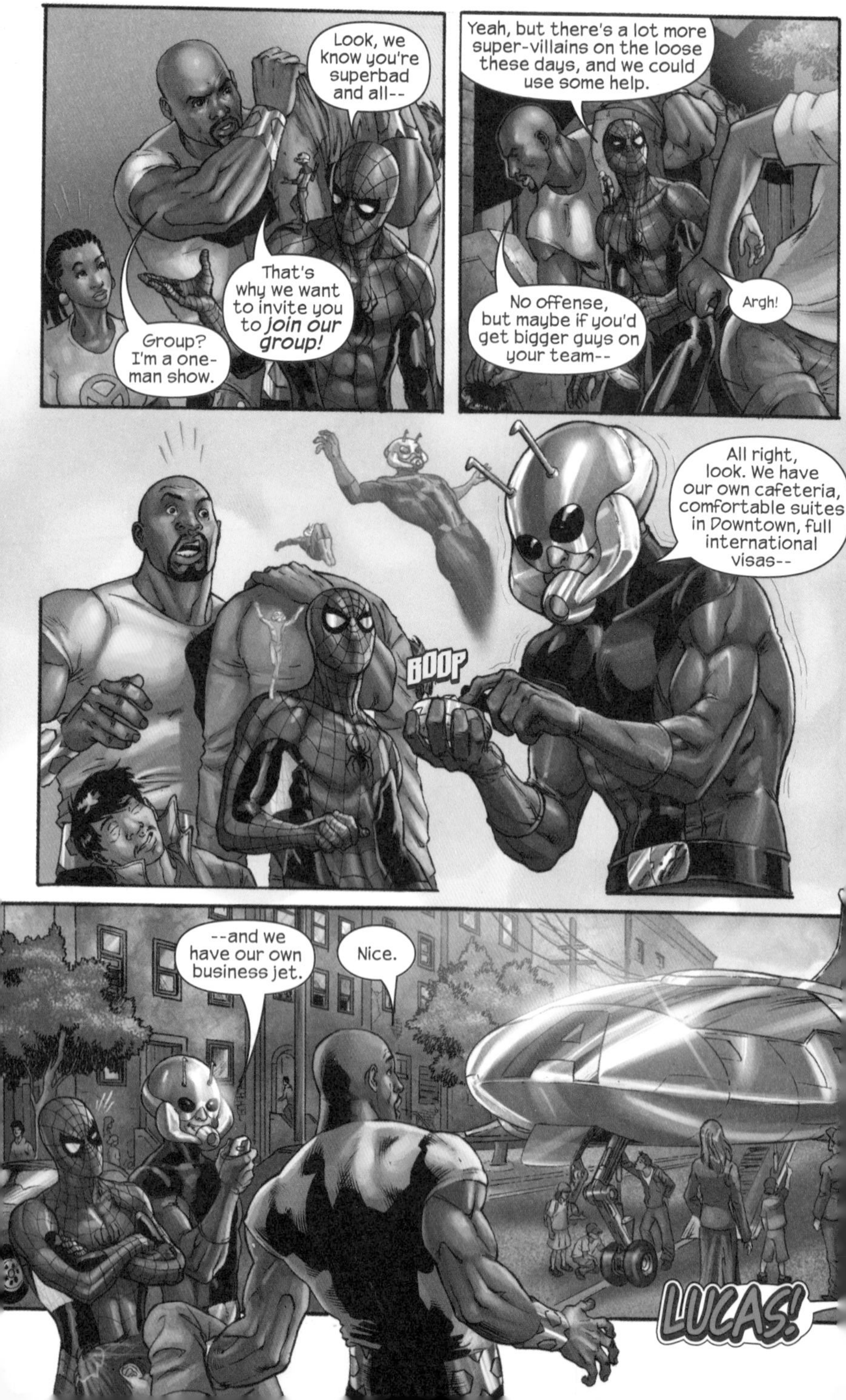
Look, we know you're superbad and all--
That's why we want to invite you to *join our group!*
Group? I'm a one-man show.
Yeah, but there's a lot more super-villains on the loose these days, and we could use some help.
No offense, but maybe if you'd get bigger guys on your team--
Argh!
All right, look. We have our own cafeteria, comfortable suites in Downtown, full international visas--
BOOP
--and we have our own business jet.
Nice.
LUCAS!

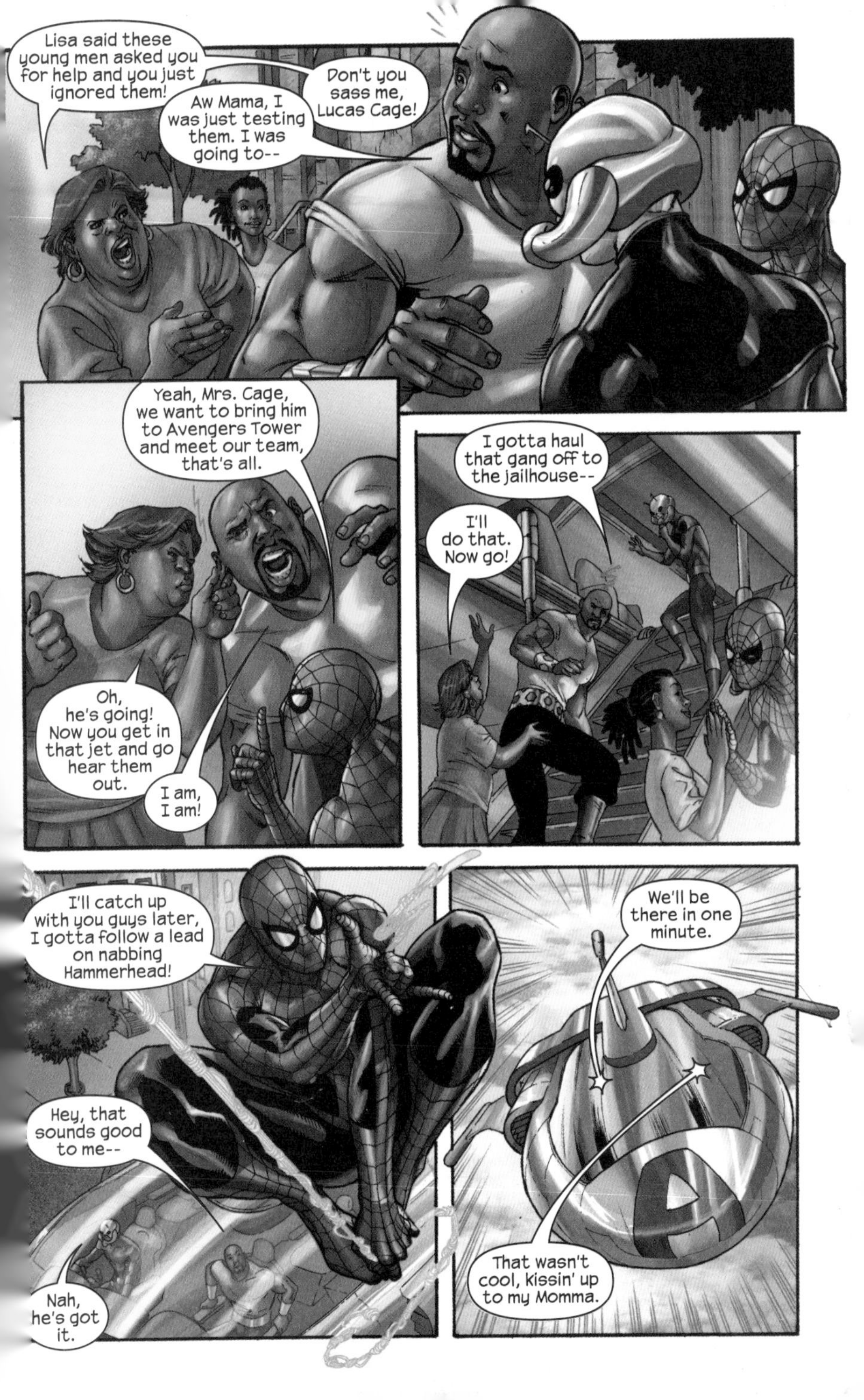
Lisa said these young men asked you for help and you just ignored them!
Aw Mama, I was just testing them. I was going to--
Don't you sass me, Lucas Cage!
Yeah, Mrs. Cage, we want to bring him to Avengers Tower and meet our team, that's all.
Oh, he's going! Now you get in that jet and go hear them out.
I am, I am!
I gotta haul that gang off to the jailhouse--
I'll do that. Now go!
I'll catch up with you guys later, I gotta follow a lead on nabbing Hammerhead!
Hey, that sounds good to me--
Nah, he's got it.
We'll be there in one minute.
That wasn't cool, kissin' up to my Momma.

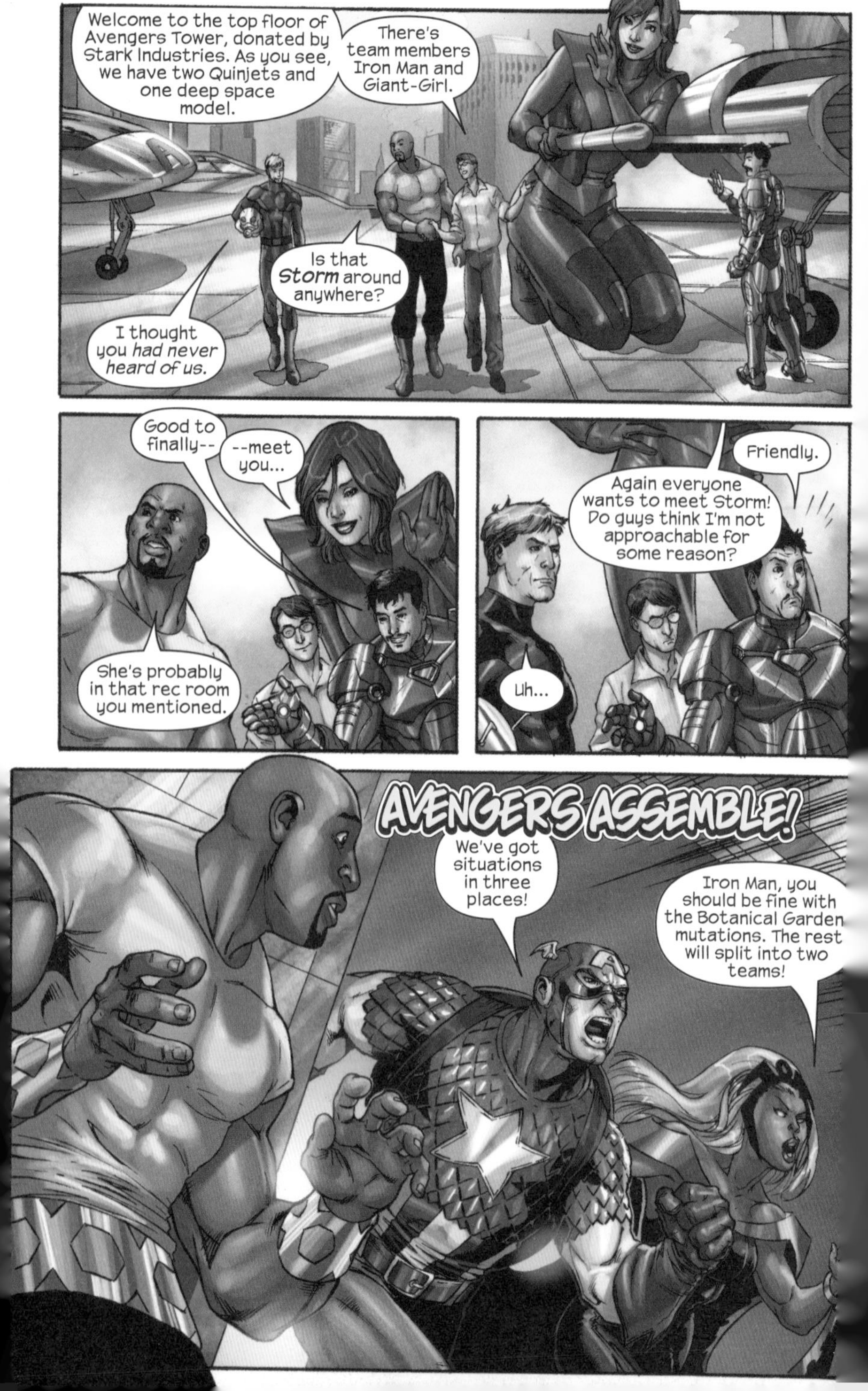
Welcome to the top floor of Avengers Tower, donated by Stark Industries. As you see, we have two Quinjets and one deep space model.
There's team members Iron Man and Giant-Girl.
Is that *Storm* around anywhere?
I thought you *had never* heard of us.
Good to finally--
--meet you...
She's probably in that rec room you mentioned.
Friendly.
Again everyone wants to meet Storm! Do guys think I'm not approachable for some reason?
Uh...
AVENGERS ASSEMBLE!
We've got situations in three places!
Iron Man, you should be fine with the Botanical Garden mutations. The rest will split into two teams!

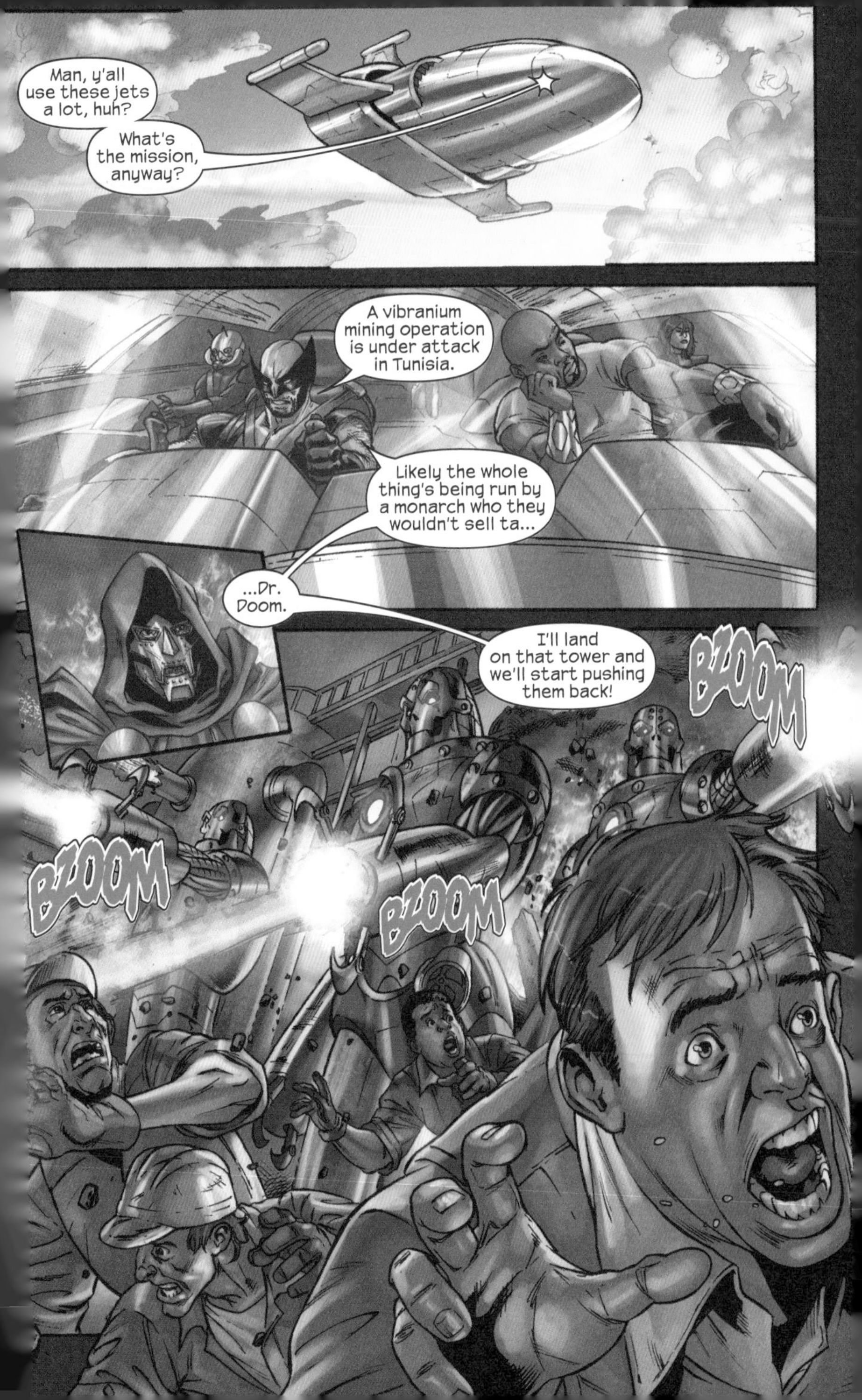

Man, y'all use these jets a lot, huh?
What's the mission, anyway?
A vibranium mining operation is under attack in Tunisia.
Likely the whole thing's being run by a monarch who they wouldn't sell ta...
...Dr. Doom.
I'll land on that tower and we'll start pushing them back!
BZOOM
BZOOM
BZOOM

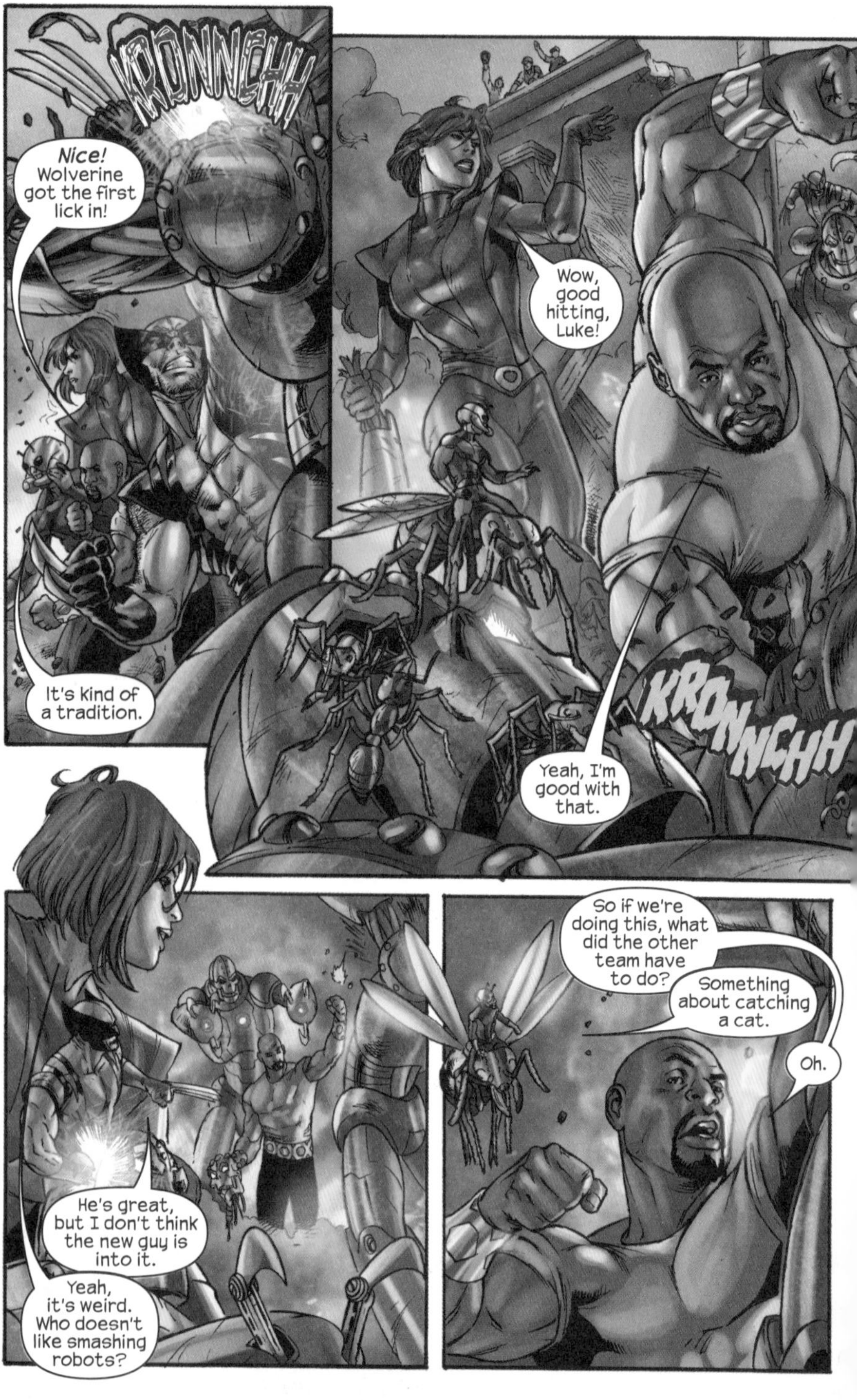
KRONNCHH
Nice! Wolverine got the first lick in!
It's kind of a tradition.
Wow, good hitting, Luke!
KRONNCHH
Yeah, I'm good with that.
He's great, but I don't think the new guy is into it.
Yeah, it's weird. Who doesn't like smashing robots?
So if we're doing this, what did the other team have to do?
Something about catching a cat.
Oh.

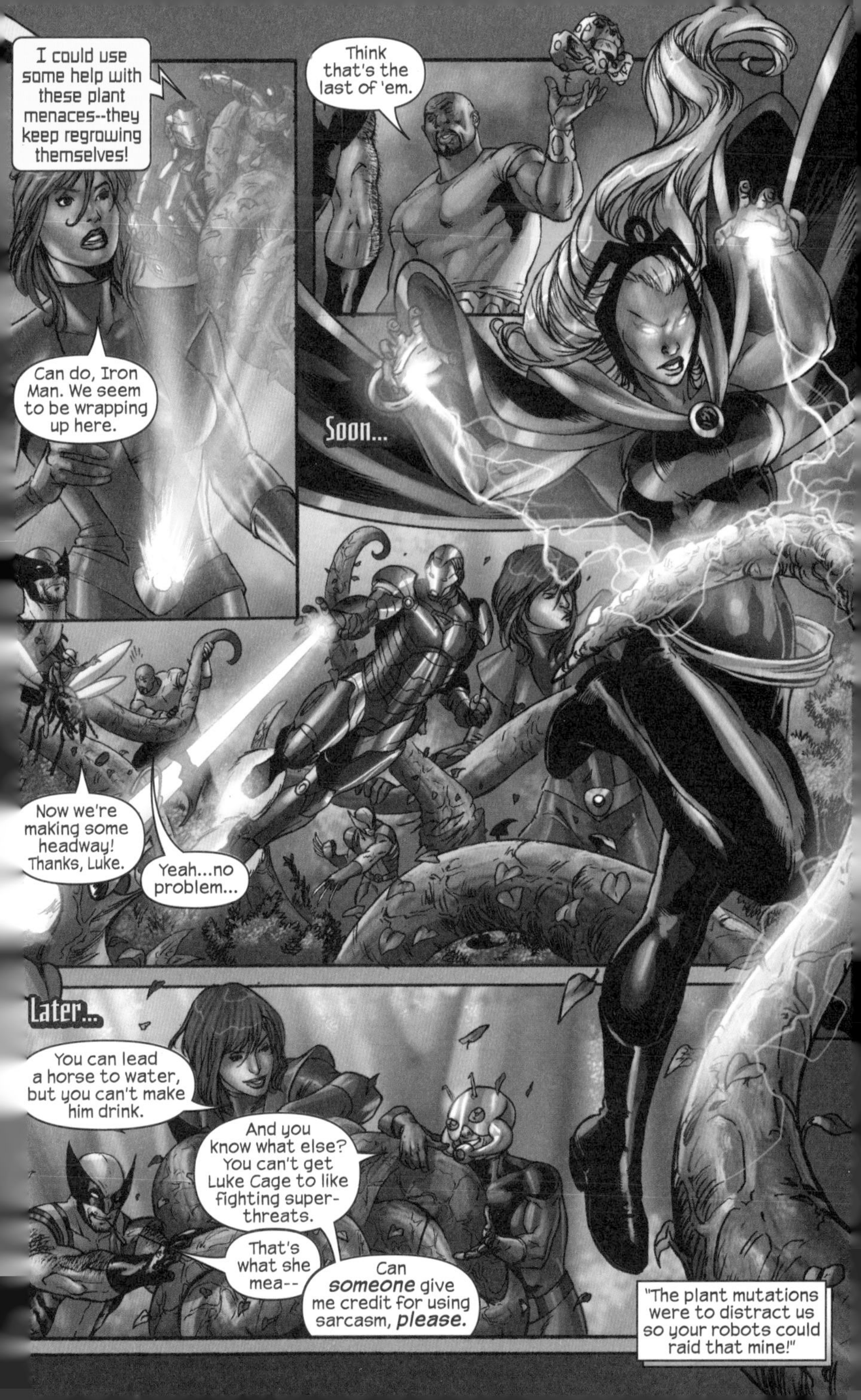
I could use some help with these plant menaces--they keep regrowing themselves!
Can do, Iron Man. We seem to be wrapping up here.
Think that's the last of 'em.
Soon...
Now we're making some headway! Thanks, Luke.
Yeah...no problem...
Later...
You can lead a horse to water, but you can't make him drink.
And you know what else? You can't get Luke Cage to like fighting super-threats.
That's what she mea--
Can *someone* give me credit for using sarcasm, *please.*
"The plant mutations were to distract us so your robots could raid that mine!"

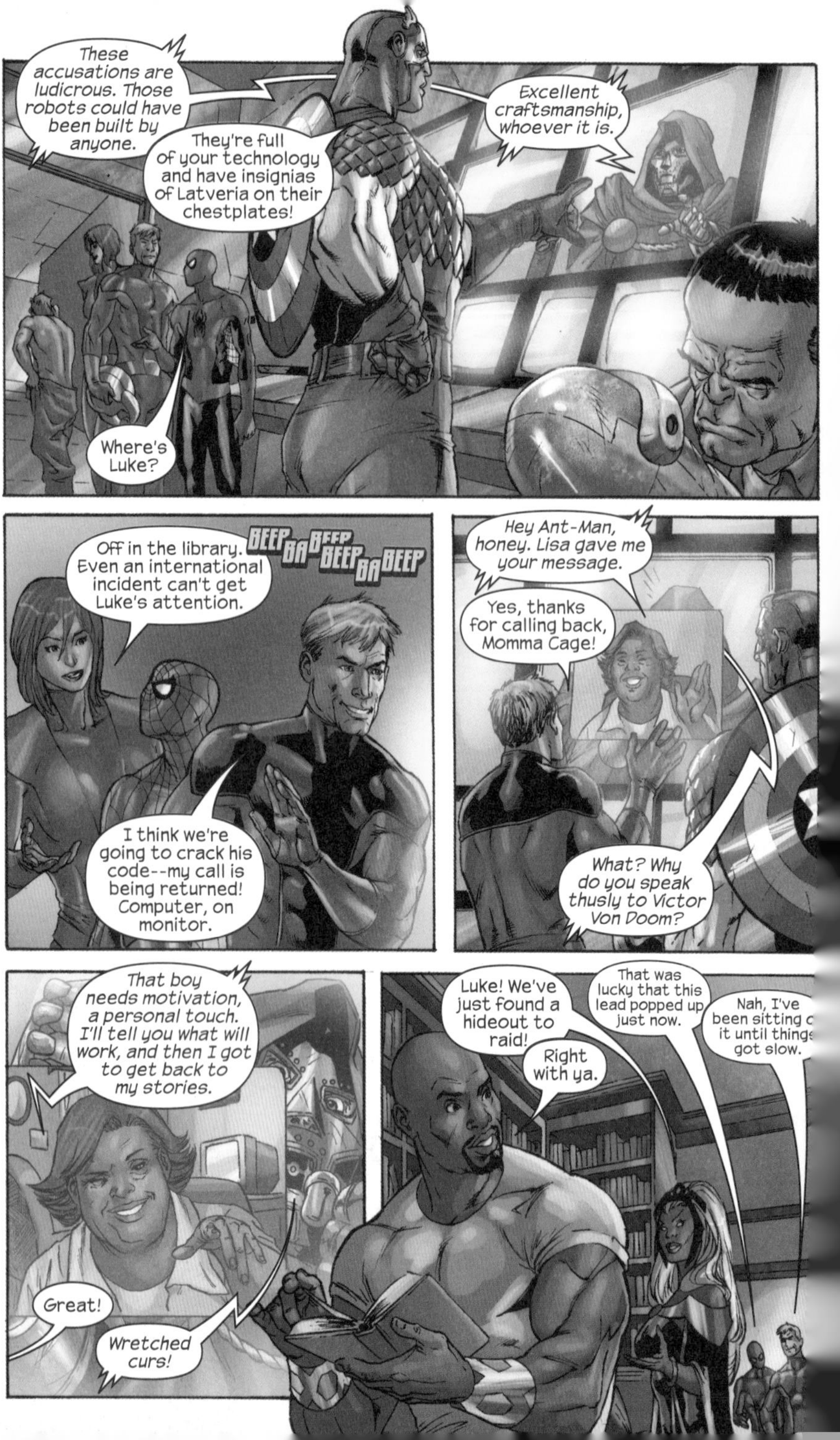
These accusations are ludicrous. Those robots could have been built by anyone.
They're full of your technology and have insignias of Latveria on their chestplates!
Excellent craftsmanship, whoever it is.
Where's Luke?
Off in the library. Even an international incident can't get Luke's attention.
BEEP BA BEEP BEEP BA BEEP
I think we're going to crack his code--my call is being returned! Computer, on monitor.
Hey Ant-Man, honey. Lisa gave me your message.
Yes, thanks for calling back, Momma Cage!
What? Why do you speak thusly to Victor Von Doom?
That boy needs motivation, a personal touch. I'll tell you what will work, and then I got to get back to my stories.
Great!
Wretched curs!
Luke! We've just found a hideout to raid!
Right with ya.
That was lucky that this lead popped up just now.

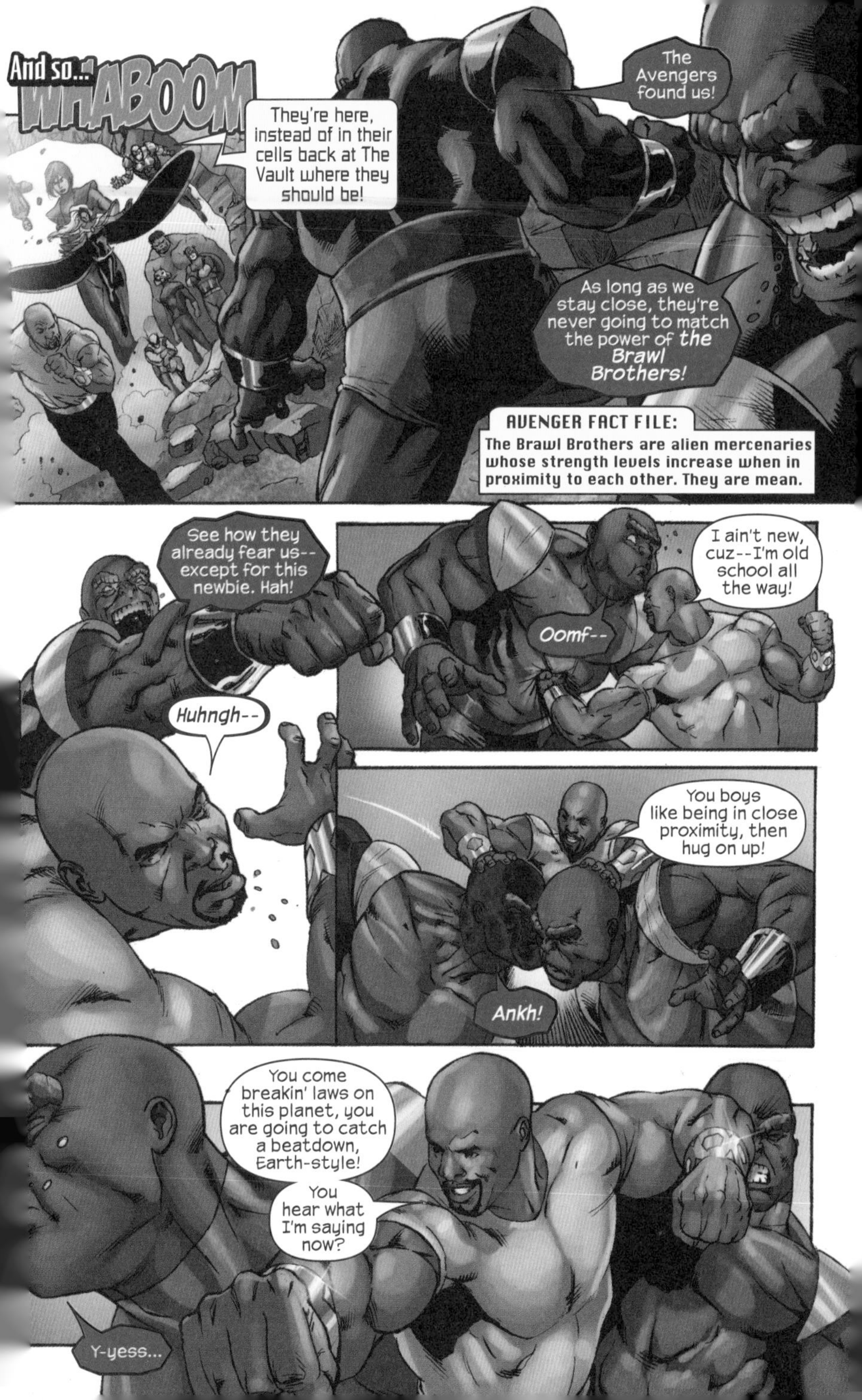
And so...!
WHABOOM
They're here, instead of in their cells back at The Vault where they should be!
The Avengers found us!
As long as we stay close, they're never going to match the power of the Brawl Brothers!
AVENGER FACT FILE:
The Brawl Brothers are alien mercenaries whose strength levels increase when in proximity to each other. They are mean.
See how they already fear us--except for this newbie. Hah!
I ain't new, cuz--I'm old school all the way!
Oomf--
Huhngh--
You boys like being in close proximity, then hug on up!
Ankh!
You come breakin' laws on this planet, you are going to catch a beatdown, Earth-style!
You hear what I'm saying now?
Y-yess...

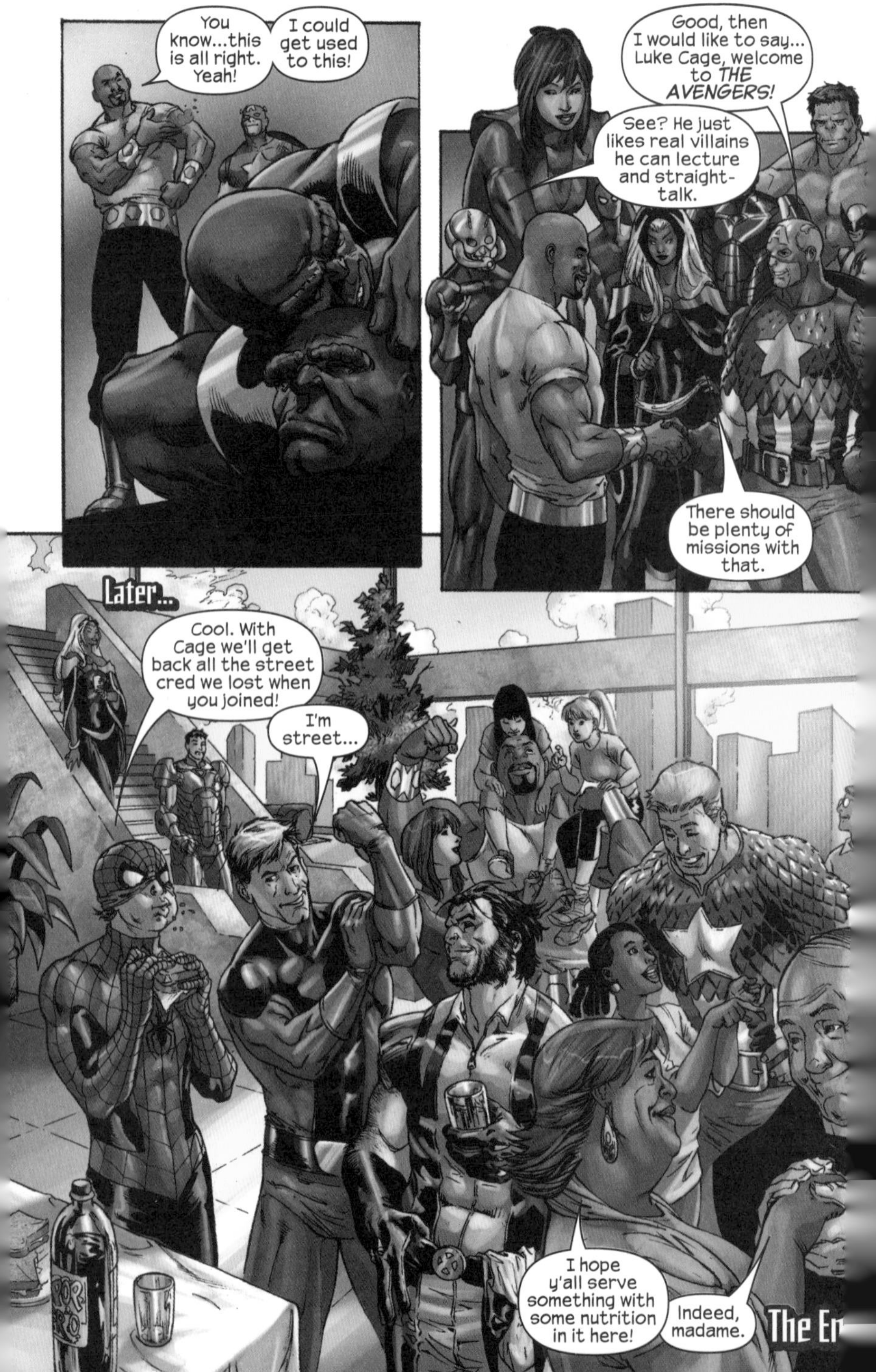

You know...this is all right. Yeah!
I could get used to this!
Good, then I would like to say... Luke Cage, welcome to THE AVENGERS!
See? He just likes real villains he can lecture and straight-talk.
There should be plenty of missions with that.
Later...
Cool. With Cage we'll get back all the street cred we lost when you joined!
I'm street...
I hope y'all serve something with some nutrition in it here!
Indeed, madame.
The En

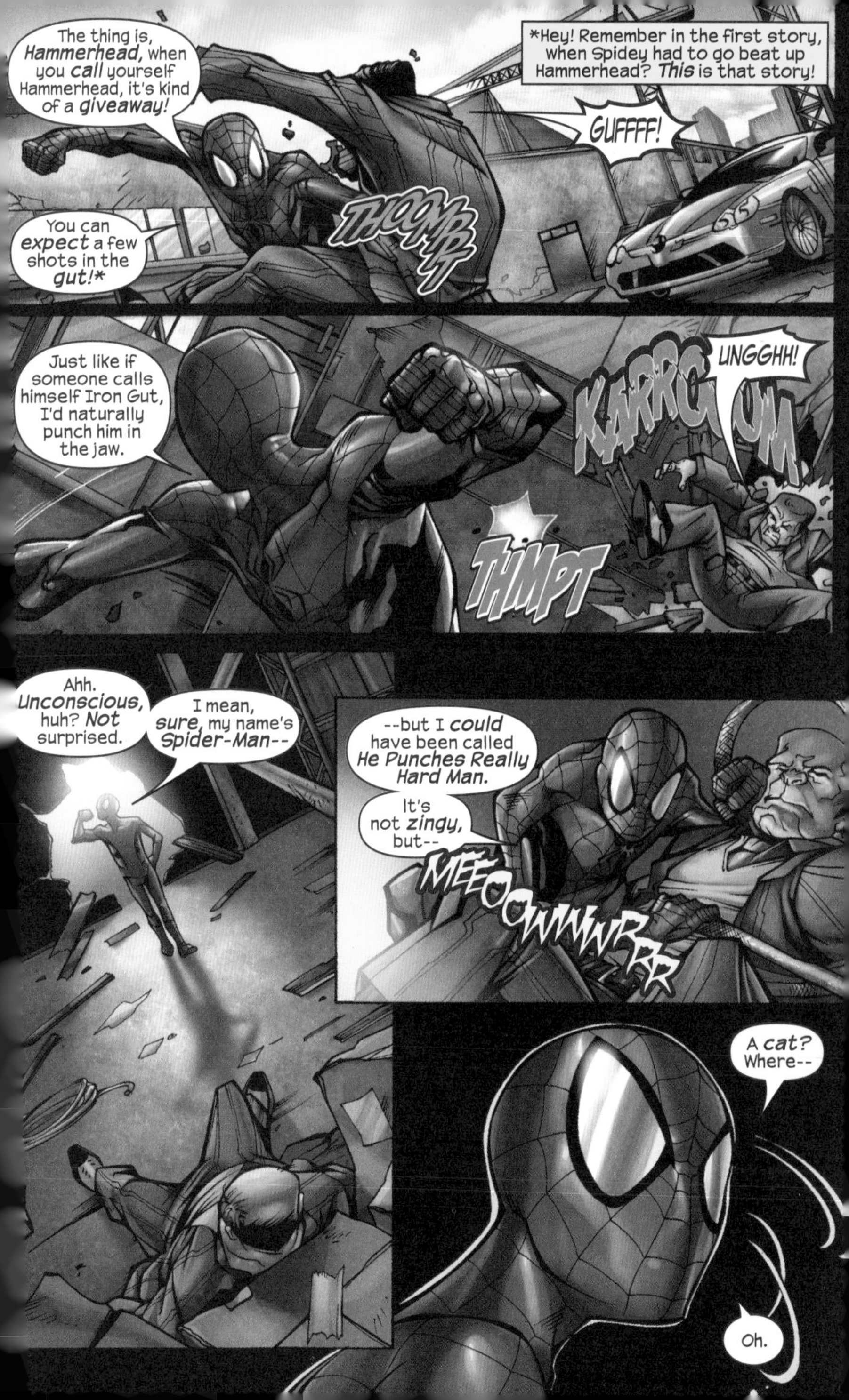
The thing is, Hammerhead, when you call yourself Hammerhead, it's kind of a giveaway!
*Hey! Remember in the first story, when Spidey had to go beat up Hammerhead? This is that story!
GUFFFF!
THOOMRR
You can expect a few shots in the gut!*
Just like if someone calls himself Iron Gut, I'd naturally punch him in the jaw.
KARRGOOM
UNGGHH!
THMPT
Ahh. Unconscious, huh? Not surprised.
I mean, sure, my name's Spider-Man--
--but I could have been called He Punches Really Hard Man.
It's not zingy, but--
MEEOOWWWRRR
A cat? Where--
Oh.

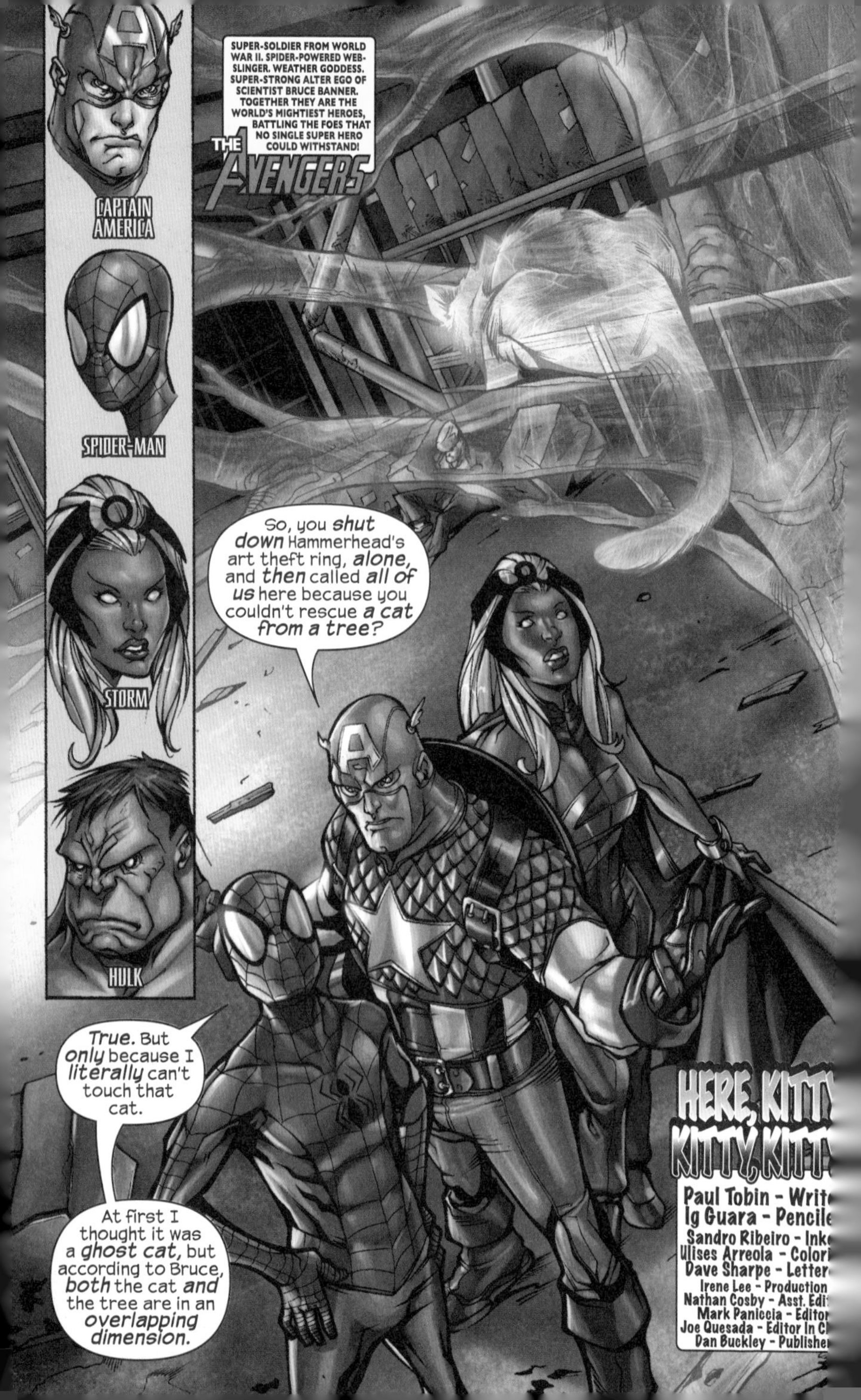

SUPER-SOLDIER FROM WORLD WAR II. SPIDER-POWERED WEB-SLINGER. WEATHER GODDESS. SUPER-STRONG ALTER EGO OF SCIENTIST BRUCE BANNER. TOGETHER THEY ARE THE WORLD'S MIGHTIEST HEROES, BATTLING THE FOES THAT NO SINGLE SUPER HERO COULD WITHSTAND!
THE AVENGERS
CAPTAIN AMERICA
SPIDER-MAN
STORM
HULK
So, you shut down Hammerhead's art theft ring, alone, and then called all of us here because you couldn't rescue a cat from a tree?
True. But only because I literally can't touch that cat.
At first I thought it was a ghost cat, but according to Bruce, both the cat and the tree are in an overlapping dimension.
HERE, KITT
KITTY, KITT
Paul Tobin - Writ
Ig Guara - Pencile
Sandro Ribeiro - Ink
Ulises Arreola - Color
Dave Sharpe - Letter
Irene Lee - Production
Nathan Cosby - Asst. Edit
Mark Paniccia - Editor
Joe Quesada - Editor In C
Dan Buckley - Publishe

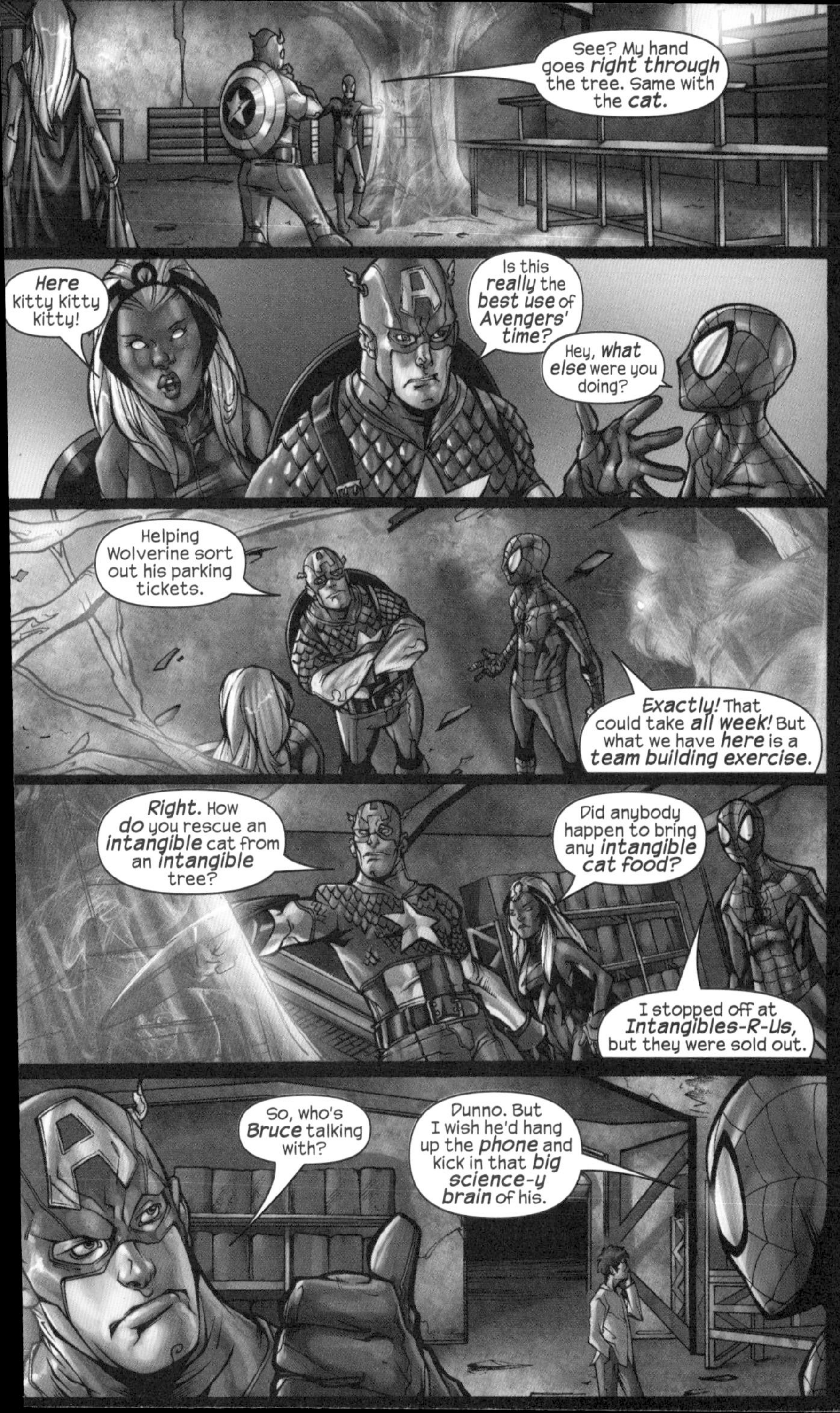
See? My hand goes right through the tree. Same with the cat.
Here kitty kitty kitty!
Is this really the best use of Avengers' time?
Hey, what else were you doing?
Helping Wolverine sort out his parking tickets.
Exactly! That could take all week! But what we have here is a team building exercise.
Right. How do you rescue an intangible cat from an intangible tree?
Did anybody happen to bring any intangible cat food?
I stopped off at Intangibles-R-Us, but they were sold out.
So, who's Bruce talking with?
Dunno. But I wish he'd hang up the phone and kick in that big science-y brain of his.

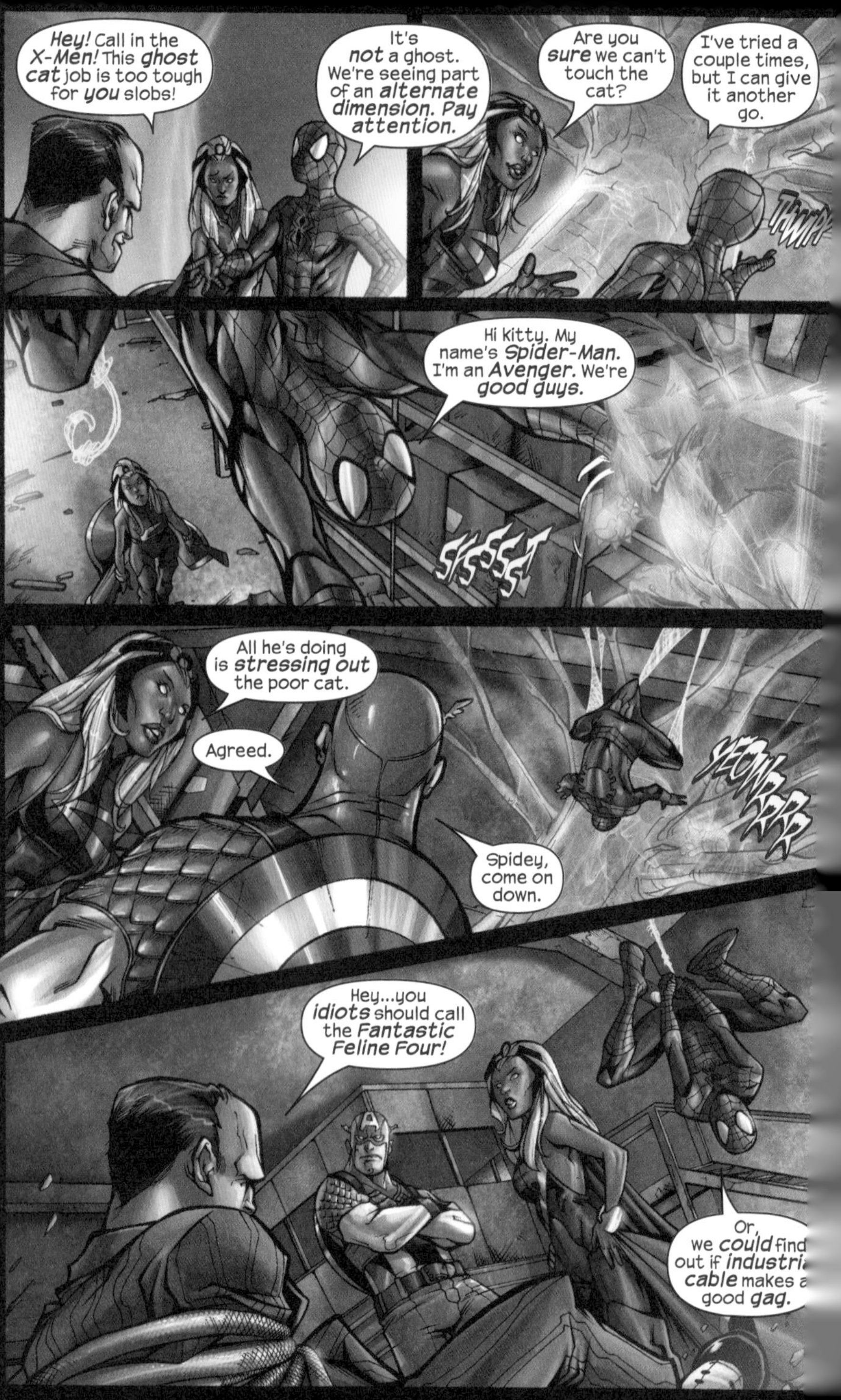
Hey! Call in the X-Men! This ghost cat job is too tough for you slobs!
It's not a ghost. We're seeing part of an alternate dimension. Pay attention.
Are you sure we can't touch the cat?
I've tried a couple times, but I can give it another go.
THWIP
Hi kitty. My name's Spider-Man. I'm an Avenger. We're good guys.
SSSSSST
All he's doing is stressing out the poor cat.
Agreed.
YEOWRRR
Spidey, come on down.
Hey...you idiots should call the Fantastic Feline Four!
Or, we could find out if industrial cable makes a good gag.

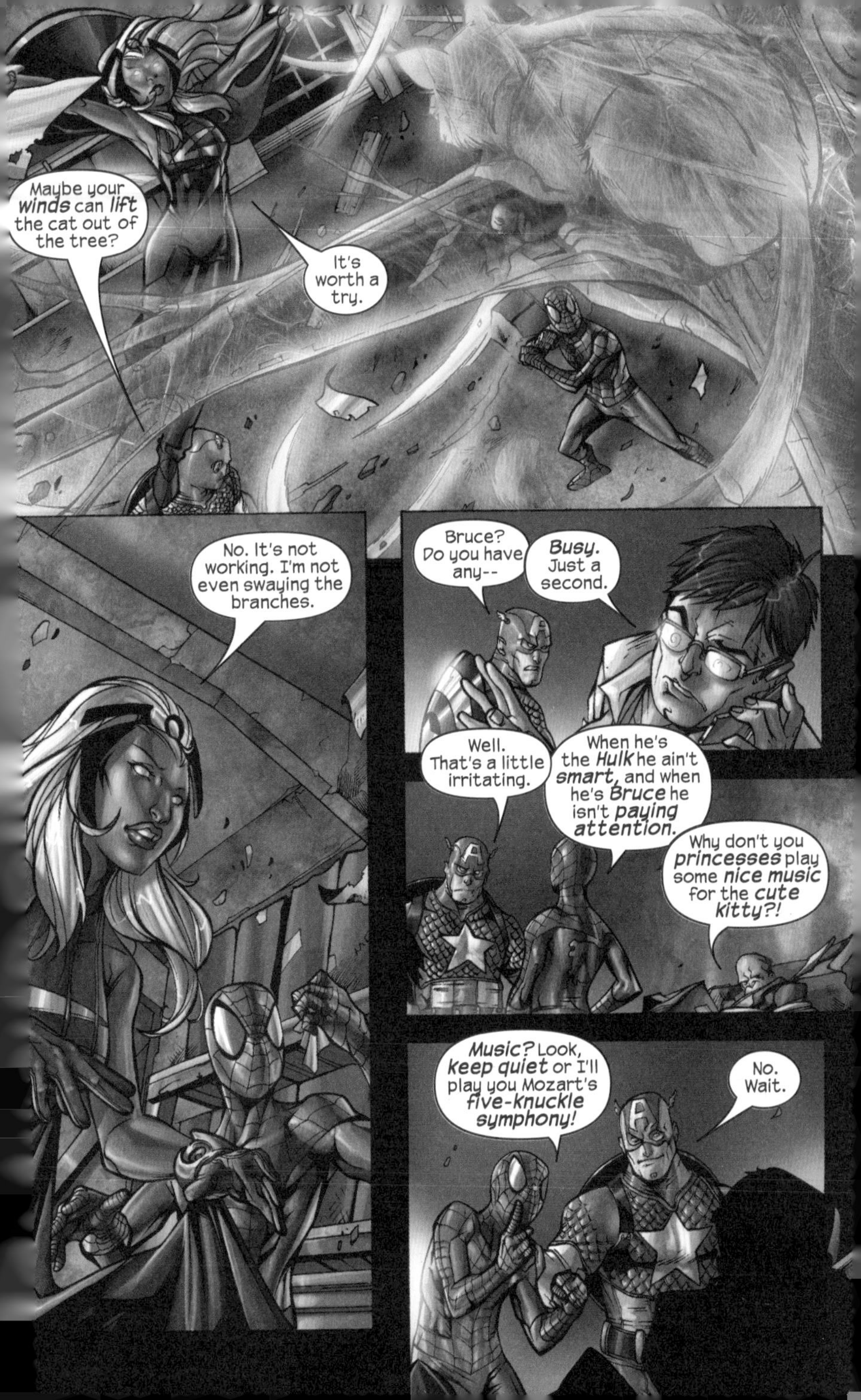
Maybe your winds can lift the cat out of the tree?
It's worth a try.
No. It's not working. I'm not even swaying the branches.
Bruce? Do you have any--
Busy. Just a second.
Well. That's a little irritating.
When he's the Hulk he ain't smart, and when he's Bruce he isn't paying attention.
Why don't you princesses play some nice music for the cute kitty?!
Music? Look, keep quiet or I'll play you Mozart's five-knuckle symphony!
No. Wait.

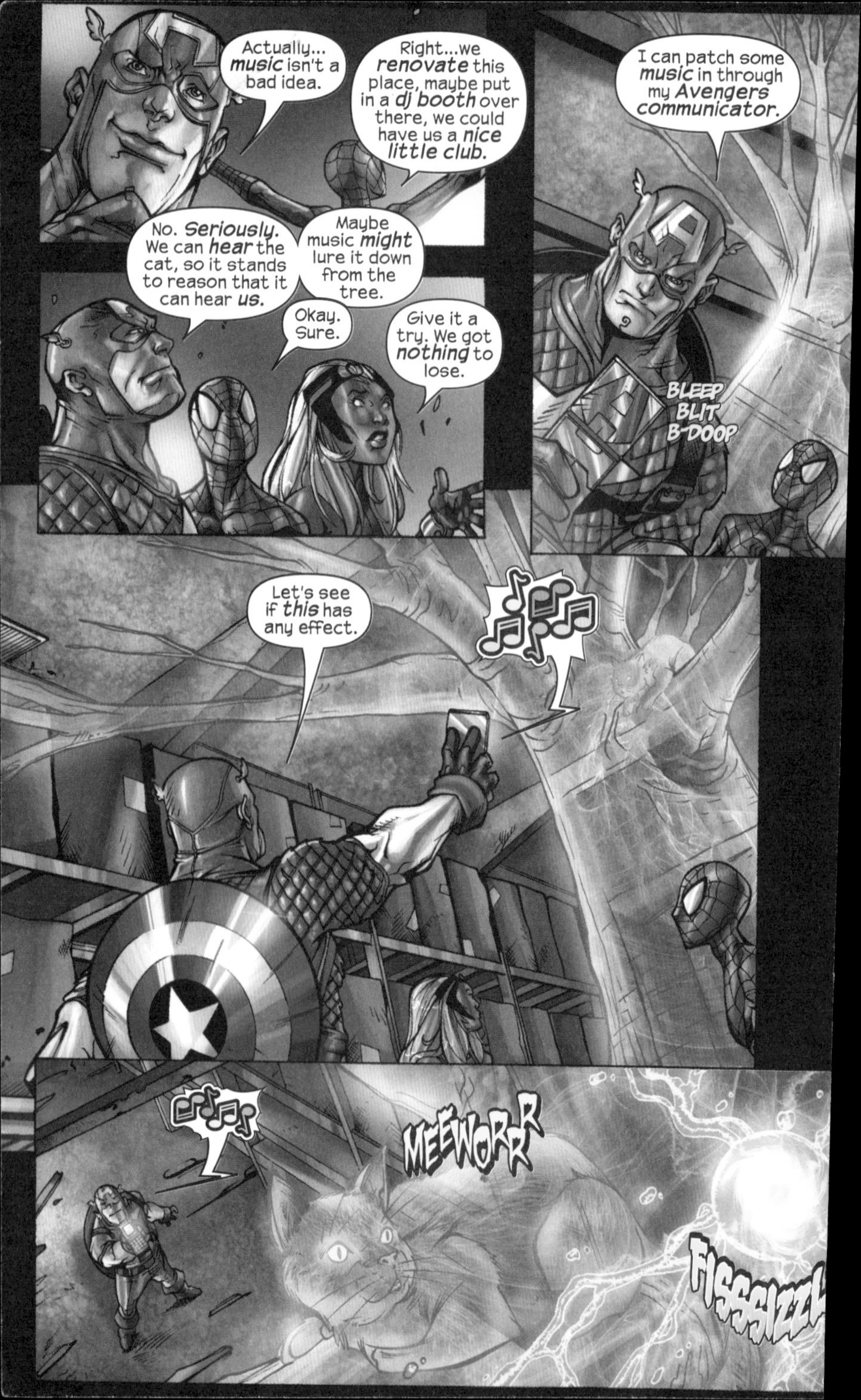
Actually... music isn't a bad idea.
Right...we renovate this place, maybe put in a dj booth over there, we could have us a nice little club.
No. Seriously. We can hear the cat, so it stands to reason that it can hear us.
Maybe music might lure it down from the tree.
Okay. Sure.
Give it a try. We got nothing to lose.
I can patch some music in through my Avengers communicator.
BLEEP BLIT B-DOOP
Let's see if this has any effect.
MEEWORRR
FISSSIZZL

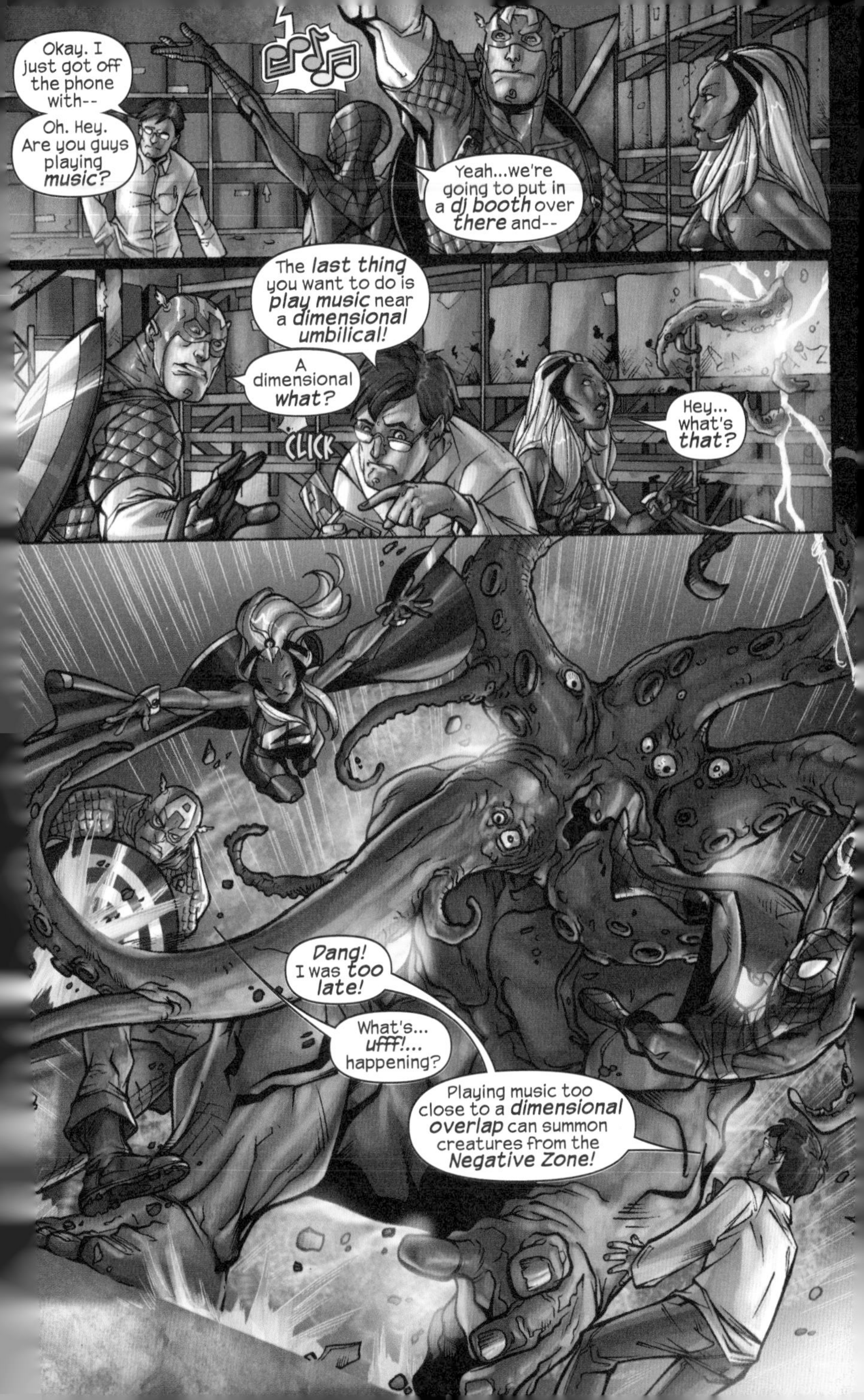
Okay. I just got off the phone with--
Oh. Hey. Are you guys playing music?
Yeah...we're going to put in a dj booth over there and--
The last thing you want to do is play music near a dimensional umbilical!
A dimensional what?
CLICK
Hey... what's that?
Dang! I was too late!
What's... ufff!... happening?
Playing music too close to a dimensional overlap can summon creatures from the Negative Zone!

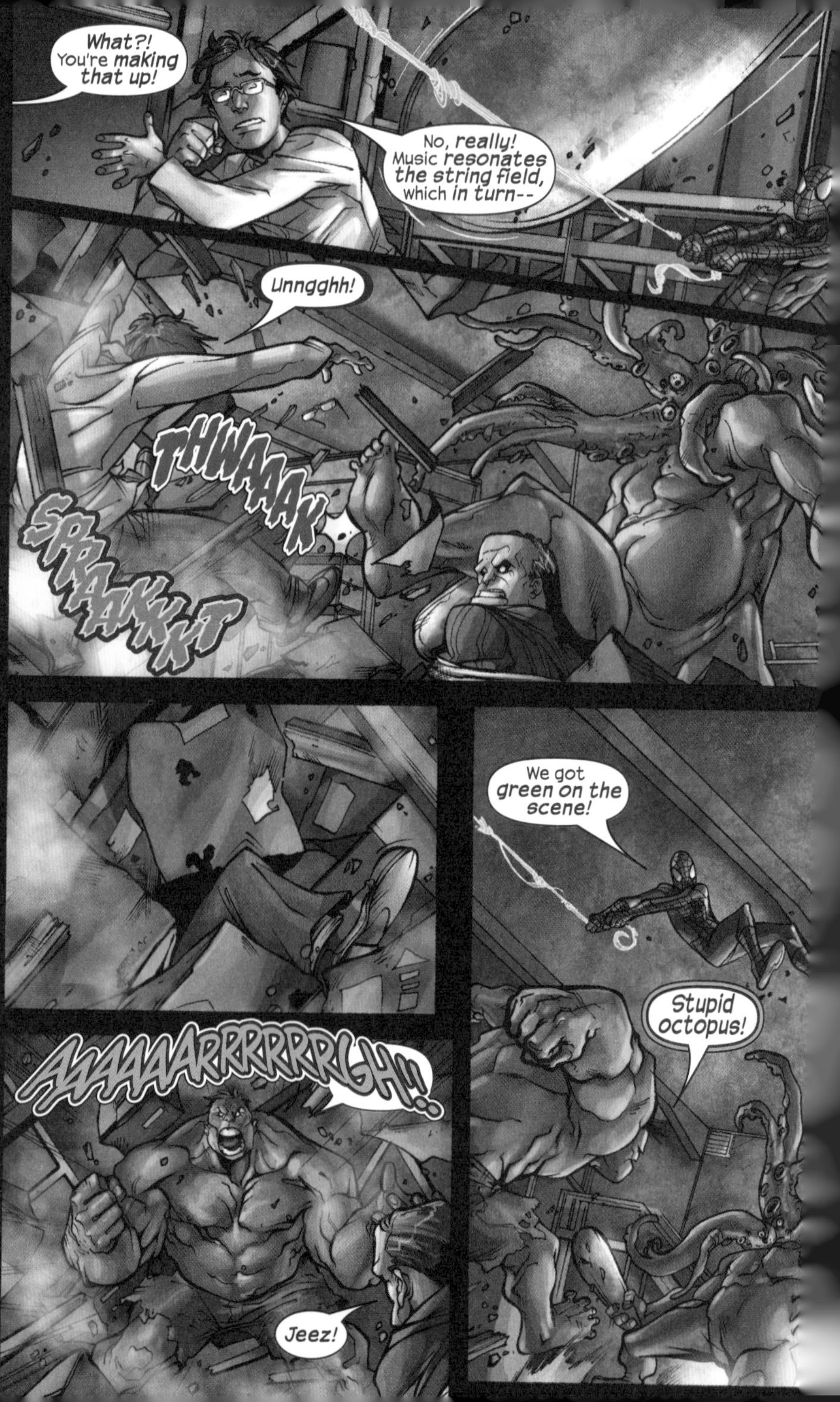
What?! You're making that up!
No, really! Music resonates the string field, which in turn--
Unngghh!
THWAAAK
SPRAAKKKT
We got green on the scene!
AAAAARRRRRGH!!
Stupid octopus!
Jeez!

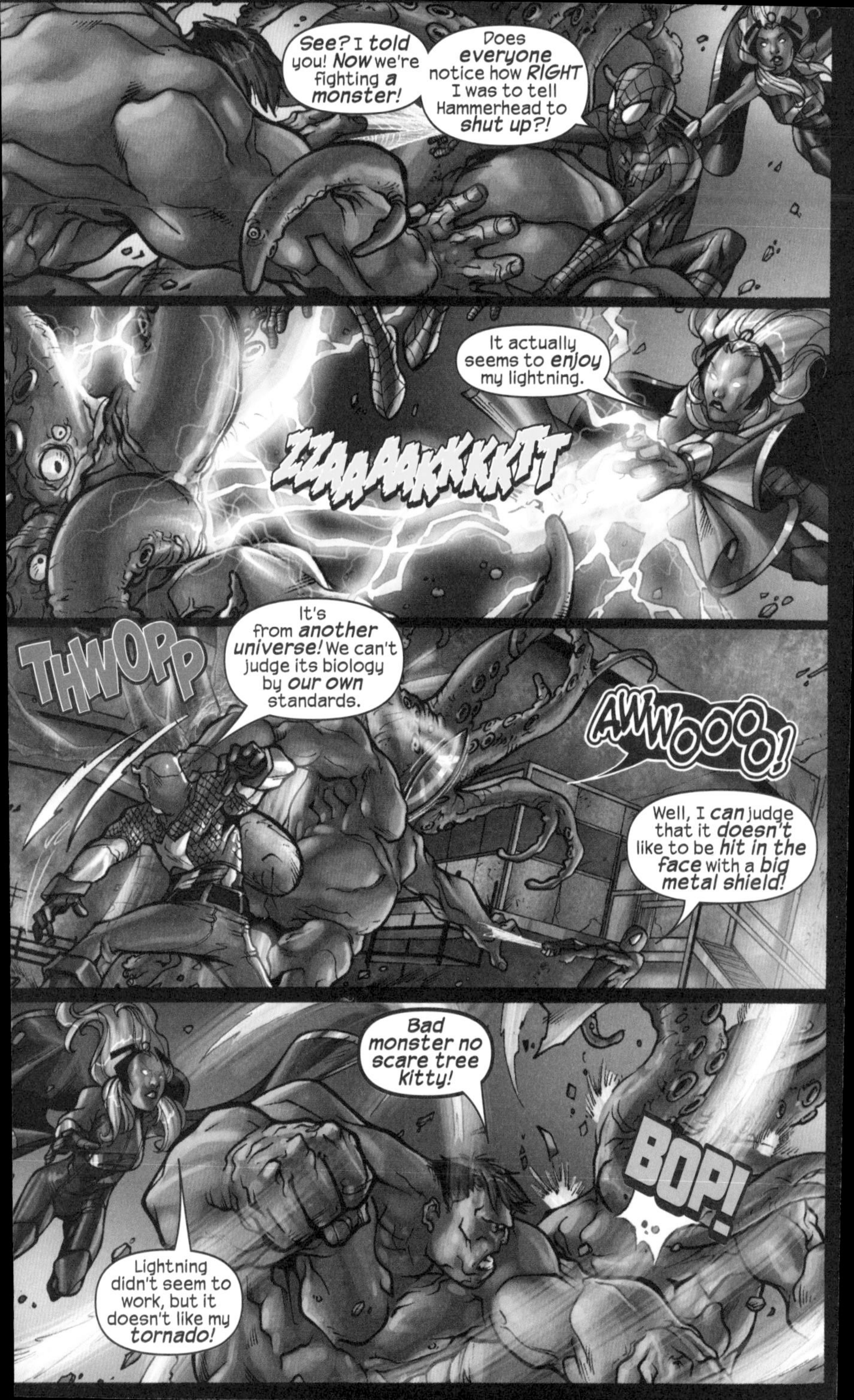
See? I told you! NOW we're fighting a monster!
Does everyone notice how RIGHT I was to tell Hammerhead to shut up?!
It actually seems to enjoy my lightning.
ZZAAAAKKKKTT
THWOPP
It's from another universe! We can't judge its biology by our own standards.
AWWOOOO!
Well, I can judge that it doesn't like to be hit in the face with a big metal shield!
Bad monster no scare tree kitty!
BOP!
Lightning didn't seem to work, but it doesn't like my tornado!

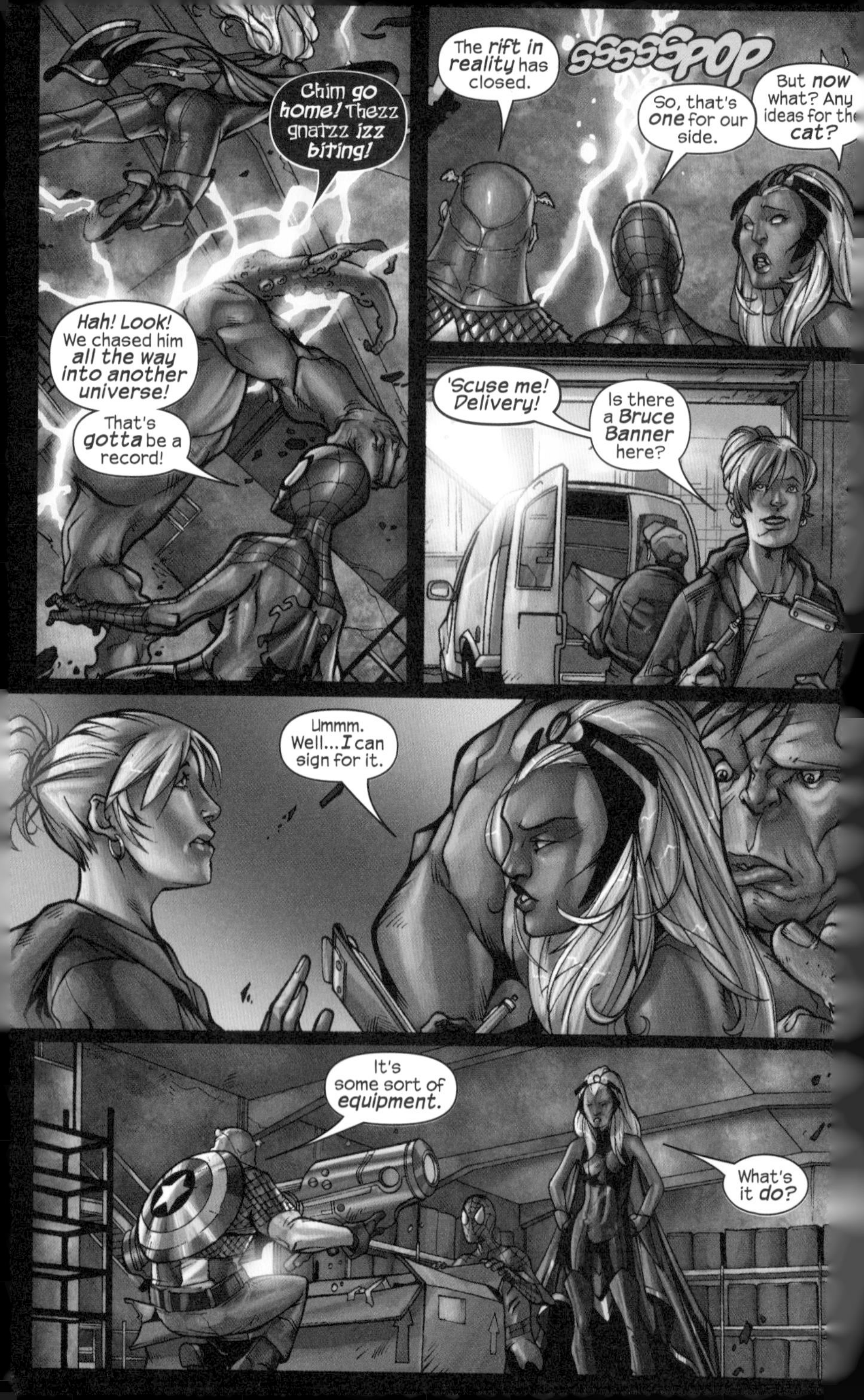
Chim go home! Thezz gnatzz izz biting!
Hah! Look! We chased him all the way into another universe!
That's gotta be a record!
The rift in reality has closed.
SSSSSPOP
So, that's one for our side.
But now what? Any ideas for the cat?
'Scuse me! Delivery!
Is there a Bruce Banner here?
Ummm. Well...I can sign for it.
It's some sort of equipment.
What's it do?

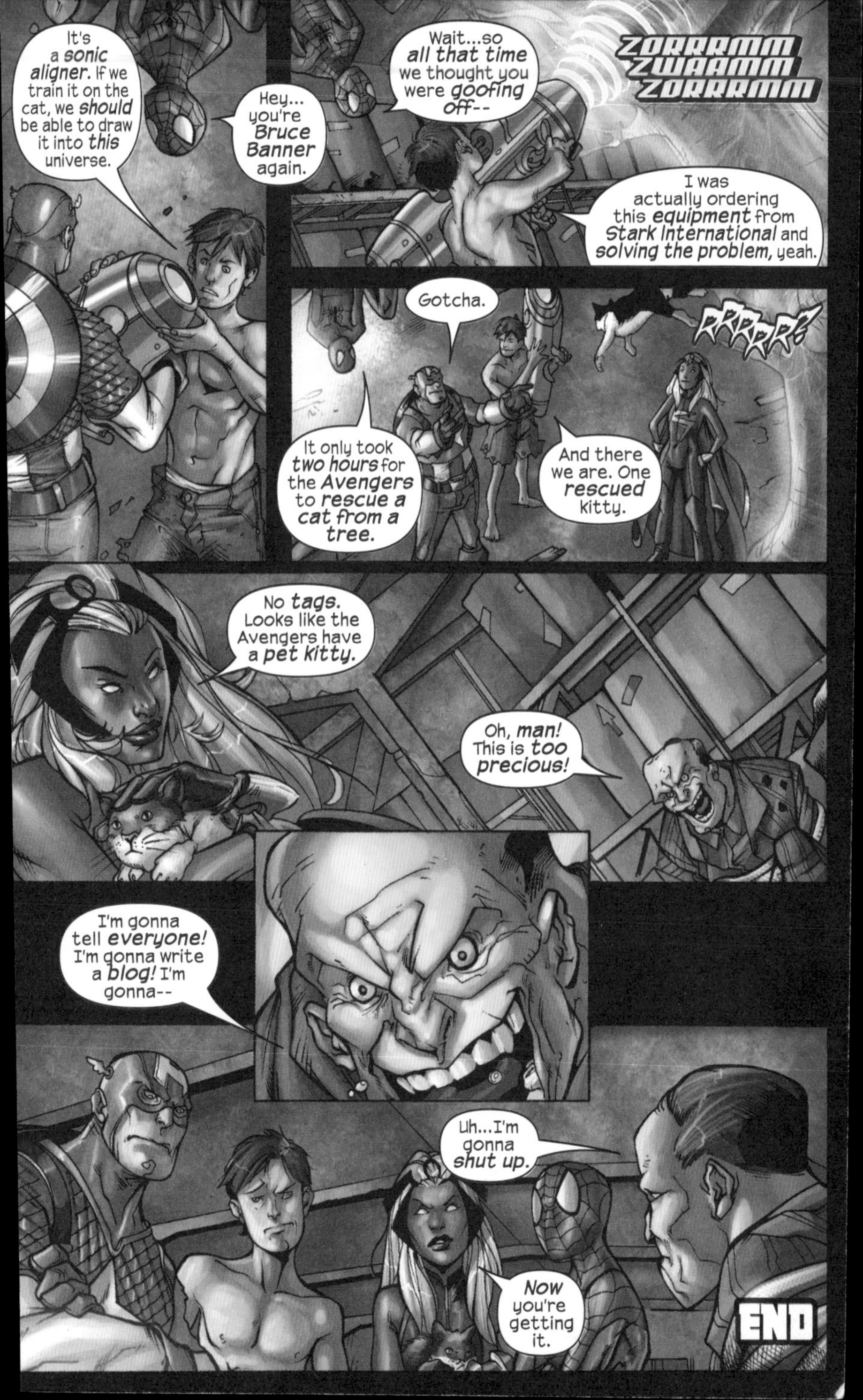

It's a sonic aligner. If we train it on the cat, we should be able to draw it into this universe.
Hey... you're Bruce Banner again.
Wait...so all that time we thought you were goofing off--
ZORRRMM ZWAAMM ZORRRMM
I was actually ordering this equipment from Stark International and solving the problem, yeah.
Gotcha.
It only took two hours for the Avengers to rescue a cat from a tree.
And there we are. One rescued kitty.
No tags. Looks like the Avengers have a pet kitty.
Oh, man! This is too precious!
I'm gonna tell everyone! I'm gonna write a blog! I'm gonna--
Uh...I'm gonna shut up.
Now you're getting it.
END

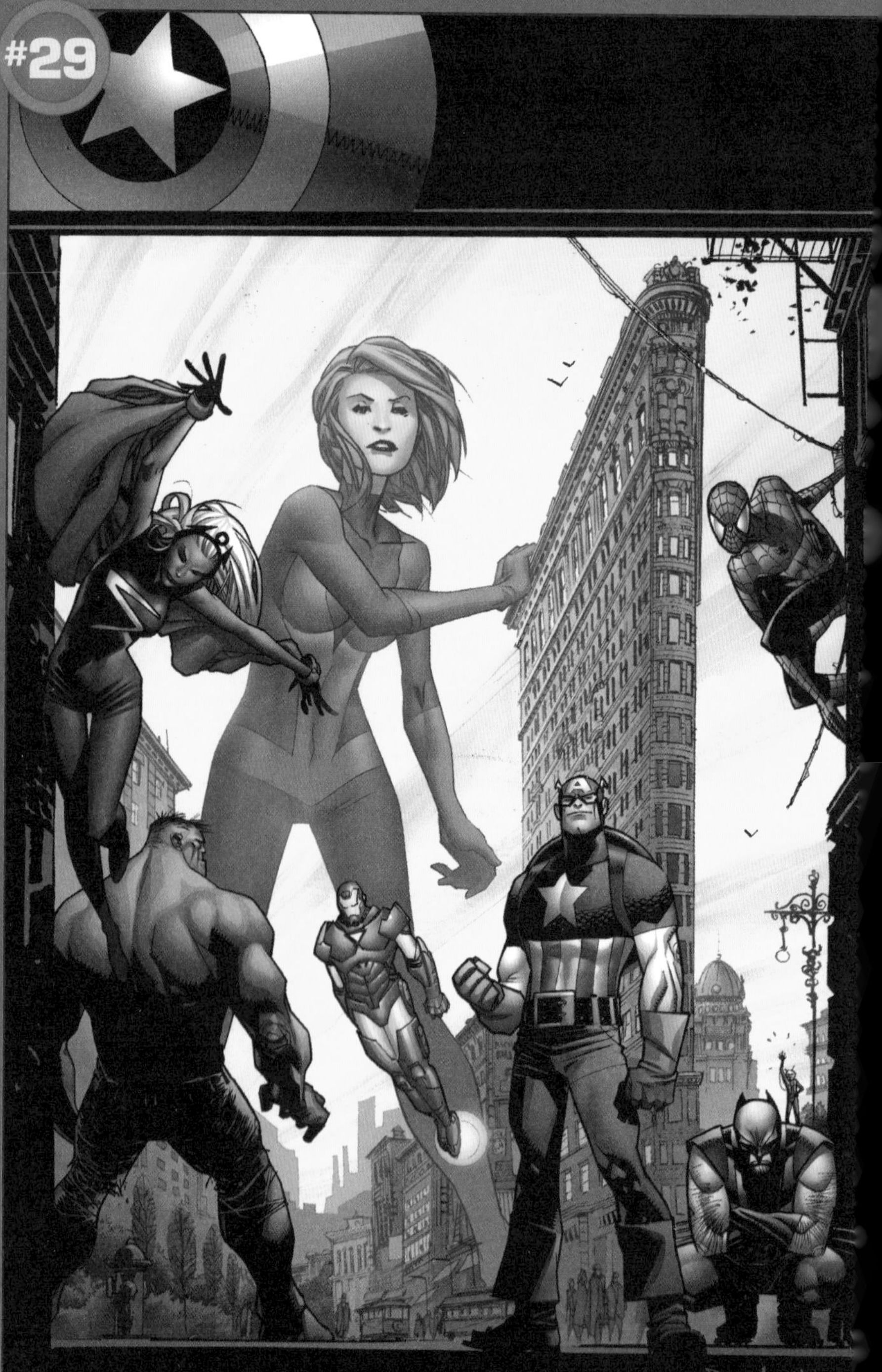
#29

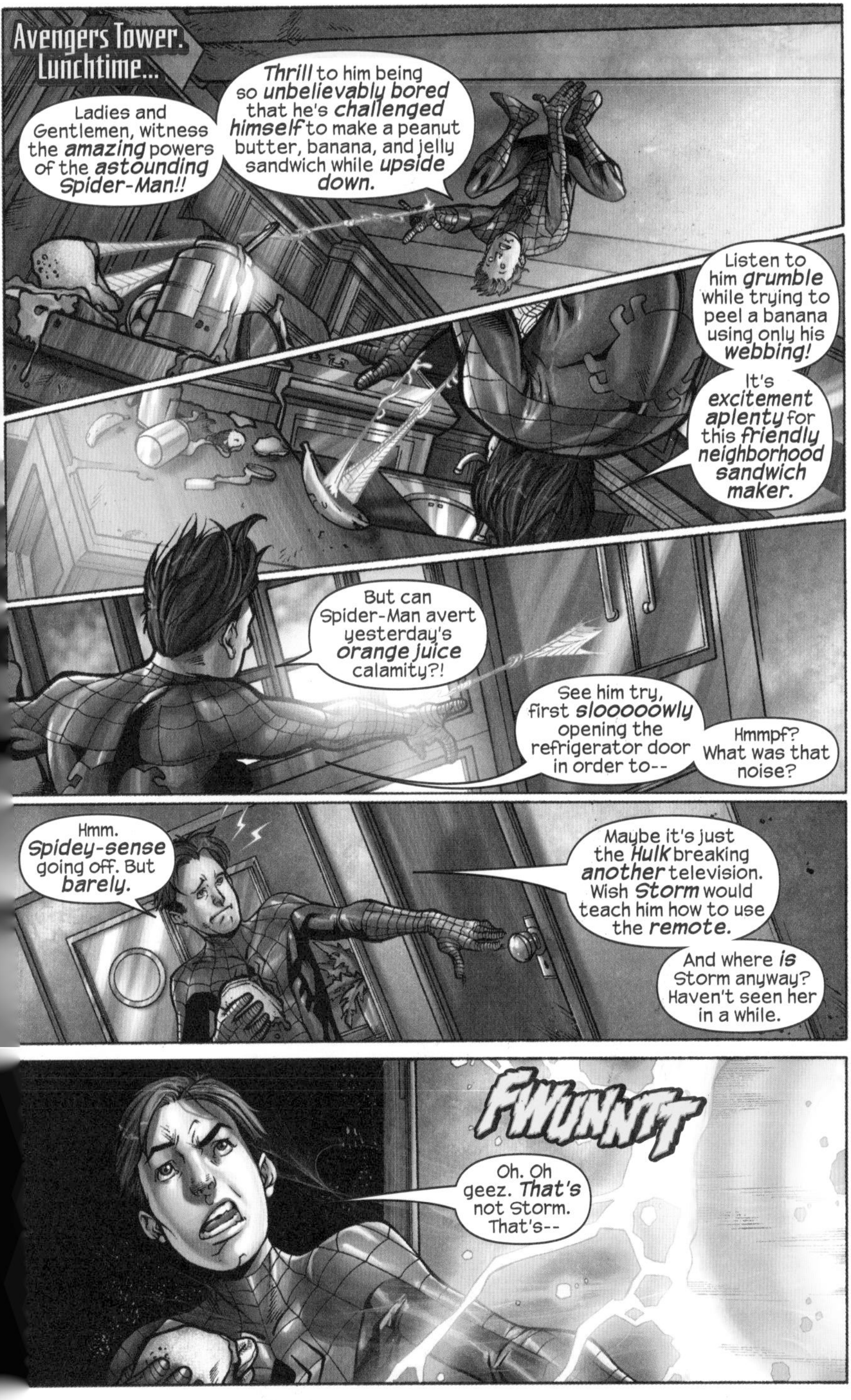
Avengers Tower. Lunchtime...
Ladies and Gentlemen, witness the amazing powers of the astounding Spider-Man!!
Thrill to him being so unbelievably bored that he's challenged himself to make a peanut butter, banana, and jelly sandwich while upside down.
Listen to him grumble while trying to peel a banana using only his webbing!
It's excitement aplenty for this friendly neighborhood sandwich maker.
But can Spider-Man avert yesterday's orange juice calamity?!
See him try, first sloooooowly opening the refrigerator door in order to--
Hmmpf? What was that noise?
Hmm. Spidey-sense going off. But barely.
Maybe it's just the Hulk breaking another television. Wish Storm would teach him how to use the remote.
And where is Storm anyway? Haven't seen her in a while.
FWUNNTT
Oh. Oh geez. That's not Storm. That's--

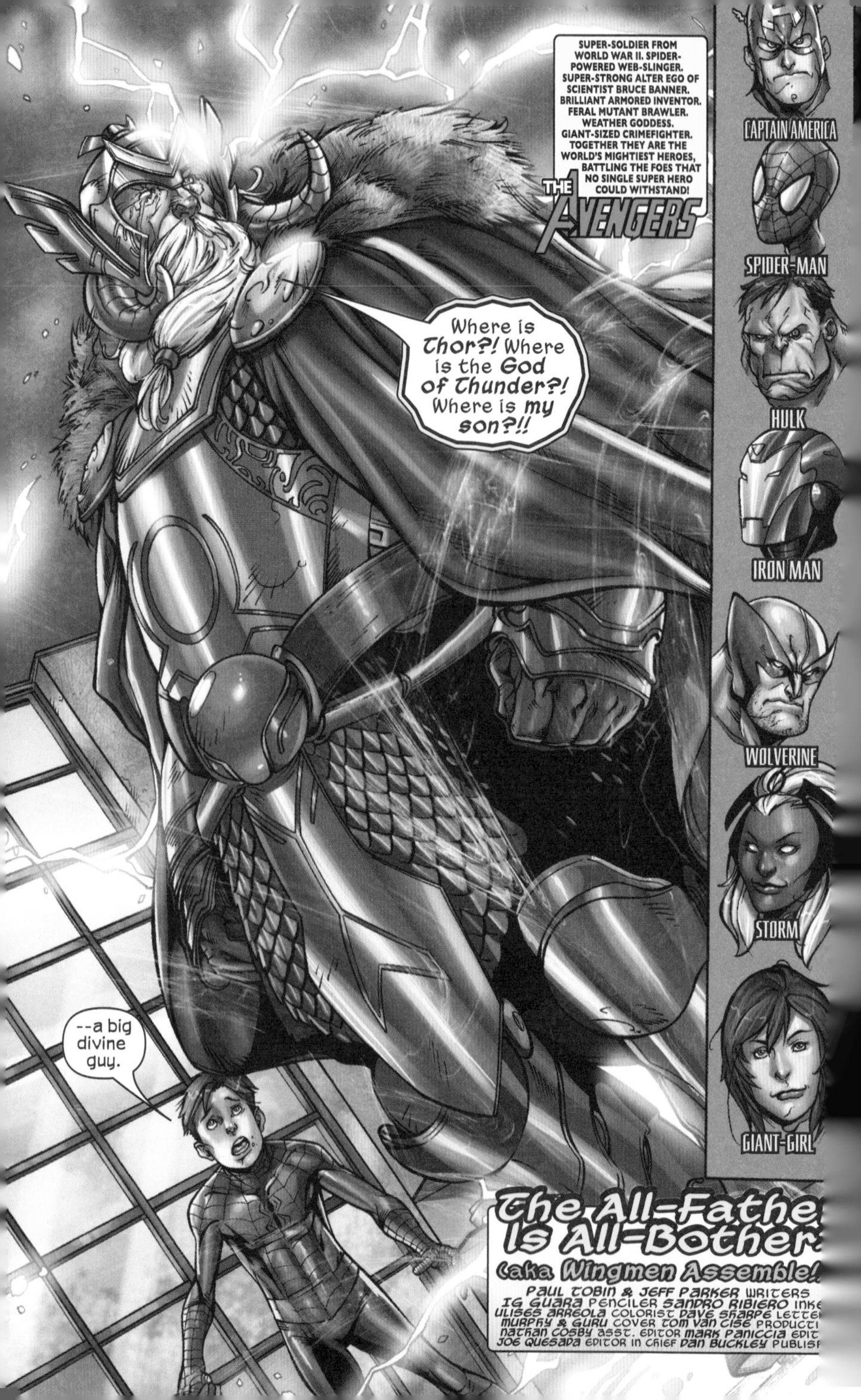
SUPER-SOLDIER FROM WORLD WAR II. SPIDER-POWERED WEB-SLINGER. SUPER-STRONG ALTER EGO OF SCIENTIST BRUCE BANNER. BRILLIANT ARMORED INVENTOR. FERAL MUTANT BRAWLER. WEATHER GODDESS. GIANT-SIZED CRIMEFIGHTER. TOGETHER THEY ARE THE WORLD'S MIGHTIEST HEROES, BATTLING THE FOES THAT NO SINGLE SUPER HERO COULD WITHSTAND!
THE AVENGERS
CAPTAIN AMERICA
SPIDER-MAN
HULK
IRON MAN
WOLVERINE
STORM
GIANT-GIRL
Where is Thor?! Where is the God of Thunder?! Where is my son?!!
--a big divine guy.
The All-Fathe
Is All-Bother
(aka Wingmen Assemble!
PAUL TOBIN & JEFF PARKER WRITERS
IG GUARA PENCILER SANDRO RIBIERO INKE
ULISES ARREOLA COLORIST DAVE SHARPE LETTE
MURPHY & GURU COVER TOM VAN CISE PRODUCTI
NATHAN COSBY ASST. EDITOR MARK PANICCIA EDIT
JOE QUESADA EDITOR IN CHIEF DAN BUCKLEY PUBLIS

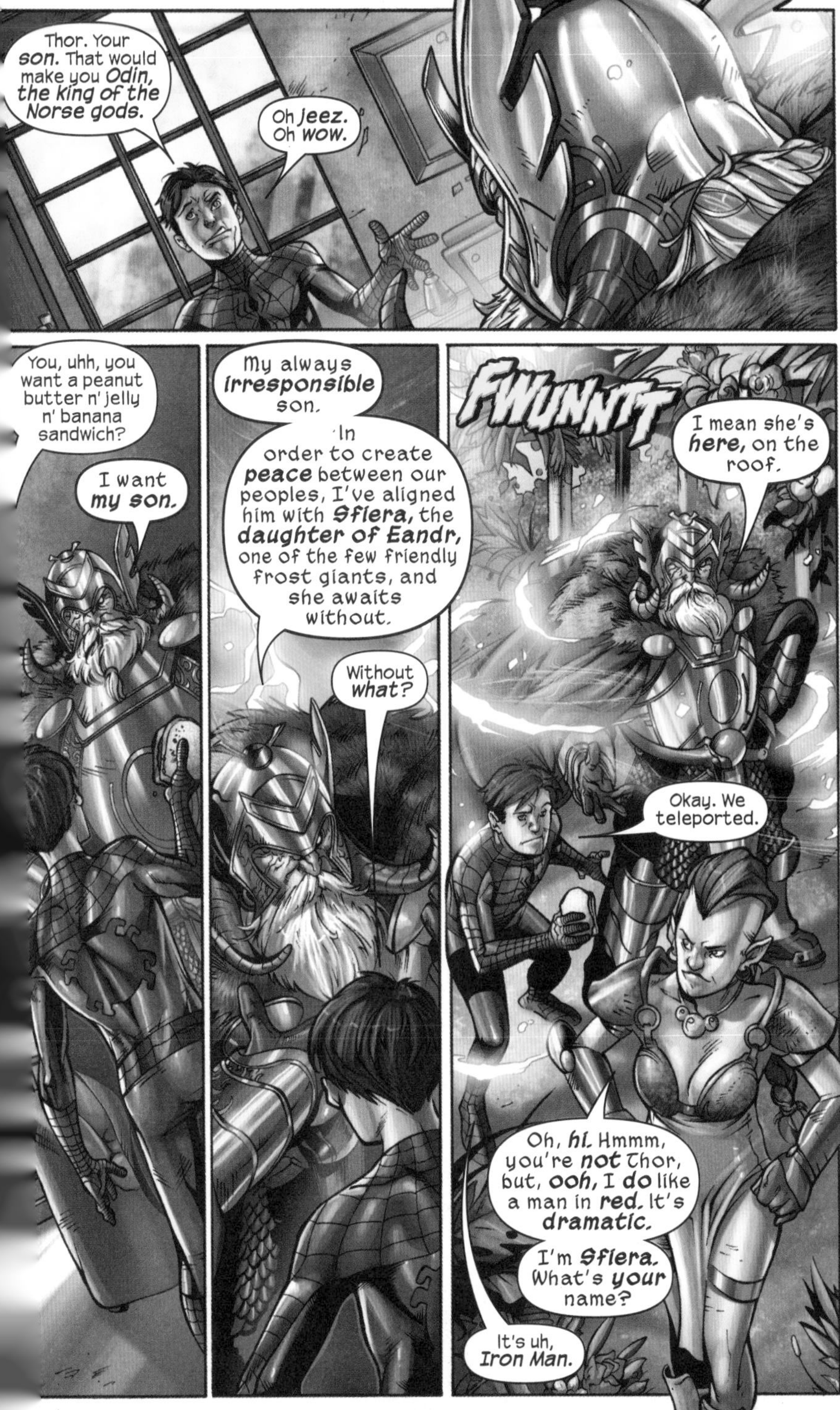
Thor. Your son. That would make you Odin, the king of the Norse gods.
Oh jeez. Oh wow.
You, uhh, you want a peanut butter n' jelly n' banana sandwich?
I want my son.
My always irresponsible son.
In order to create peace between our peoples, I've aligned him with Sfiera, the daughter of Eandr, one of the few friendly frost giants, and she awaits without.
Without what?
FWUNNTT
I mean she's here, on the roof.
Okay. We teleported.
Oh, hi. Hmmm, you're not Thor, but, ooh, I do like a man in red. It's dramatic.
I'm Sfiera. What's your name?
It's uh, Iron Man.

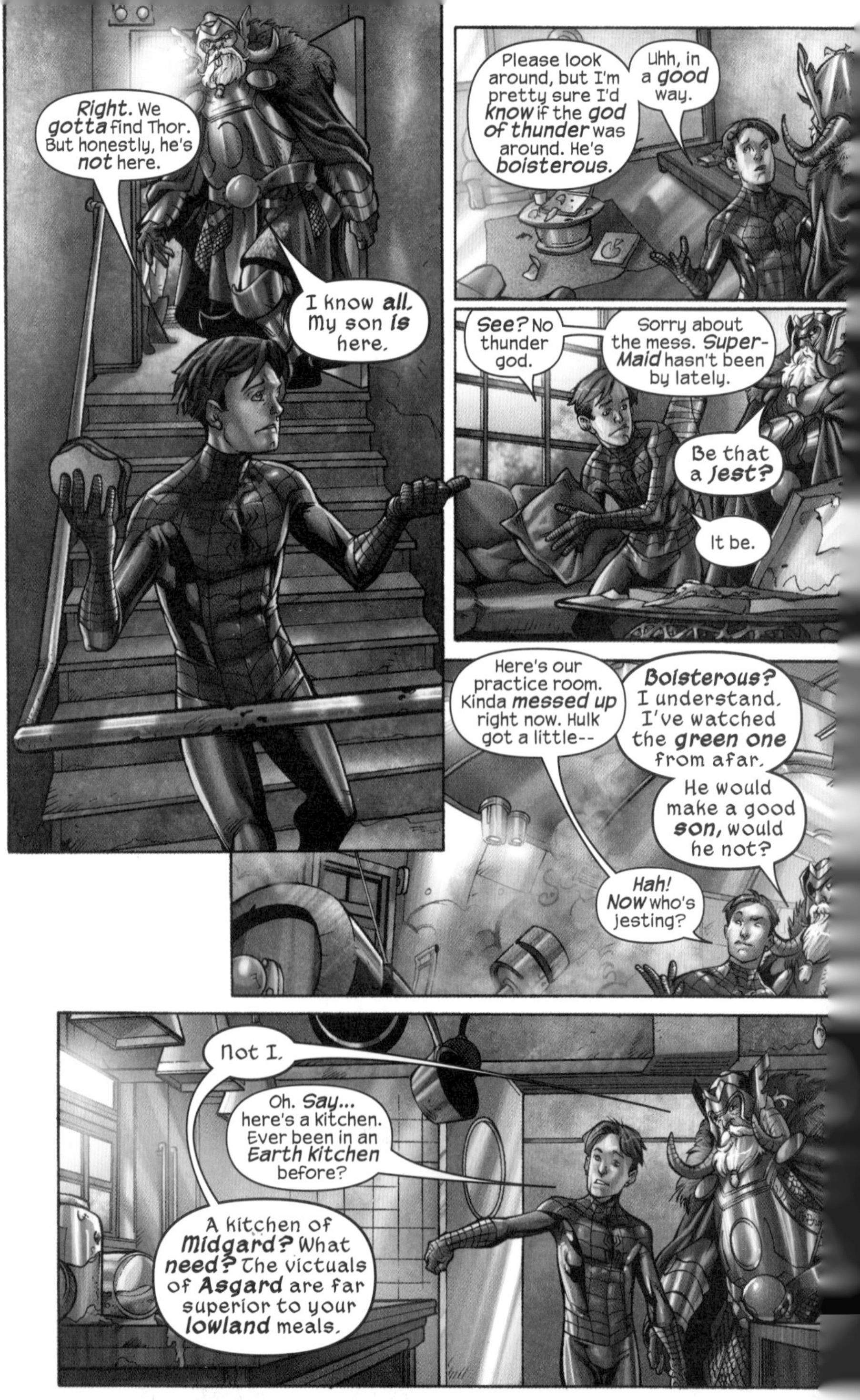
Right. We gotta find Thor. But honestly, he's not here.
I know all. My son is here.
Please look around, but I'm pretty sure I'd know if the god of thunder was around. He's boisterous.
Uhh, in a good way.
See? No thunder god.
Sorry about the mess. Super-Maid hasn't been by lately.
Be that a jest?
It be.
Here's our practice room. Kinda messed up right now. Hulk got a little--
Boisterous? I understand. I've watched the green one from afar.
He would make a good son, would he not?
Hah! Now who's jesting?
Not I.
Oh. Say... here's a kitchen. Ever been in an Earth kitchen before?
A kitchen of Midgard? What need? The victuals of Asgard are far superior to your lowland meals.

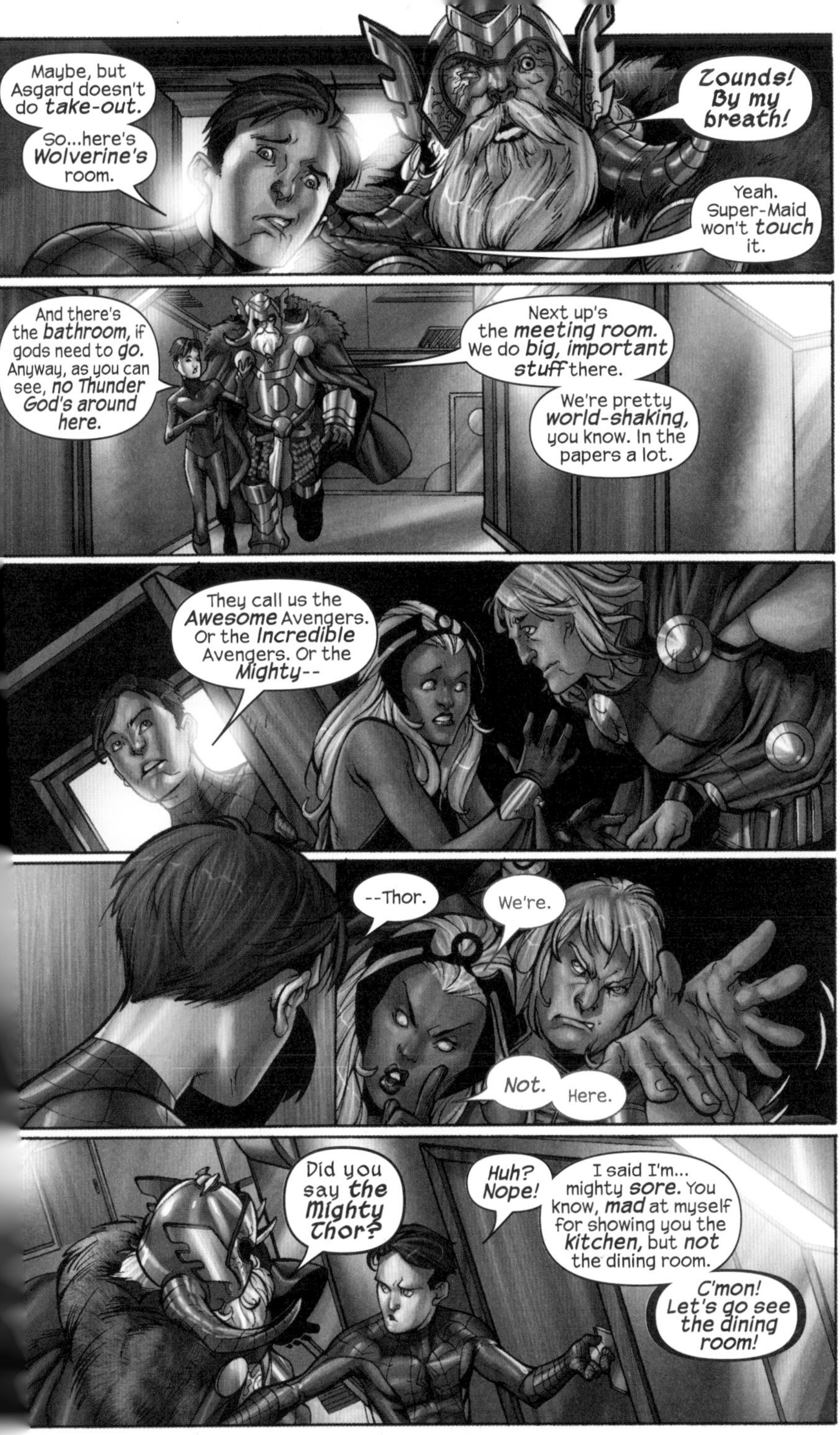
Maybe, but Asgard doesn't do take-out.
So...here's Wolverine's room.
Zounds! By my breath!
Yeah. Super-Maid won't touch it.
And there's the bathroom, if gods need to go. Anyway, as you can see, no Thunder God's around here.
Next up's the meeting room. We do big, important stuff there.
We're pretty world-shaking, you know. In the papers a lot.
They call us the Awesome Avengers. Or the Incredible Avengers. Or the Mighty--
--Thor.
We're.
Not.
Here.
Did you say the Mighty Thor?
Huh? Nope!
I said I'm... mighty sore. You know, mad at myself for showing you the kitchen, but not the dining room.
C'mon! Let's go see the dining room!

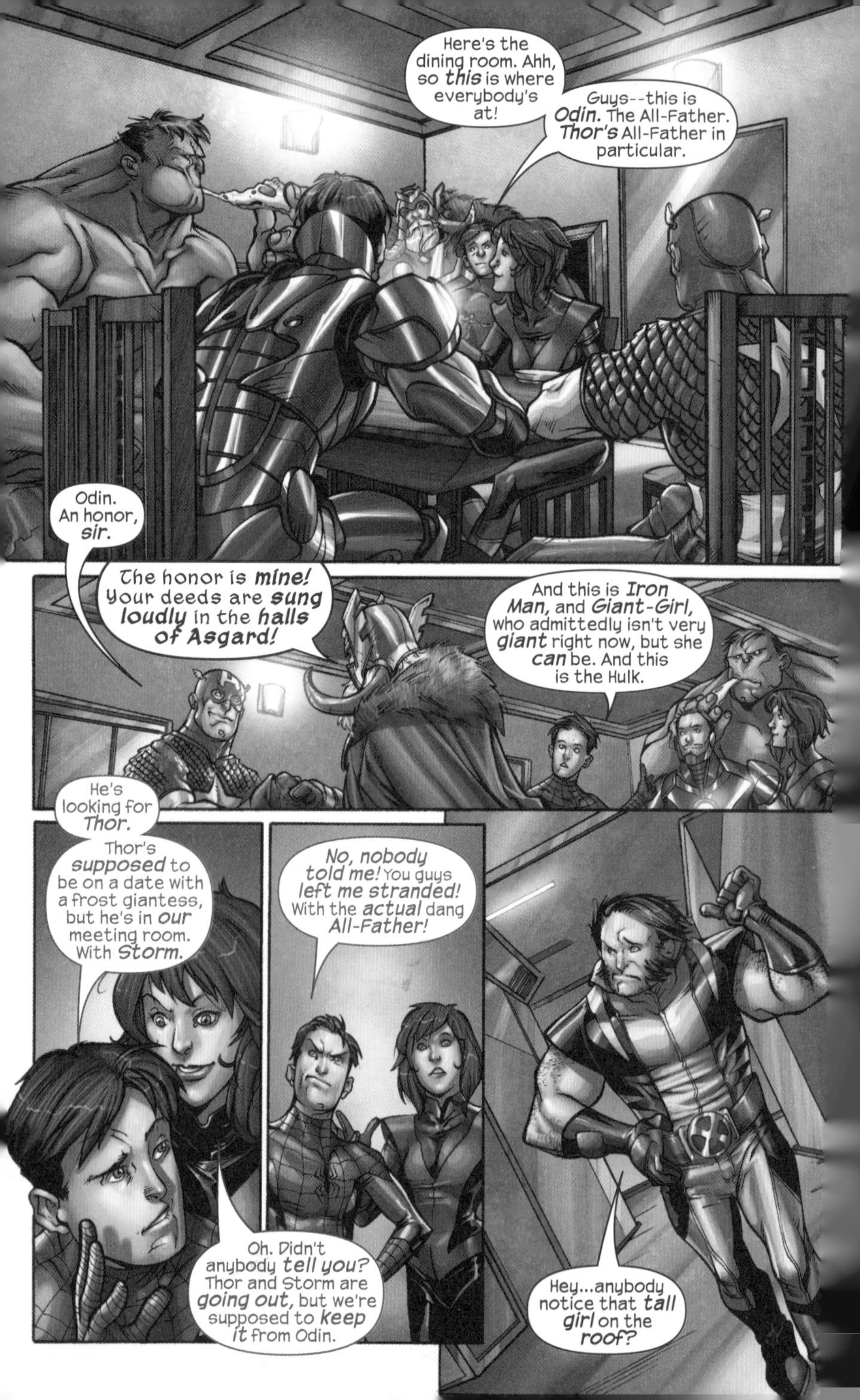
Here's the dining room. Ahh, so this is where everybody's at!
Guys--this is Odin. The All-Father. Thor's All-Father in particular.
Odin. An honor, sir.
The honor is mine! Your deeds are sung loudly in the halls of Asgard!
And this is Iron Man, and Giant-Girl, who admittedly isn't very giant right now, but she can be. And this is the Hulk.
He's looking for Thor.
Thor's supposed to be on a date with a frost giantess, but he's in our meeting room. With Storm.
No, nobody told me! You guys left me stranded! With the actual dang All-Father!
Oh. Didn't anybody tell you? Thor and Storm are going out, but we're supposed to keep it from Odin.
Hey...anybody notice that tall girl on the roof?

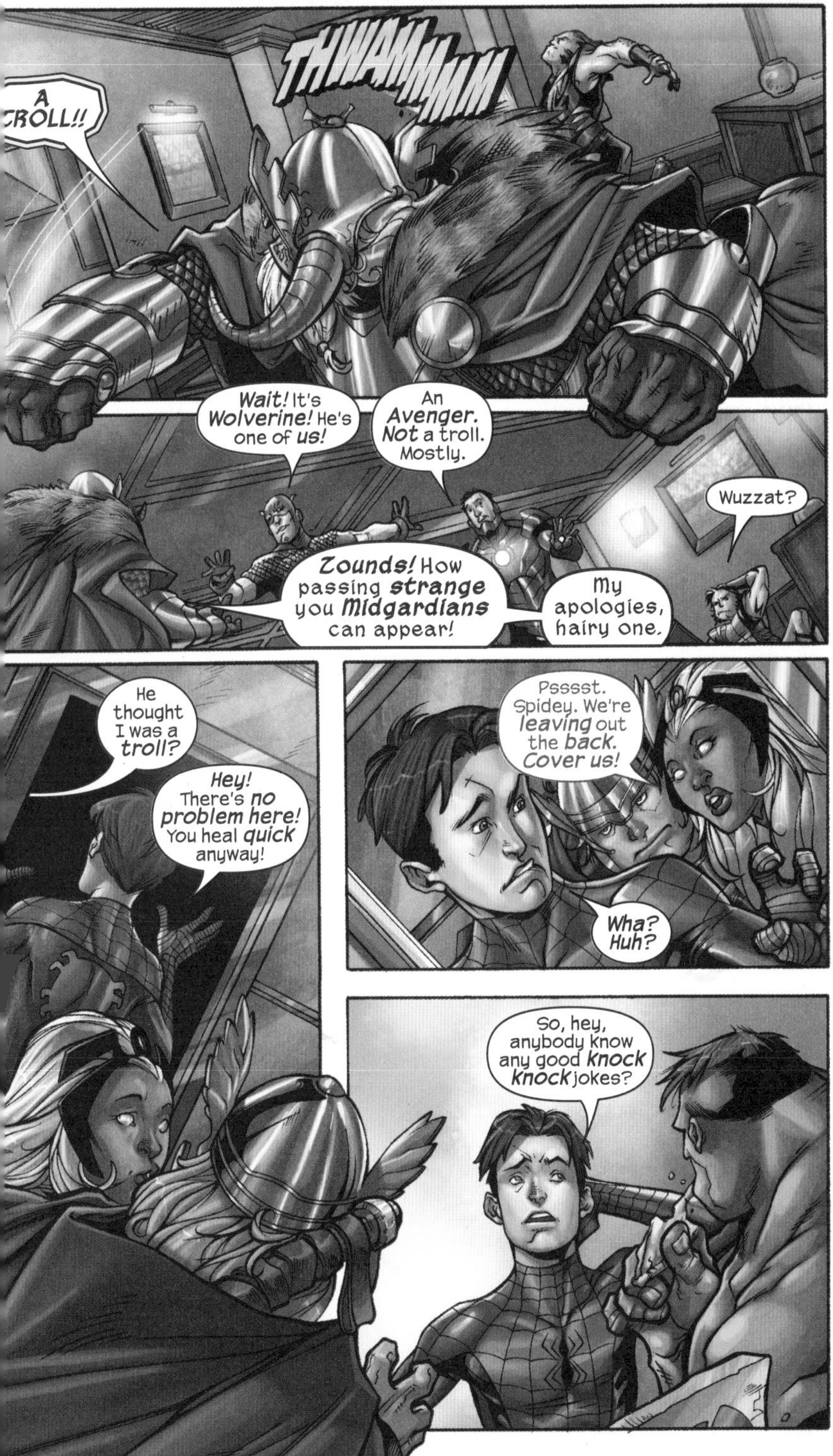
THWAMMMM
A TROLL!!
Wait! It's Wolverine! He's one of us!
An Avenger. Not a troll. Mostly.
Wuzzat?
Zounds! How passing strange you Midgardians can appear!
My apologies, hairy one.
He thought I was a troll?
Hey! There's no problem here! You heal quick anyway!
Psssst. Spidey. We're leaving out the back. Cover us!
Wha? Huh?
So, hey, anybody know any good knock knock jokes?

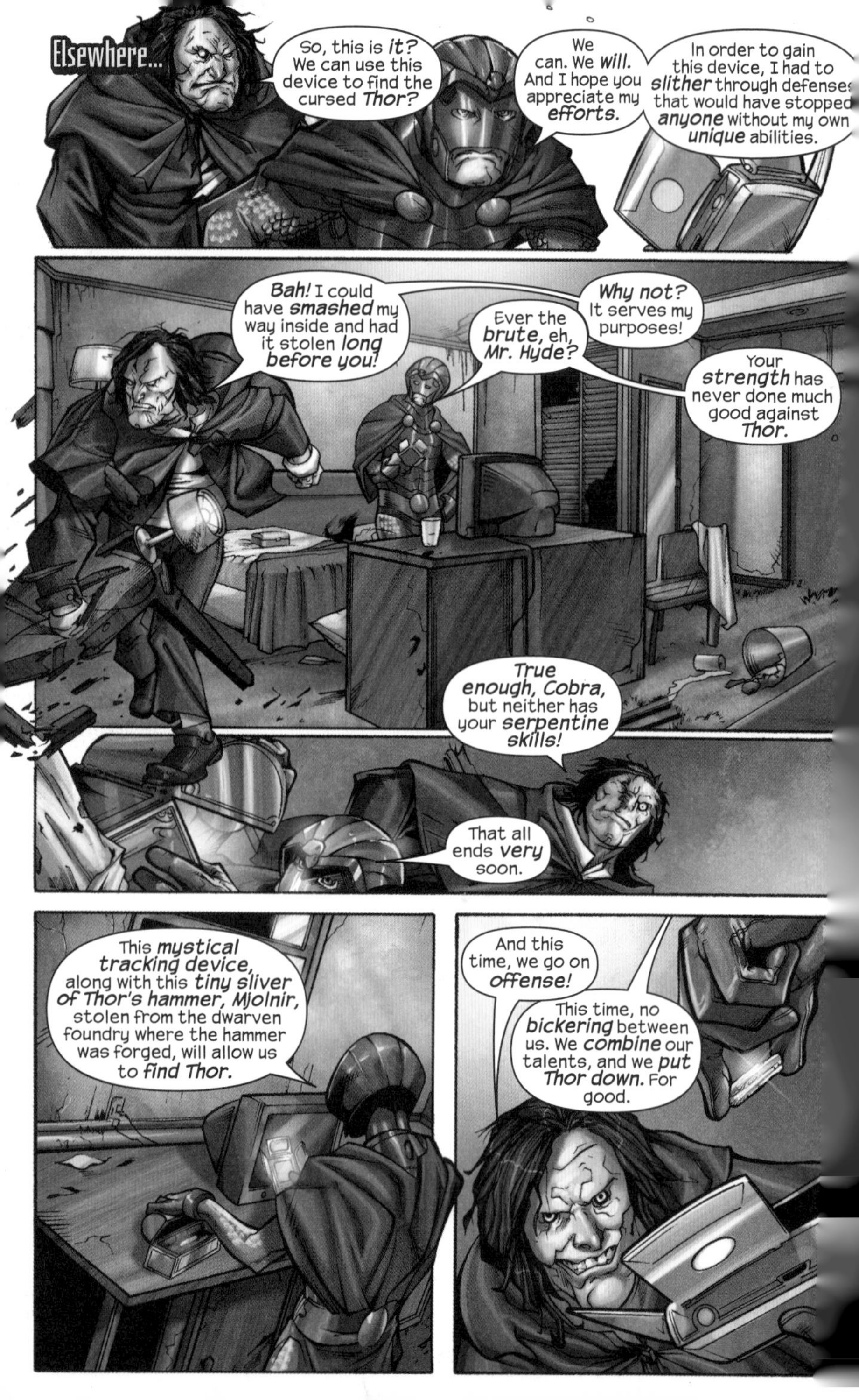
Elsewhere...
So, this is *it*? We can use this device to find the cursed *Thor*?
We can. We *will*. And I hope you appreciate my *efforts*.
In order to gain this device, I had to *slither* through defenses that would have stopped *anyone* without my own *unique* abilities.
Bah! I could have *smashed* my way inside and had it stolen *long before you!*
Why not? It serves my purposes!
Ever the *brute*, eh, *Mr. Hyde*?
Your *strength* has never done much good against *Thor*.
True enough, Cobra, but neither has your *serpentine skills!*
That all ends *very* soon.
This *mystical tracking device,* along with this *tiny sliver of Thor's hammer, Mjolnir,* stolen from the dwarven foundry where the hammer was forged, will allow us to *find Thor*.
And this time, we go on *offense!*
This time, no *bickering* between us. We *combine* our talents, and we *put Thor down*. For good.

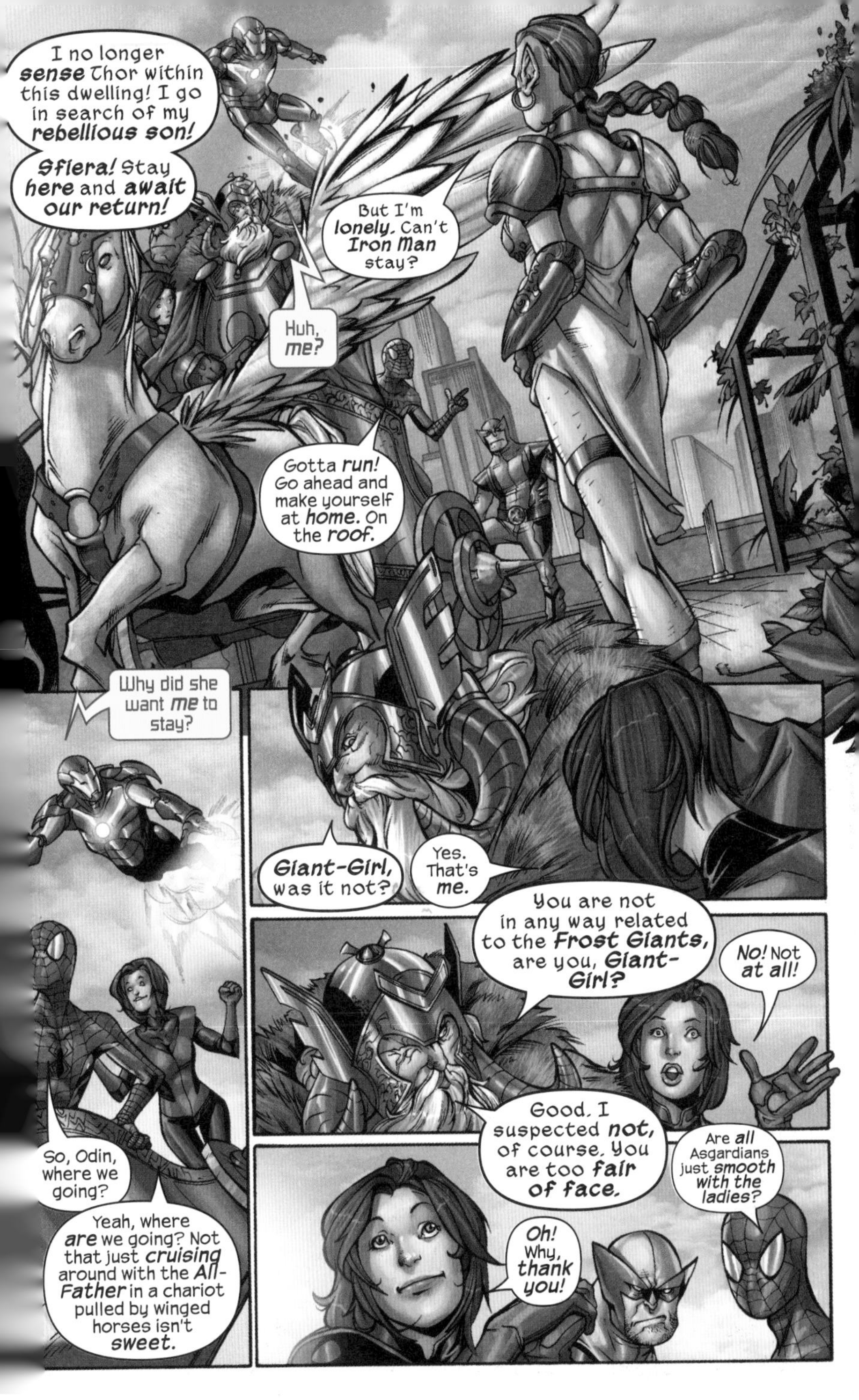

I no longer sense Thor within this dwelling! I go in search of my rebellious son!
Sfiera! Stay here and await our return!
But I'm lonely. Can't Iron Man stay?
Huh, me?
Gotta run! Go ahead and make yourself at home. On the roof.
Why did she want me to stay?
Giant-Girl, was it not?
Yes. That's me.
You are not in any way related to the Frost Giants, are you, Giant-Girl?
No! Not at all!
Good. I suspected not, of course. You are too fair of face.
Oh! Why, thank you!
Are all Asgardians just smooth with the ladies?
So, Odin, where we going?
Yeah, where are we going? Not that just cruising around with the All-Father in a chariot pulled by winged horses isn't sweet.

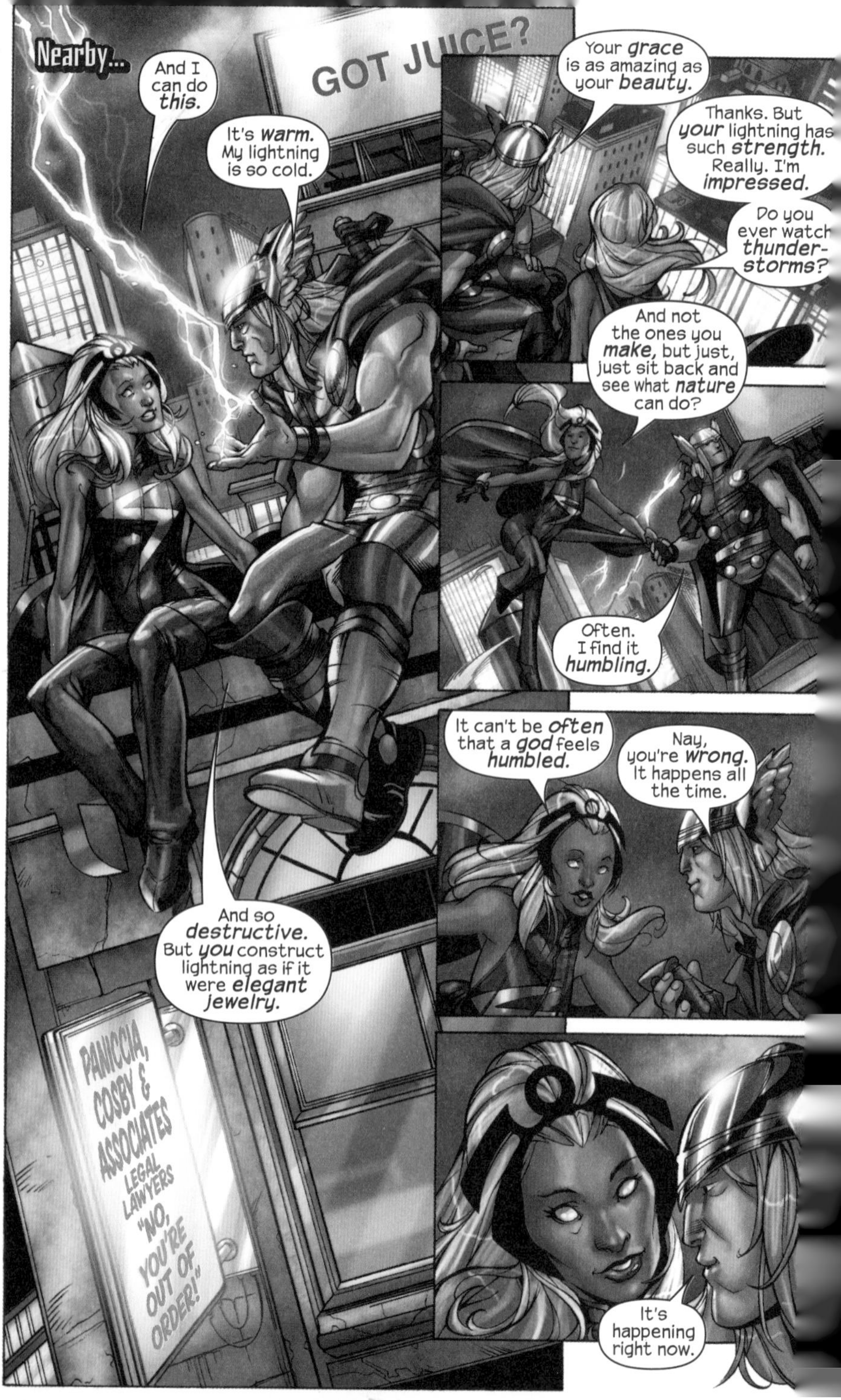

Nearby...
And I can do this.
It's warm. My lightning is so cold.
GOT JUICE?
And so destructive. But you construct lightning as if it were elegant jewelry.
PANICCIA, COSBY & ASSOCIATES LEGAL LAWYERS "NO, YOU'RE OUT OF ORDER!"
Your grace is as amazing as your beauty.
Thanks. But your lightning has such strength. Really. I'm impressed.
Do you ever watch thunder-storms?
And not the ones you make, but just, just sit back and see what nature can do?
Often. I find it humbling.
It can't be often that a god feels humbled.
Nay, you're wrong. It happens all the time.
It's happening right now.

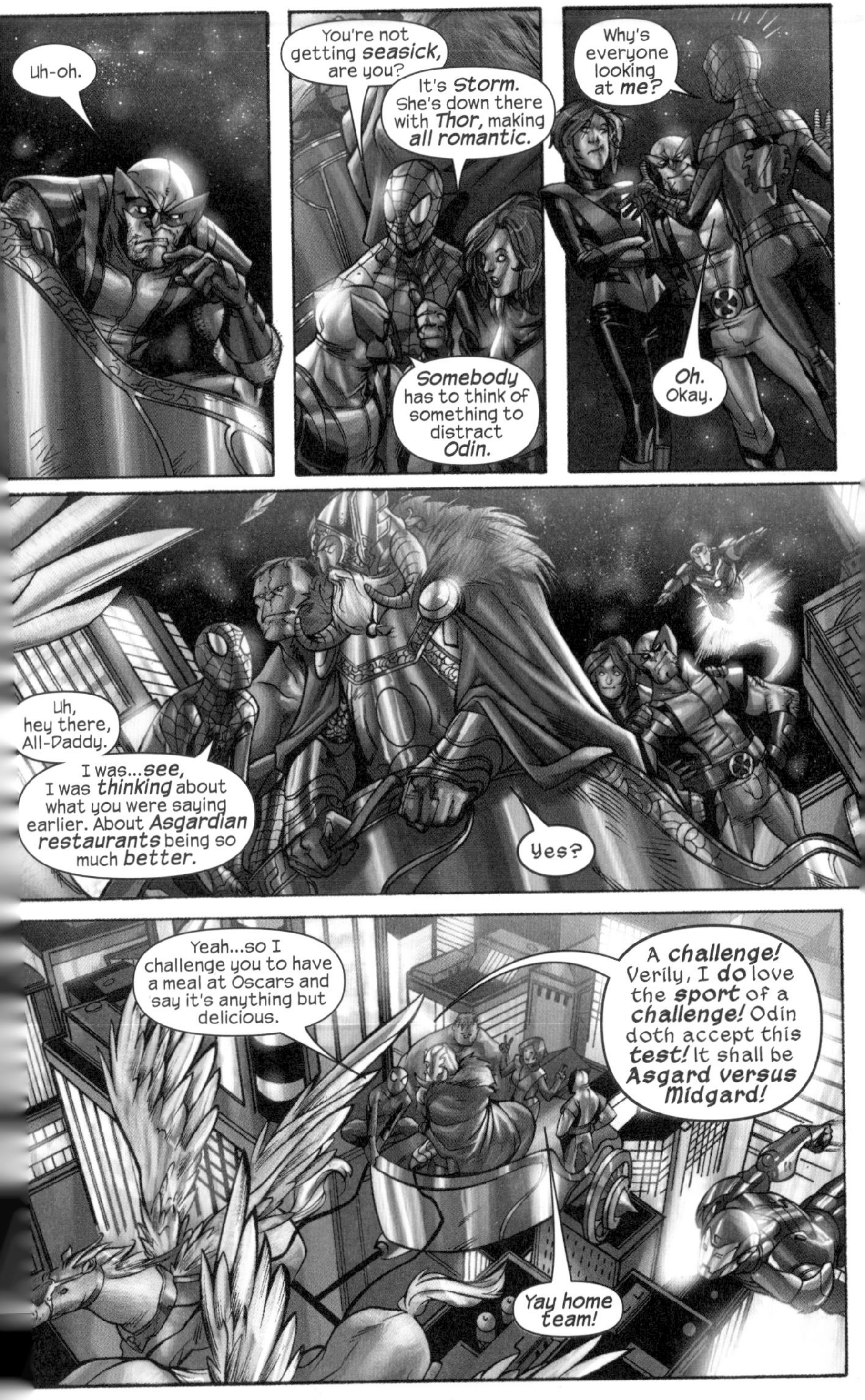
Uh-oh.
You're not getting seasick, are you?
It's Storm. She's down there with Thor, making all romantic.
Somebody has to think of something to distract Odin.
Why's everyone looking at me?
Oh. Okay.
Uh, hey there, All-Daddy.
I was...see, I was thinking about what you were saying earlier. About Asgardian restaurants being so much better.
Yes?
Yeah...so I challenge you to have a meal at Oscars and say it's anything but delicious.
A challenge! Verily, I do love the sport of a challenge! Odin doth accept this test! It shall be Asgard versus Midgard!
Yay home team!

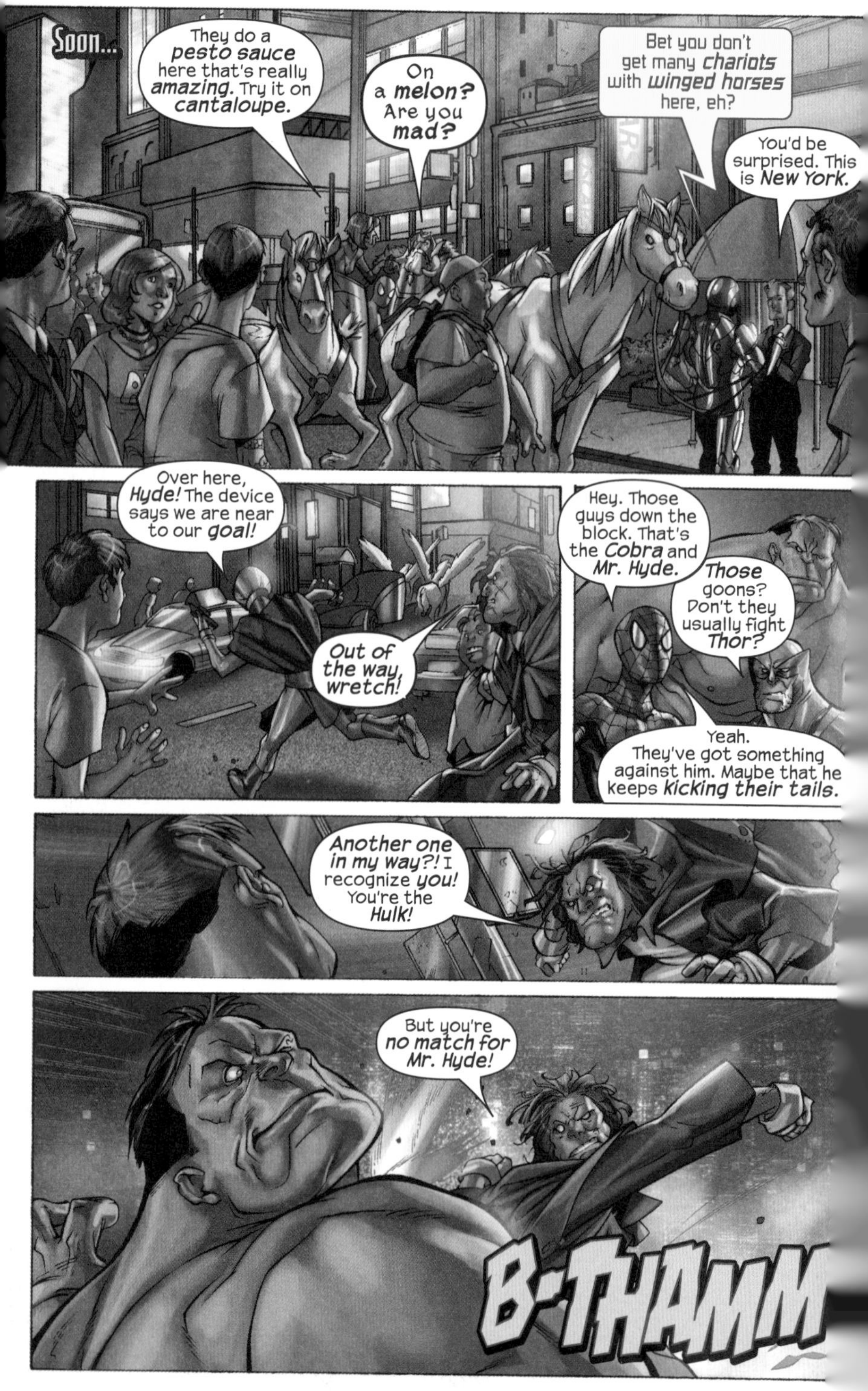
Soon...
They do a pesto sauce here that's really amazing. Try it on cantaloupe.
On a melon? Are you mad?
Bet you don't get many chariots with winged horses here, eh?
You'd be surprised. This is New York.
Over here, Hyde! The device says we are near to our goal!
Out of the way, wretch!
Hey. Those guys down the block. That's the Cobra and Mr. Hyde.
Those goons? Don't they usually fight Thor?
Yeah. They've got something against him. Maybe that he keeps kicking their tails.
Another one in my way?! I recognize you! You're the Hulk!
But you're no match for Mr. Hyde!
B-THAMM

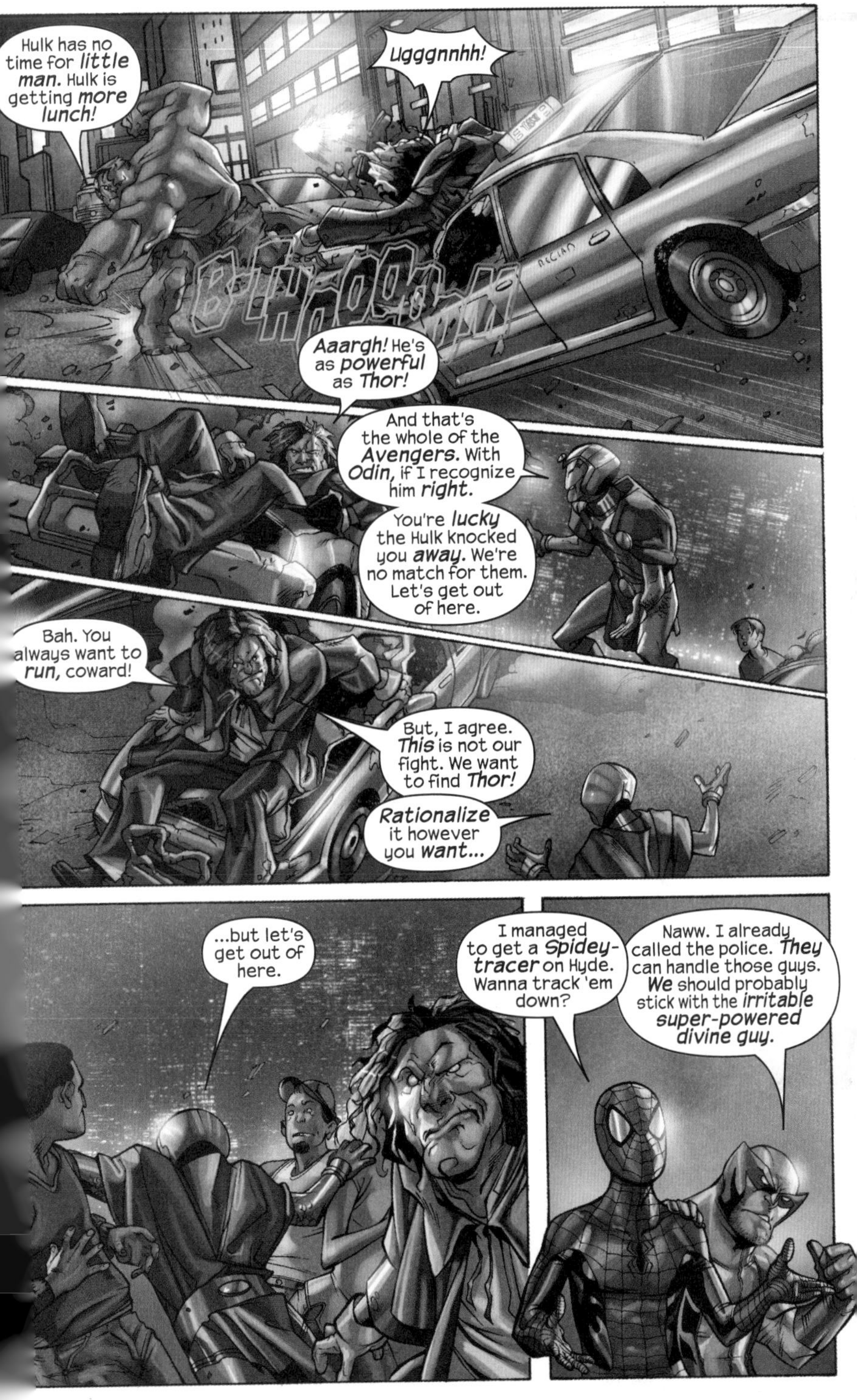
Hulk has no time for little man. Hulk is getting more lunch!
Ugggnnhh!
B'WHOOOM
Aaargh! He's as powerful as Thor!
And that's the whole of the Avengers. With Odin, if I recognize him right.
You're lucky the Hulk knocked you away. We're no match for them. Let's get out of here.
Bah. You always want to run, coward!
But, I agree. This is not our fight. We want to find Thor!
Rationalize it however you want...
...but let's get out of here.
I managed to get a Spidey-tracer on Hyde. Wanna track 'em down?
Naww. I already called the police. They can handle those guys. We should probably stick with the irritable super-powered divine guy.

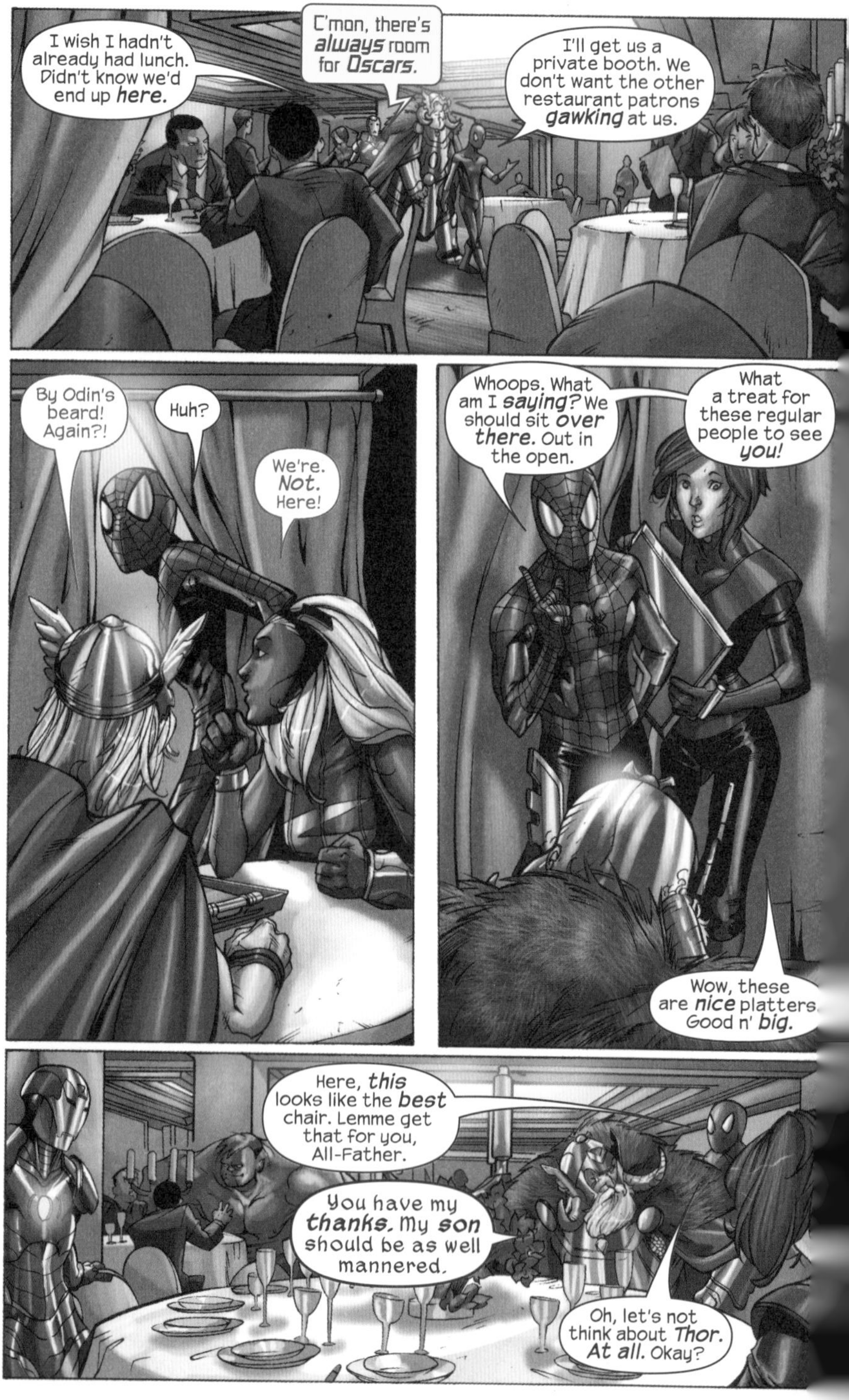
I wish I hadn't already had lunch. Didn't know we'd end up here.
C'mon, there's always room for Oscars.
I'll get us a private booth. We don't want the other restaurant patrons gawking at us.
By Odin's beard! Again?!
Huh?
We're. Not. Here!
Whoops. What am I saying? We should sit over there. Out in the open.
What a treat for these regular people to see you!
Wow, these are nice platters. Good n' big.
Here, this looks like the best chair. Lemme get that for you, All-Father.
You have my thanks. My son should be as well mannered.
Oh, let's not think about Thor. At all. Okay?

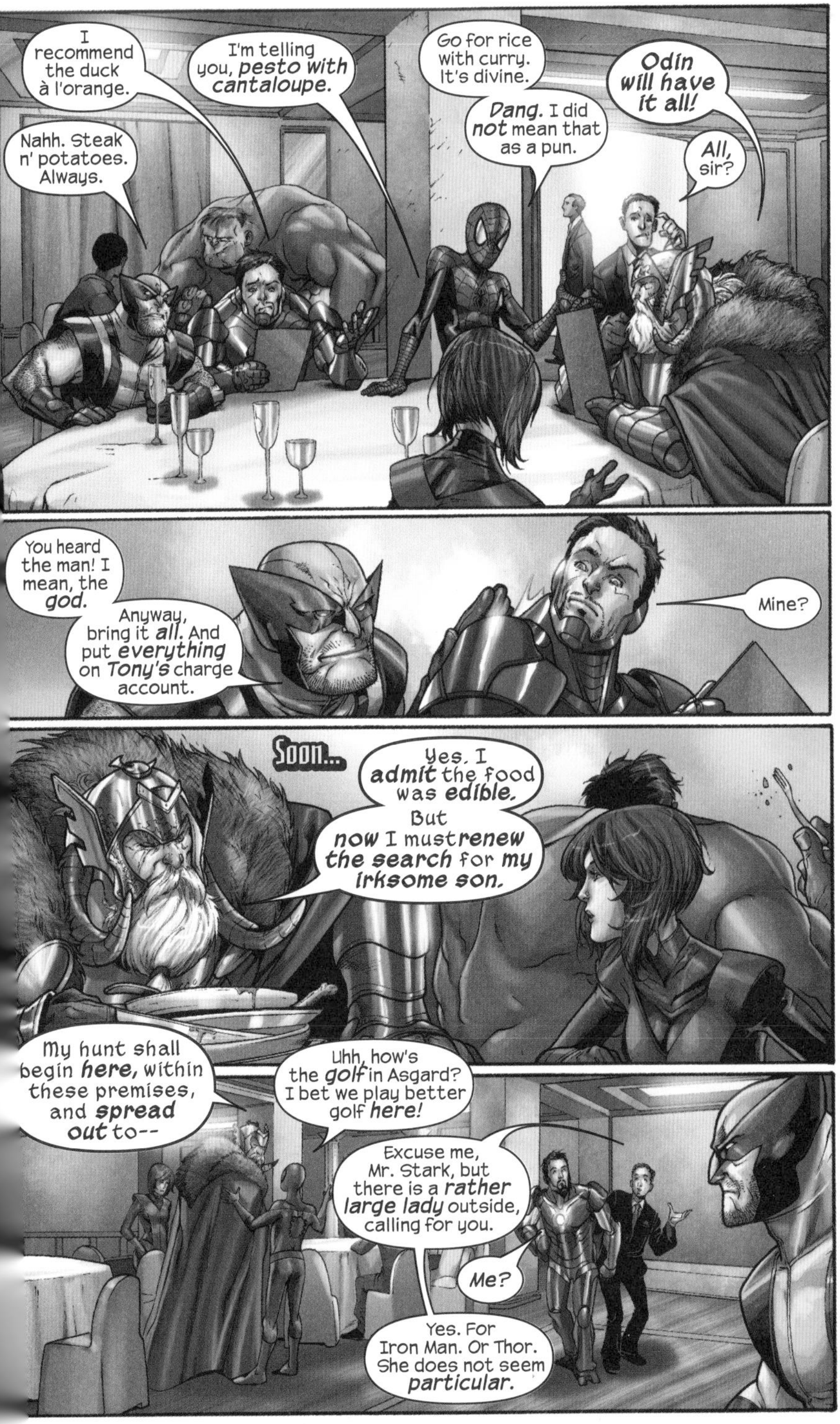
I recommend the duck à l'orange.
Nahh. Steak n' potatoes. Always.
I'm telling you, pesto with cantaloupe.
Go for rice with curry. It's divine.
Dang. I did not mean that as a pun.
Odin will have it all!
All, sir?
You heard the man! I mean, the god.
Anyway, bring it all. And put everything on Tony's charge account.
Mine?
Soon...
Yes. I admit the food was edible.
But now I must renew the search for my irksome son.
My hunt shall begin here, within these premises, and spread out to--
Uhh, how's the golf in Asgard? I bet we play better golf here!
Excuse me, Mr. Stark, but there is a rather large lady outside, calling for you.
Me?
Yes. For Iron Man. Or Thor. She does not seem particular.

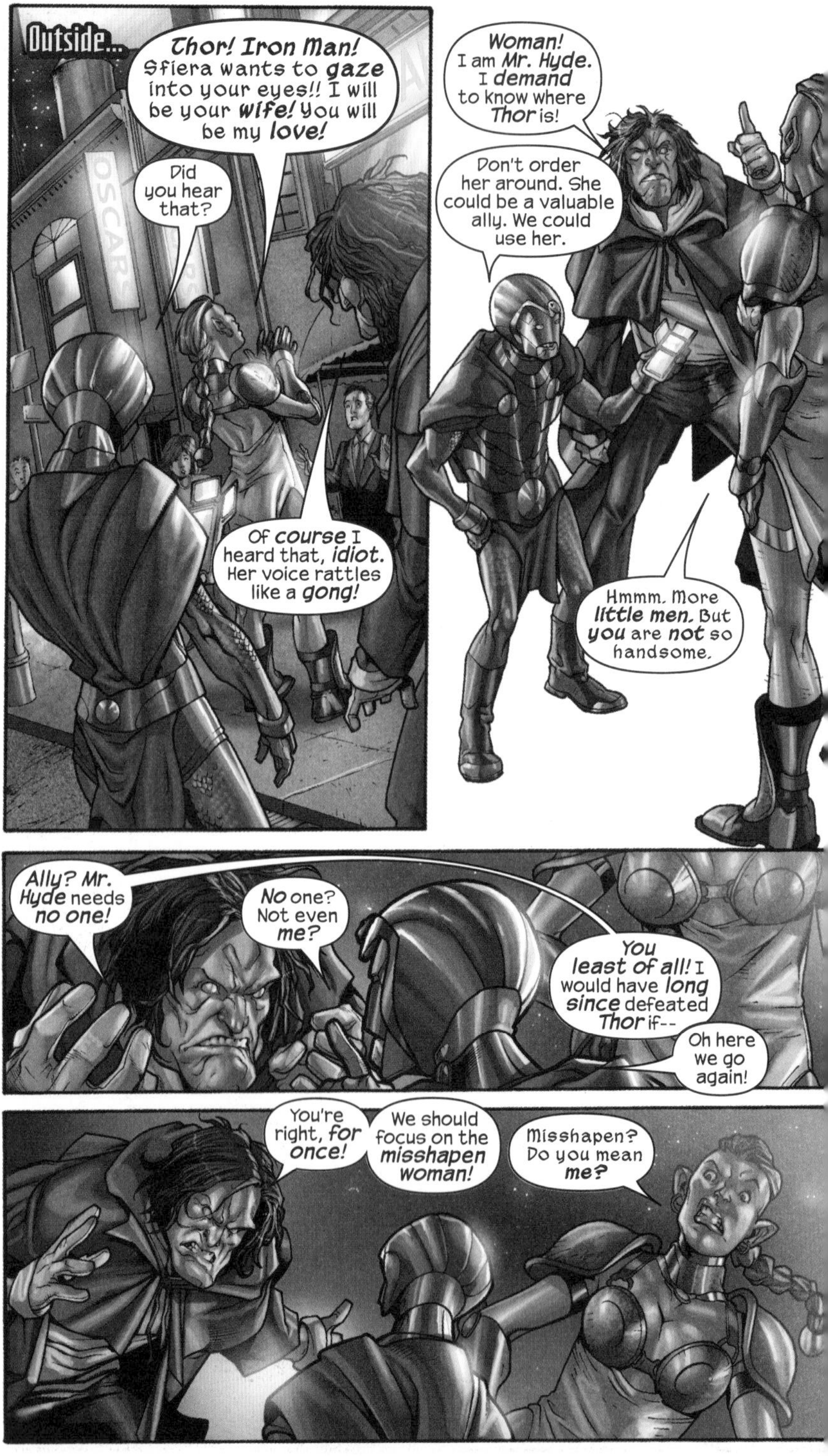
Outside...
Thor! Iron Man! Sfiera wants to gaze into your eyes!! I will be your wife! You will be my love!
Did you hear that?
Of course I heard that, idiot. Her voice rattles like a gong!
Woman! I am Mr. Hyde. I demand to know where Thor is!
Don't order her around. She could be a valuable ally. We could use her.
Hmmm. More little men. But you are not so handsome.
Ally? Mr. Hyde needs no one!
No one? Not even me?
You least of all! I would have long since defeated Thor if--
Oh here we go again!
You're right, for once!
We should focus on the misshapen woman!
Misshapen? Do you mean me?

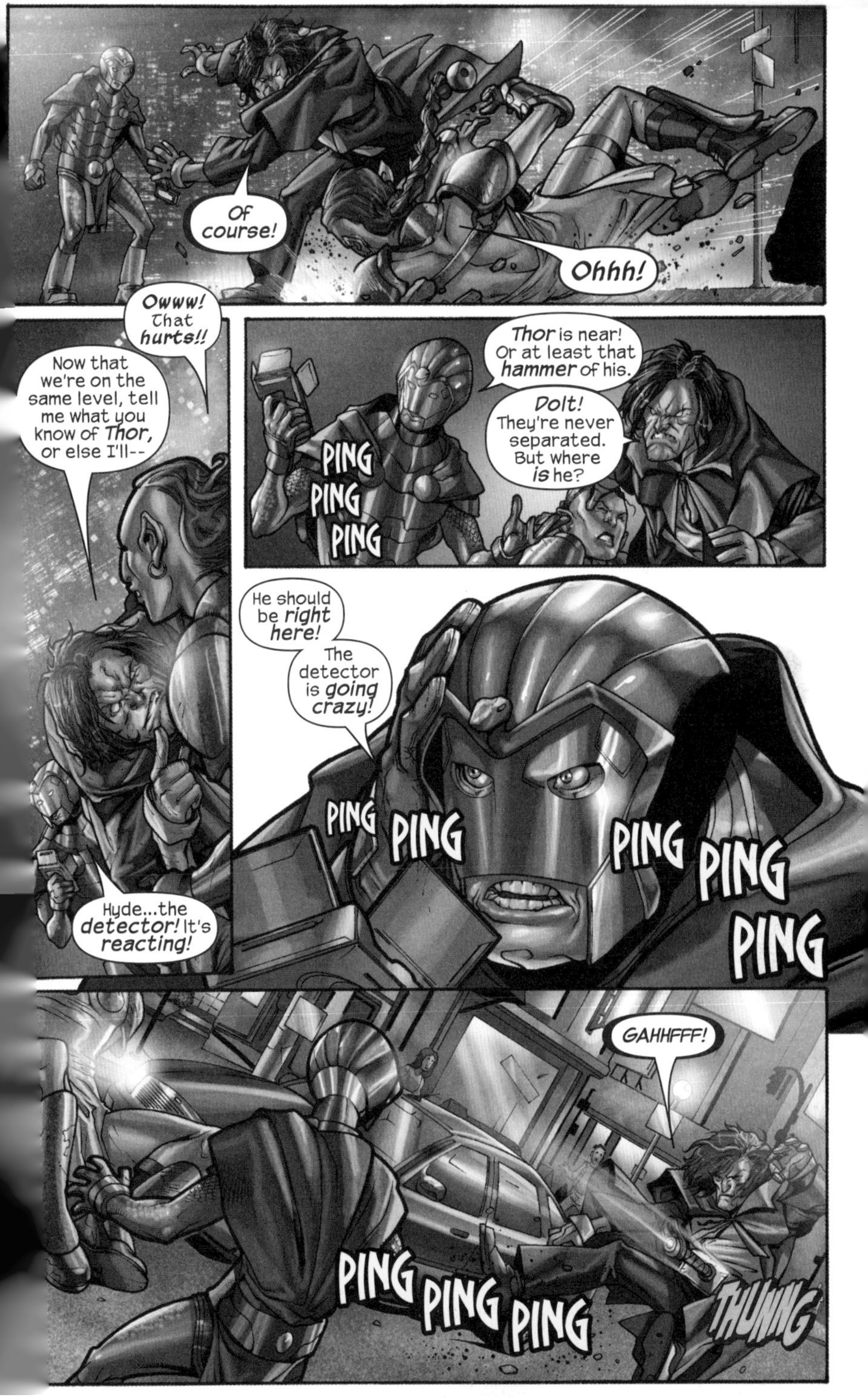
Of course!
Ohhh!
Owww! That hurts!!
Now that we're on the same level, tell me what you know of Thor, or else I'll--
Hyde...the detector! It's reacting!
Thor is near! Or at least that hammer of his.
PING PING PING
Dolt! They're never separated. But where is he?
He should be right here!
The detector is going crazy!
PING PING PING PING PING
GAHHFFF!
PING PING PING
THUNNG

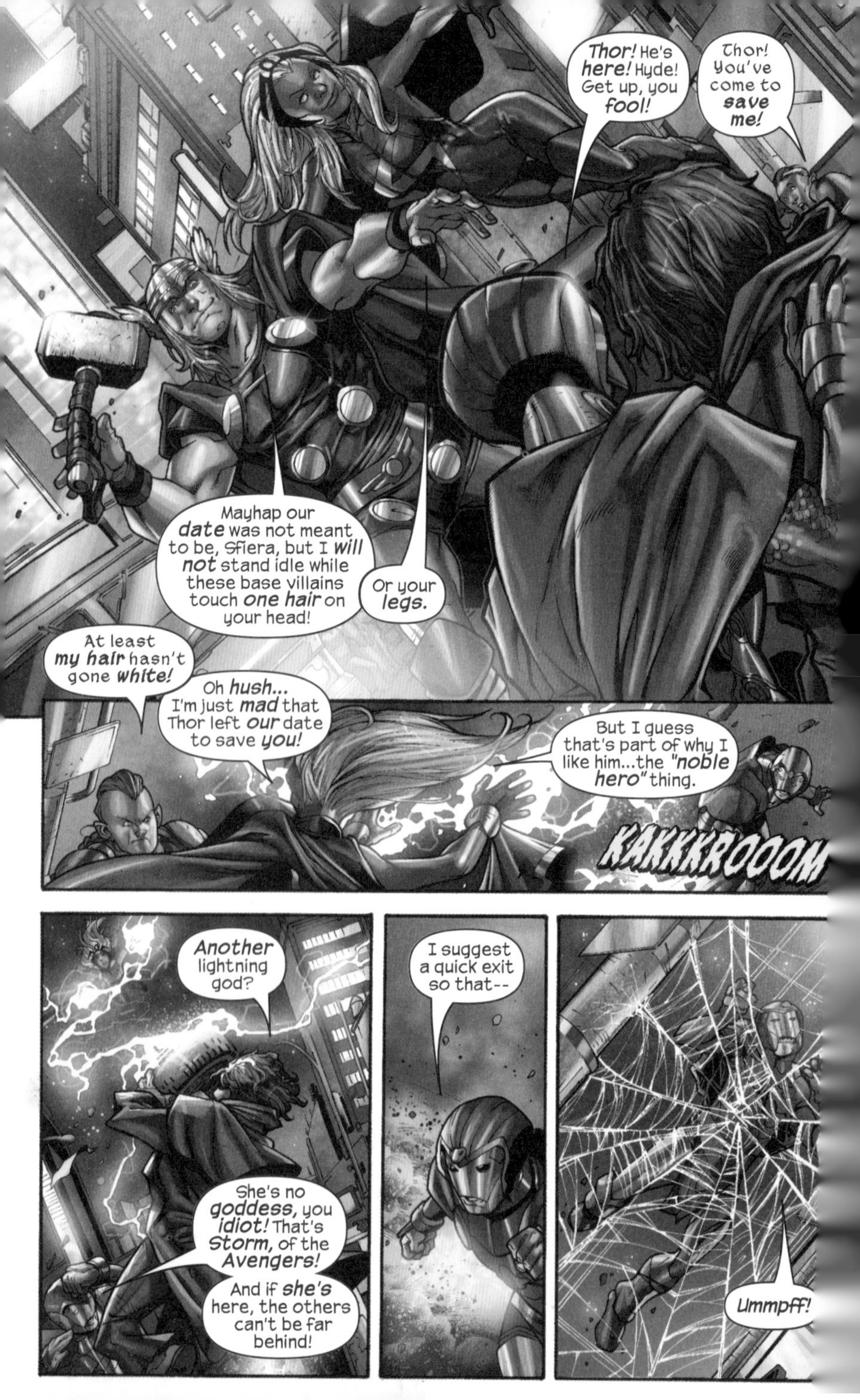
Thor! He's here! Hyde! Get up, you fool!
Thor! You've come to save me!
Mayhap our date was not meant to be, Sfiera, but I will not stand idle while these base villains touch one hair on your head!
Or your legs.
At least my hair hasn't gone white!
Oh hush... I'm just mad that Thor left our date to save you!
But I guess that's part of why I like him...the "noble hero" thing.
KAKKKROOOM
Another lightning god?
She's no goddess, you idiot! That's Storm, of the Avengers!
And if she's here, the others can't be far behind!
I suggest a quick exit so that--
Ummpff!

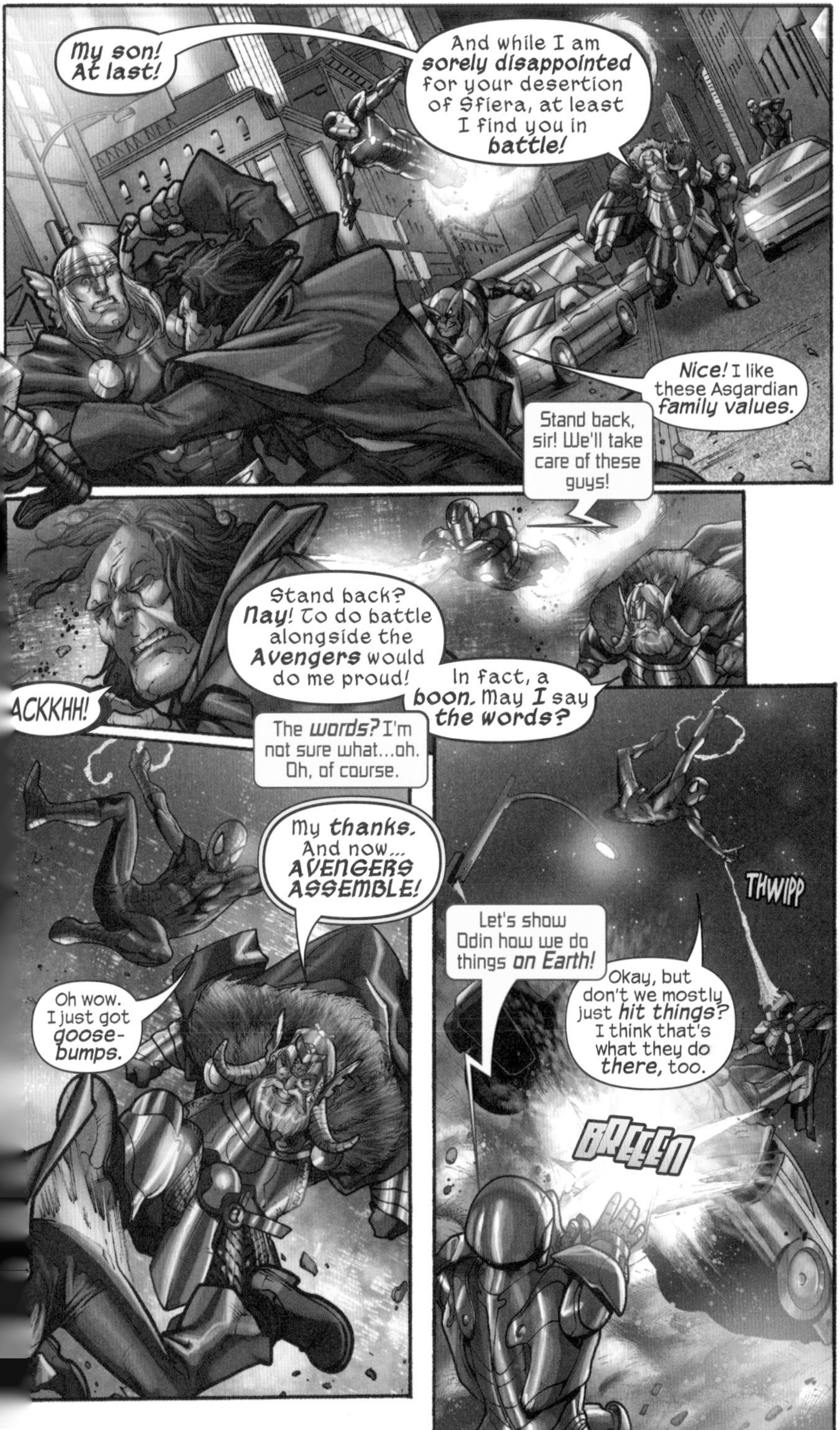
My son! At last!
And while I am sorely disappointed for your desertion of Sfiera, at least I find you in battle!
Nice! I like these Asgardian family values.
Stand back, sir! We'll take care of these guys!
Stand back? Nay! To do battle alongside the Avengers would do me proud!
ACKKHH!
In fact, a boon. May I say the words?
The words? I'm not sure what...oh. Oh, of course.
My thanks. And now... AVENGERS ASSEMBLE!
Oh wow. I just got goose-bumps.
THWIPP
Let's show Odin how we do things on Earth!
Okay, but don't we mostly just hit things? I think that's what they do there, too.
BREEEN

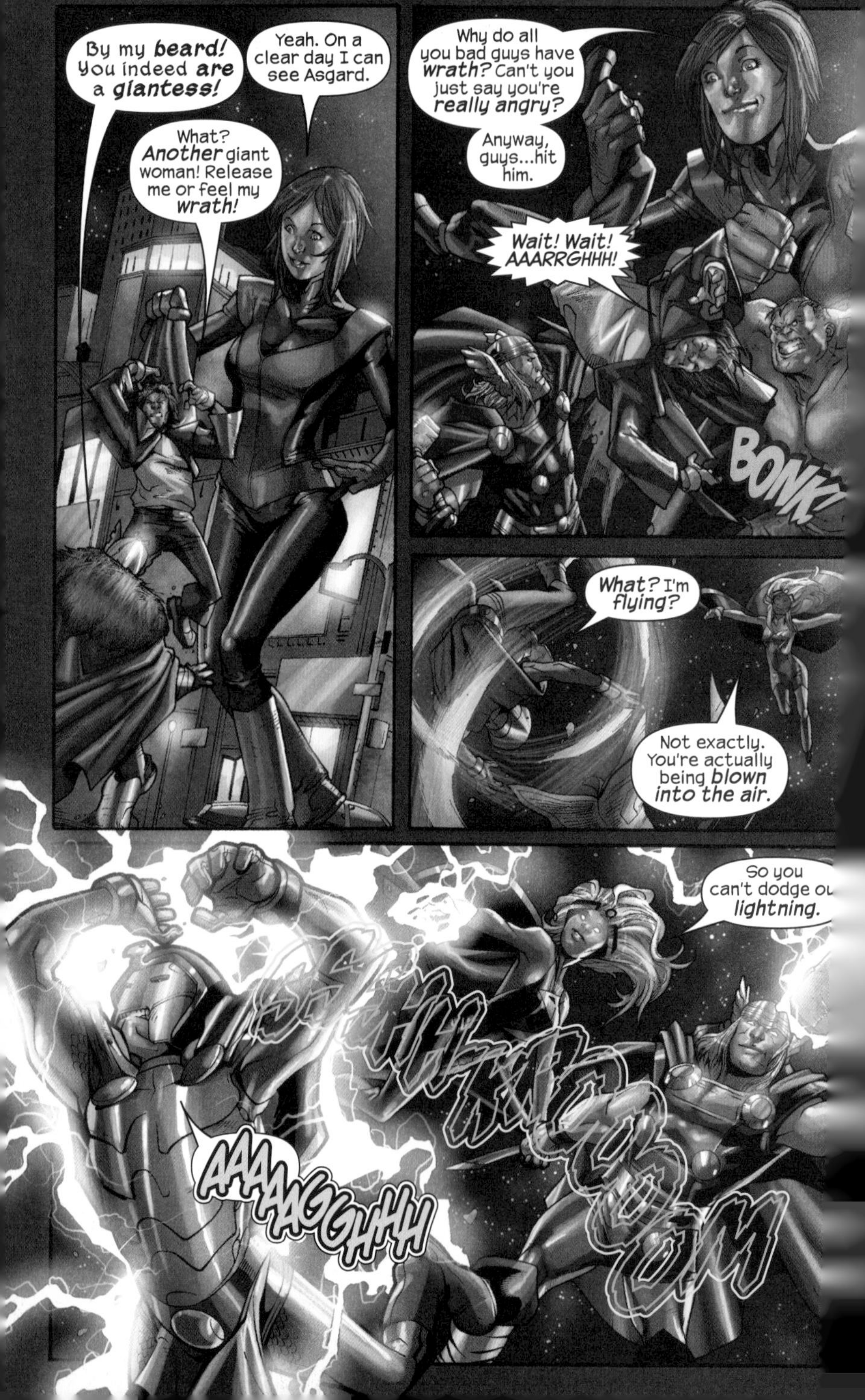
By my beard! You indeed are a giantess!
Yeah. On a clear day I can see Asgard.
What? Another giant woman! Release me or feel my wrath!
Why do all you bad guys have wrath? Can't you just say you're really angry?
Anyway, guys...hit him.
Wait! Wait! AAARRGHHH!
BONK!
What? I'm flying?
Not exactly. You're actually being blown into the air.
So you can't dodge ou
lightning.
AAAAAGGHHH

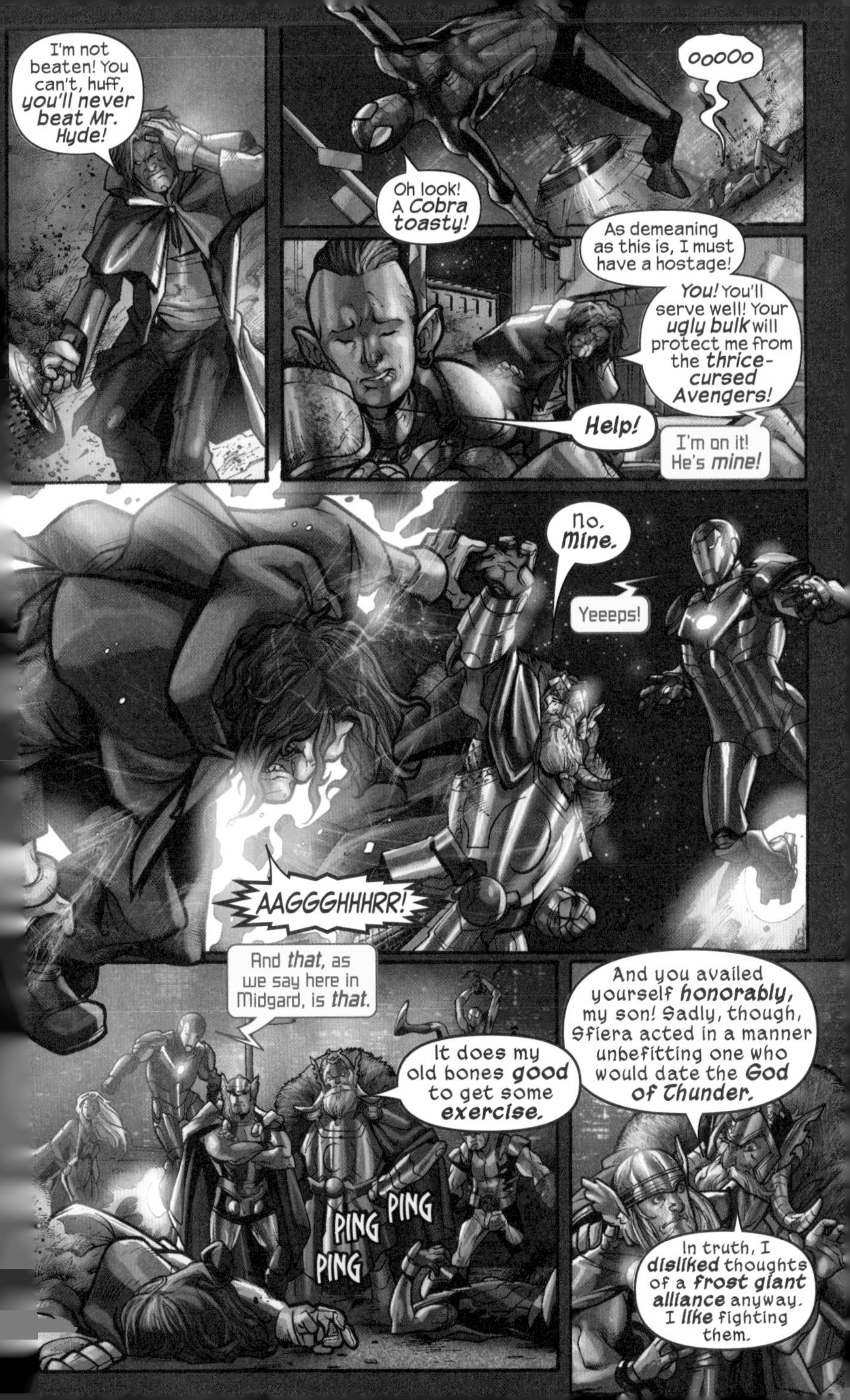
I'm not beaten! You can't, huff, you'll never beat Mr. Hyde!
OOOOO
Oh look! A Cobra toasty!
As demeaning as this is, I must have a hostage!
You! You'll serve well! Your ugly bulk will protect me from the thrice-cursed Avengers!
Help!
I'm on it! He's mine!
No. Mine.
Yeeeps!
AAGGGHHHRR!
And that, as we say here in Midgard, is that.
It does my old bones good to get some exercise.
PING
PING
PING
And you availed yourself honorably, my son! Sadly, though, Sfiera acted in a manner unbefitting one who would date the God of Thunder.
In truth, I disliked thoughts of a frost giant alliance anyway. I like fighting them.

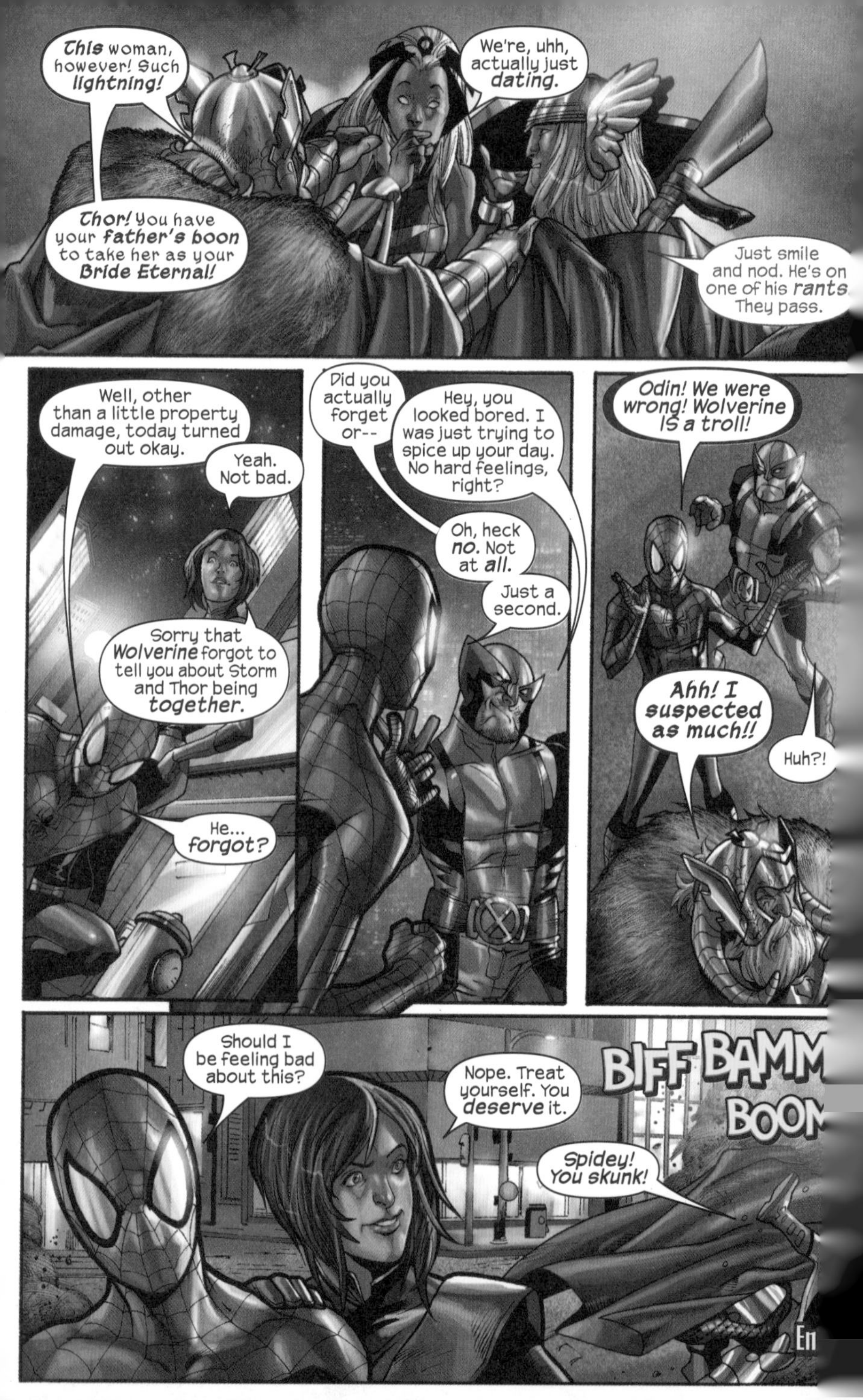
This woman, however! Such lightning!
We're, uhh, actually just dating.
Thor! You have your father's boon to take her as your Bride Eternal!
Just smile and nod. He's on one of his rants. They pass.
Well, other than a little property damage, today turned out okay.
Yeah. Not bad.
Sorry that Wolverine forgot to tell you about Storm and Thor being together.
He... forgot?
Did you actually forget or--
Hey, you looked bored. I was just trying to spice up your day. No hard feelings, right?
Oh, heck no. Not at all.
Just a second.
Odin! We were wrong! Wolverine IS a troll!
Ahh! I suspected as much!!
Huh?!
Should I be feeling bad about this?
Nope. Treat yourself. You deserve it.
BIFF BAMM
BOO
Spidey! You skunk!
En

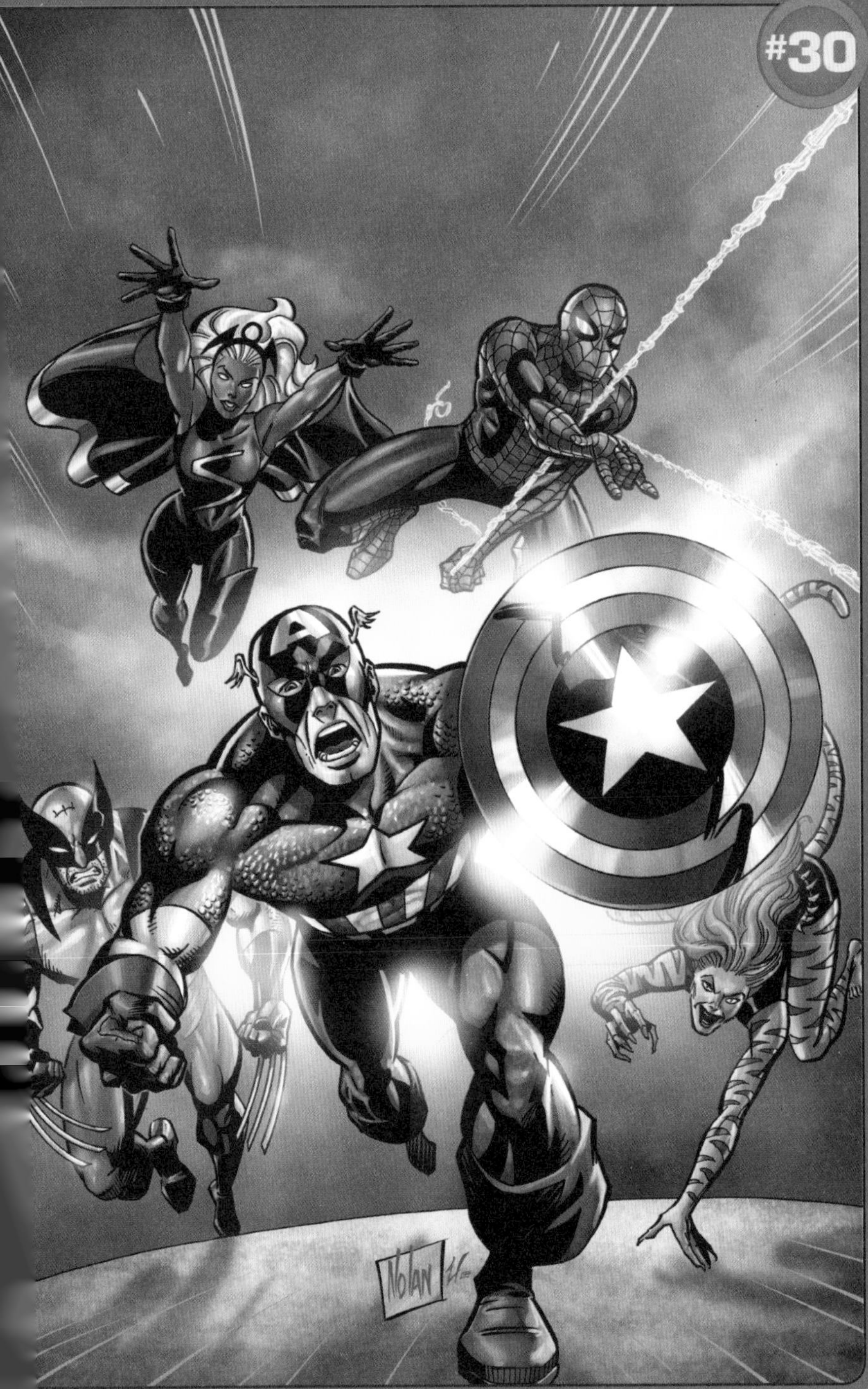

#30
NOLAN

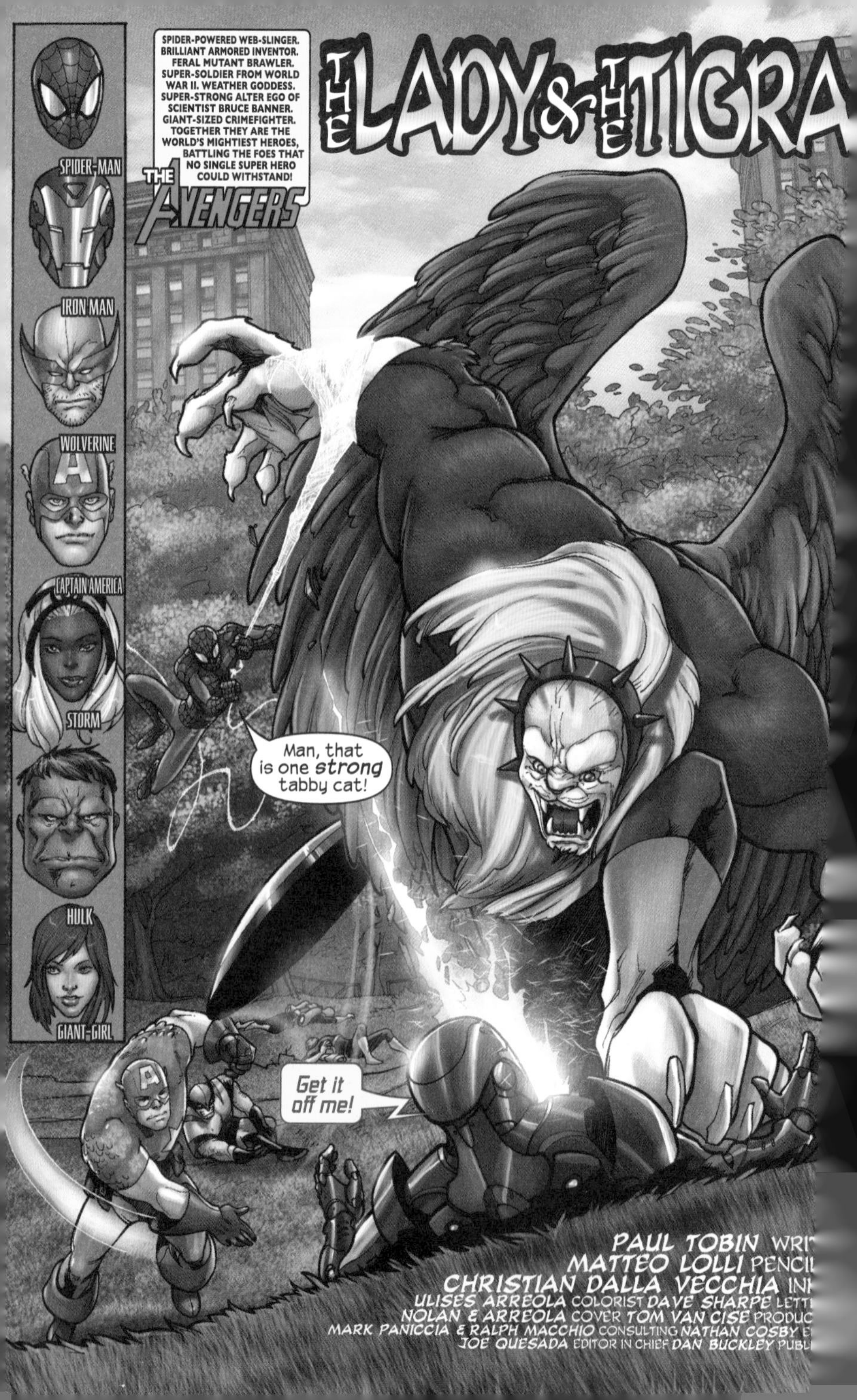
SPIDER-POWERED WEB-SLINGER. BRILLIANT ARMORED INVENTOR. FERAL MUTANT BRAWLER. SUPER-SOLDIER FROM WORLD WAR II. WEATHER GODDESS. SUPER-STRONG ALTER EGO OF SCIENTIST BRUCE BANNER. GIANT-SIZED CRIMEFIGHTER. TOGETHER THEY ARE THE WORLD'S MIGHTIEST HEROES, BATTLING THE FOES THAT NO SINGLE SUPER HERO COULD WITHSTAND!
THE AVENGERS
THE LADY & THE TIGRA
SPIDER-MAN
IRON MAN
WOLVERINE
CAPTAIN AMERICA
STORM
HULK
GIANT-GIRL
Man, that is one strong tabby cat!
Get it off me!
PAUL TOBIN WRIT
MATTEO LOLLI PENCIL
CHRISTIAN DALLA VECCHIA INK
ULISES ARREOLA COLORIST DAVE SHARPE LETTE
NOLAN & ARREOLA COVER TOM VAN CISE PRODUC
MARK PANICCIA & RALPH MACCHIO CONSULTING NATHAN COSBY E
JOE QUESADA EDITOR IN CHIEF DAN BUCKLEY PUBL

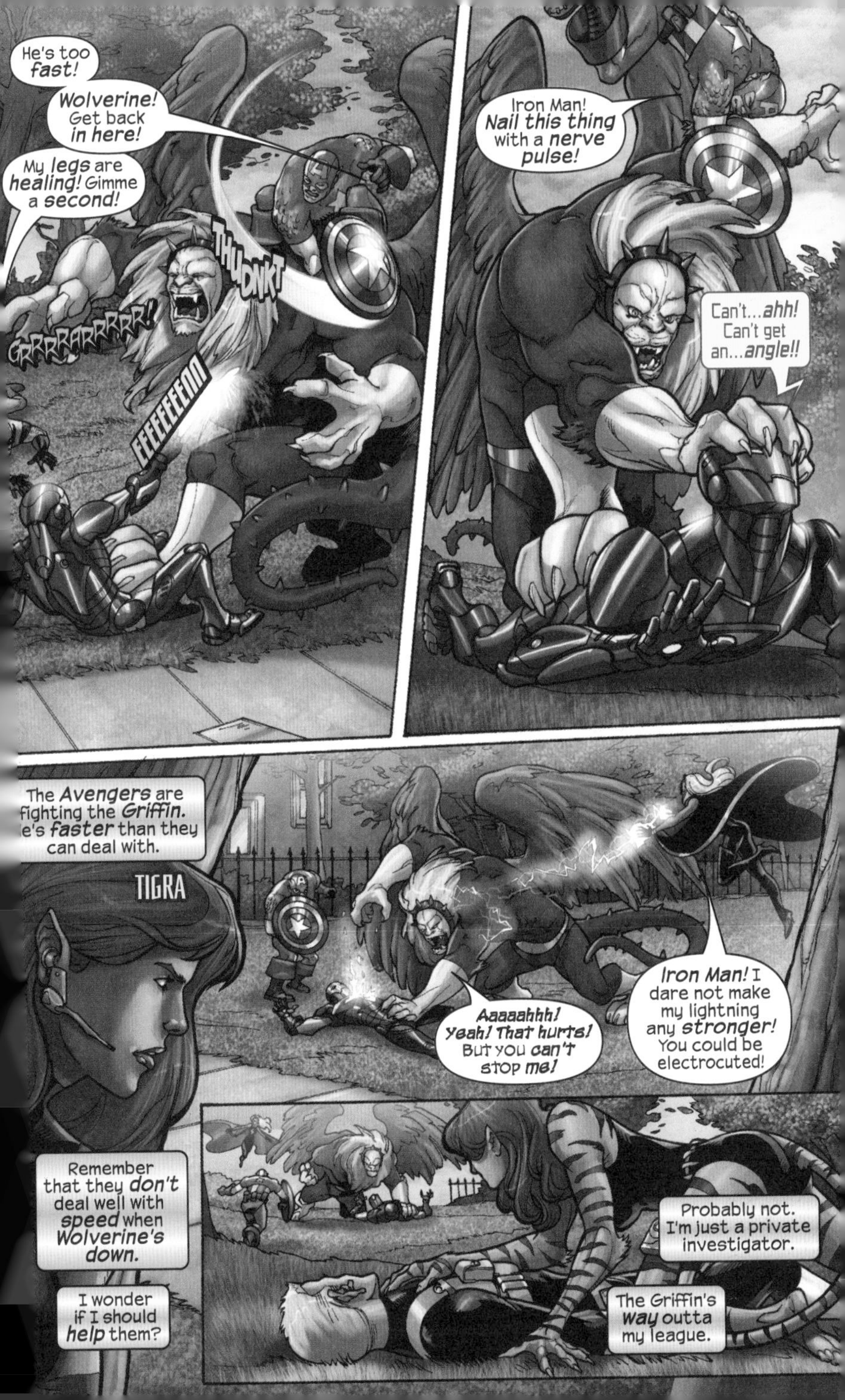

He's too fast!
Wolverine! Get back in here!
My legs are healing! Gimme a second!
THUDNKT
GRRRARRRRR!
EEEEEEEENN
Iron Man! Nail this thing with a nerve pulse!
Can't...ahh! Can't get an...angle!!
The Avengers are fighting the Griffin. e's faster than they can deal with.
TIGRA
Aaaaahhh! Yeah! That hurts! But you can't stop me!
Iron Man! I dare not make my lightning any stronger! You could be electrocuted!
Remember that they don't deal well with speed when Wolverine's down.
I wonder if I should help them?
Probably not. I'm just a private investigator.
The Griffin's way outta my league.

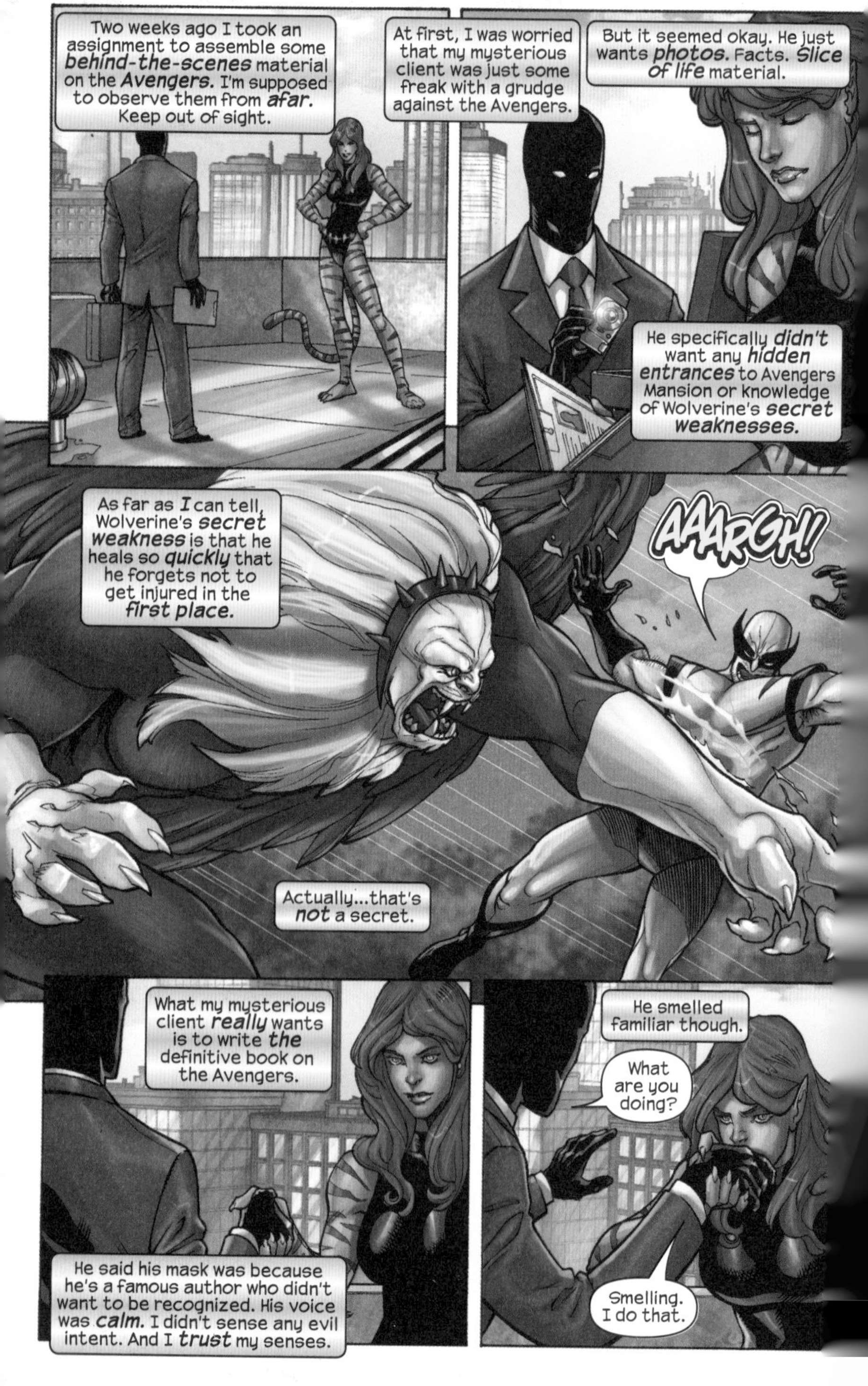
Two weeks ago I took an assignment to assemble some behind-the-scenes material on the Avengers. I'm supposed to observe them from afar. Keep out of sight.
At first, I was worried that my mysterious client was just some freak with a grudge against the Avengers.
But it seemed okay. He just wants photos. Facts. Slice of life material.
He specifically didn't want any hidden entrances to Avengers Mansion or knowledge of Wolverine's secret weaknesses.
As far as I can tell, Wolverine's secret weakness is that he heals so quickly that he forgets not to get injured in the first place.
AAARGH!
Actually...that's not a secret.
What my mysterious client really wants is to write the definitive book on the Avengers.
He said his mask was because he's a famous author who didn't want to be recognized. His voice was calm. I didn't sense any evil intent. And I trust my senses.
He smelled familiar though.
What are you doing?
Smelling. I do that.

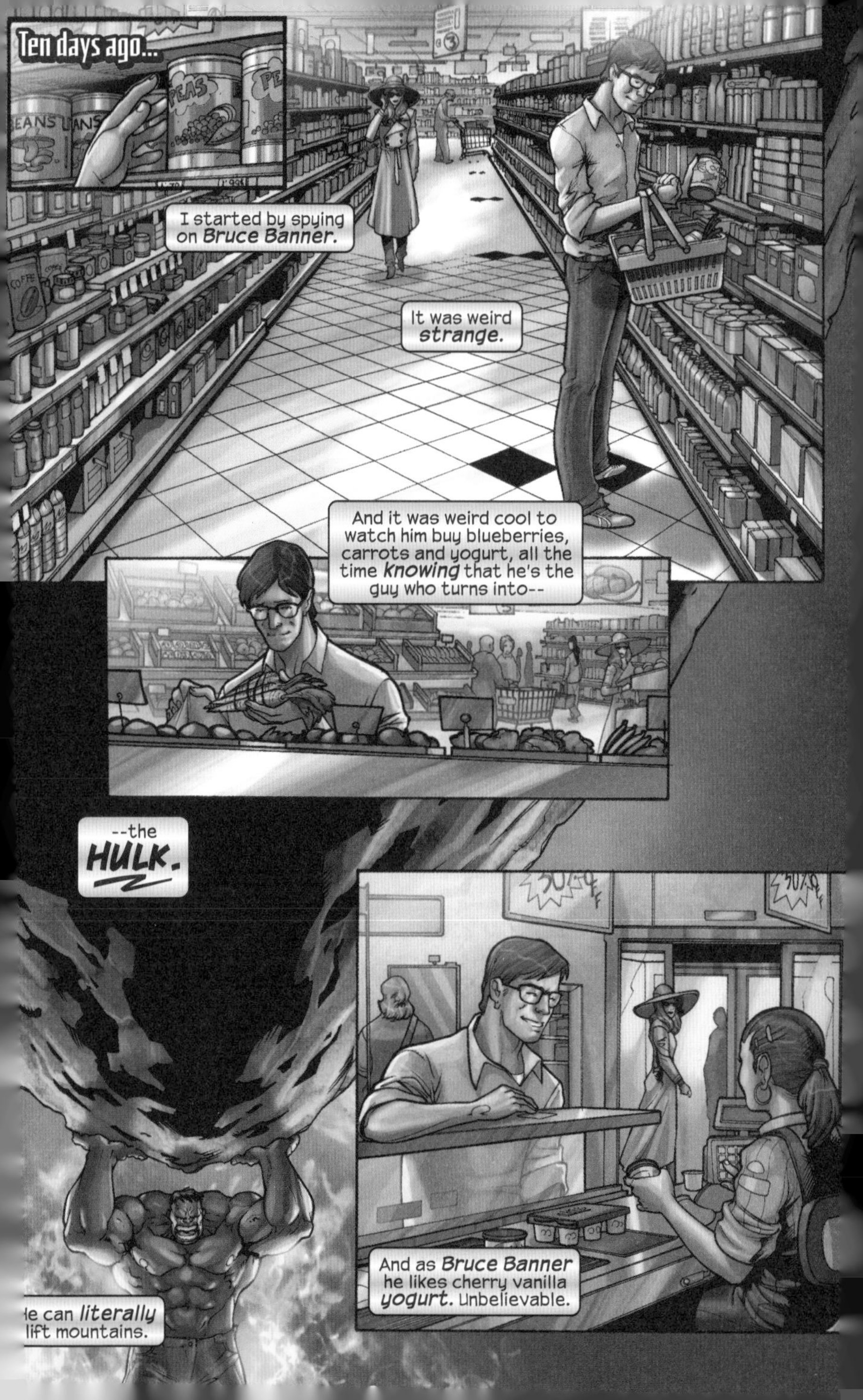

Ten days ago...
BEANS
PEAS
I started by spying on Bruce Banner.
It was weird strange.
And it was weird cool to watch him buy blueberries, carrots and yogurt, all the time knowing that he's the guy who turns into--
--the HULK.
He can literally lift mountains.
And as Bruce Banner he likes cherry vanilla yogurt. Unbelievable.

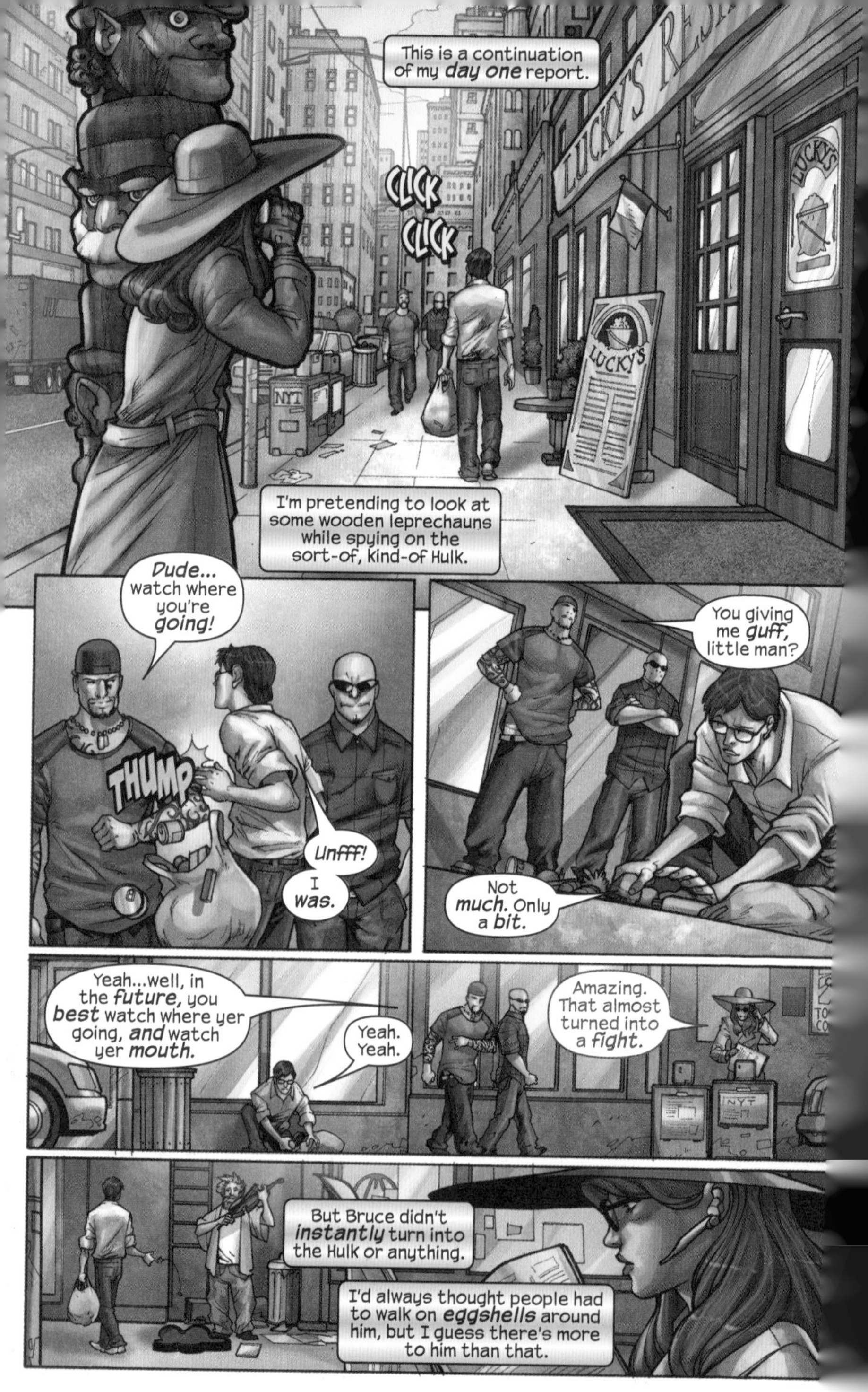

This is a continuation of my *day one* report.
LUCKY'S RES
LUCKY'S
CLICK
CLICK
NYT
LUCKY'S
I'm pretending to look at some wooden leprechauns while spying on the sort-of, kind-of Hulk.
Dude... watch where you're *going!*
THUMP
Unfff!
I *was.*
You giving me *guff,* little man?
Not *much.* Only a *bit.*
Yeah...well, in the *future,* you *best* watch where yer going, *and* watch yer *mouth.*
Yeah. Yeah.
Amazing. That almost turned into a *fight.*
NYT
But Bruce didn't *instantly* turn into the Hulk or anything.
I'd always thought people had to walk on *eggshells* around him, but I guess there's more to him than that.

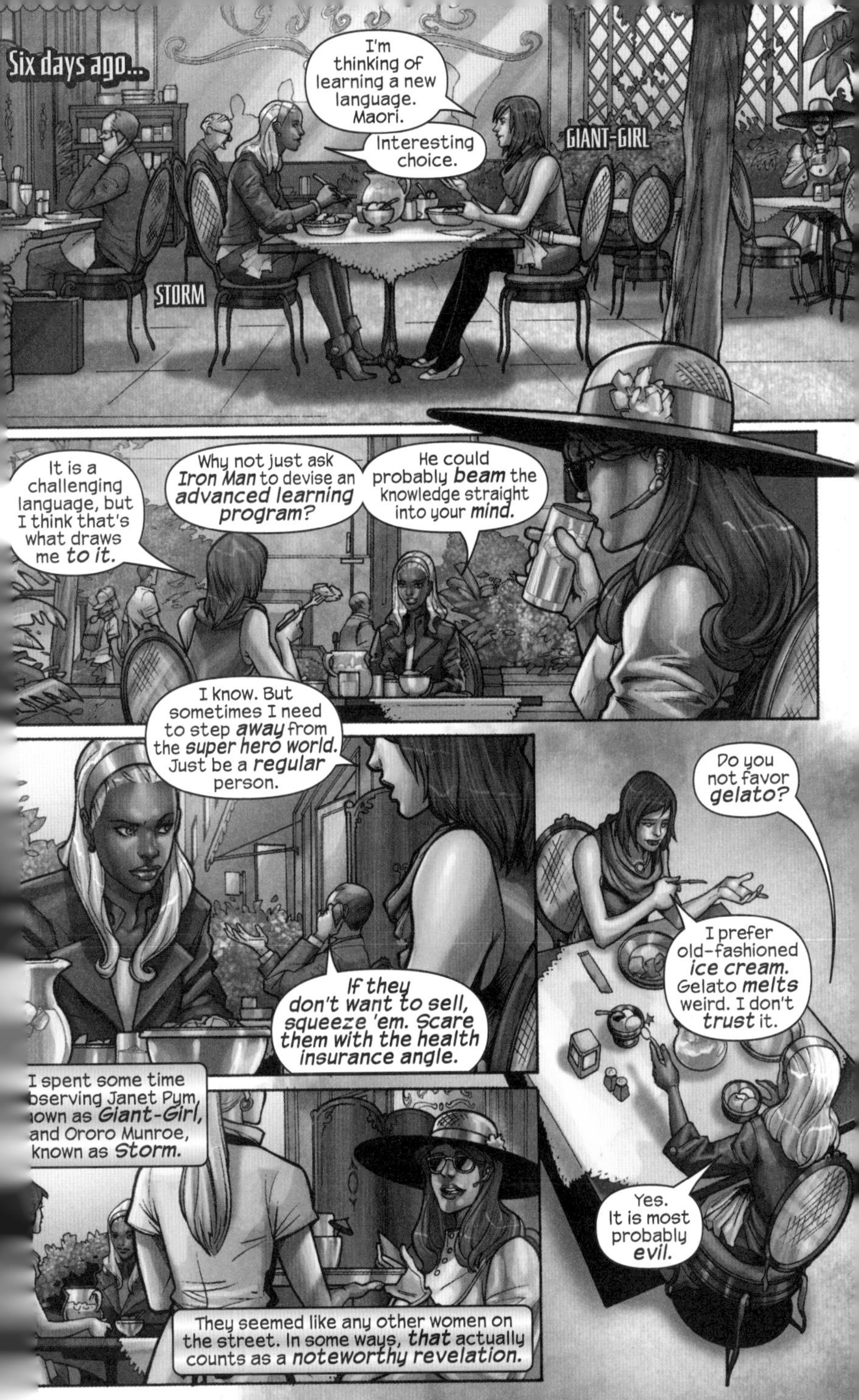

Six days ago...
I'm thinking of learning a new language. Maori.
Interesting choice.
GIANT-GIRL
STORM
It is a challenging language, but I think that's what draws me to it.
Why not just ask Iron Man to devise an advanced learning program?
He could probably beam the knowledge straight into your mind.
I know. But sometimes I need to step away from the super hero world. Just be a regular person.
If they don't want to sell, squeeze 'em. Scare them with the health insurance angle.
Do you not favor gelato?
I prefer old-fashioned ice cream. Gelato melts weird. I don't trust it.
Yes. It is most probably evil.
I spent some time observing Janet Pym, known as Giant-Girl, and Ororo Munroe, known as Storm.
They seemed like any other women on the street. In some ways, that actually counts as a noteworthy revelation.

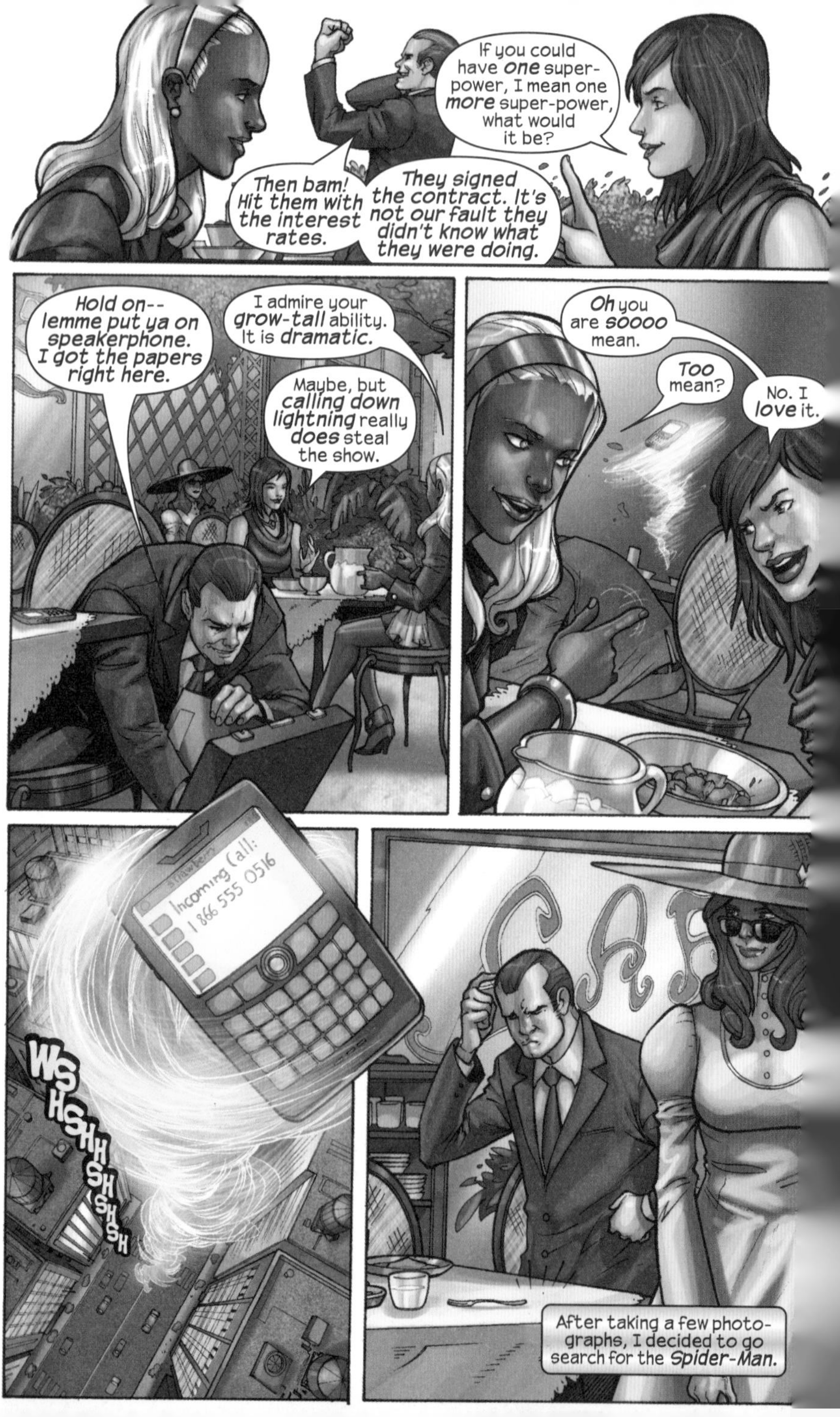

If you could have one super-power, I mean one more super-power, what would it be?
Then bam! Hit them with the interest rates.
They signed the contract. It's not our fault they didn't know what they were doing.
Hold on-- lemme put ya on speakerphone. I got the papers right here.
I admire your grow-tall ability. It is dramatic.
Maybe, but calling down lightning really does steal the show.
Oh you are soooo mean.
Too mean?
No. I love it.
Incoming Call: 1 866 555 0516
WSHSHHSHSH
After taking a few photo-graphs, I decided to go search for the Spider-Man.

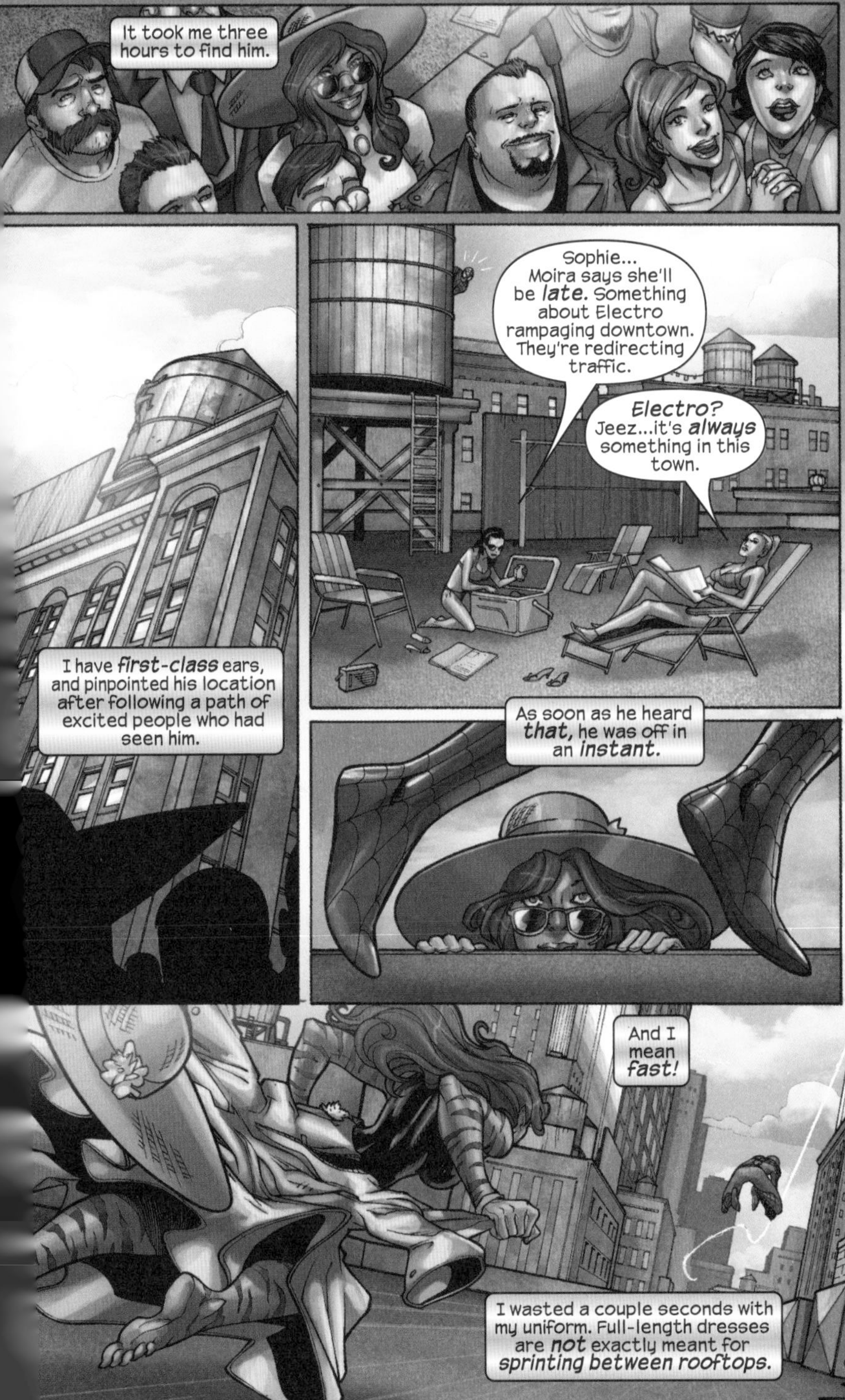
It took me three hours to find him.
I have first-class ears, and pinpointed his location after following a path of excited people who had seen him.
Sophie... Moira says she'll be late. Something about Electro rampaging downtown. They're redirecting traffic.
Electro? Jeez...it's always something in this town.
As soon as he heard that, he was off in an instant.
And I mean fast!
I wasted a couple seconds with my uniform. Full-length dresses are not exactly meant for sprinting between rooftops.

Later, I heard that the "Electro" report was false.

Just the usual exaggerated story of a downed power line.

But right then, I was running. Full speed.

THWAPPP

Akkpttt

K-THUMPT

My only consolation was that nobody witnessed my total defeat at the hands (make that wings) of a panicked pigeon.

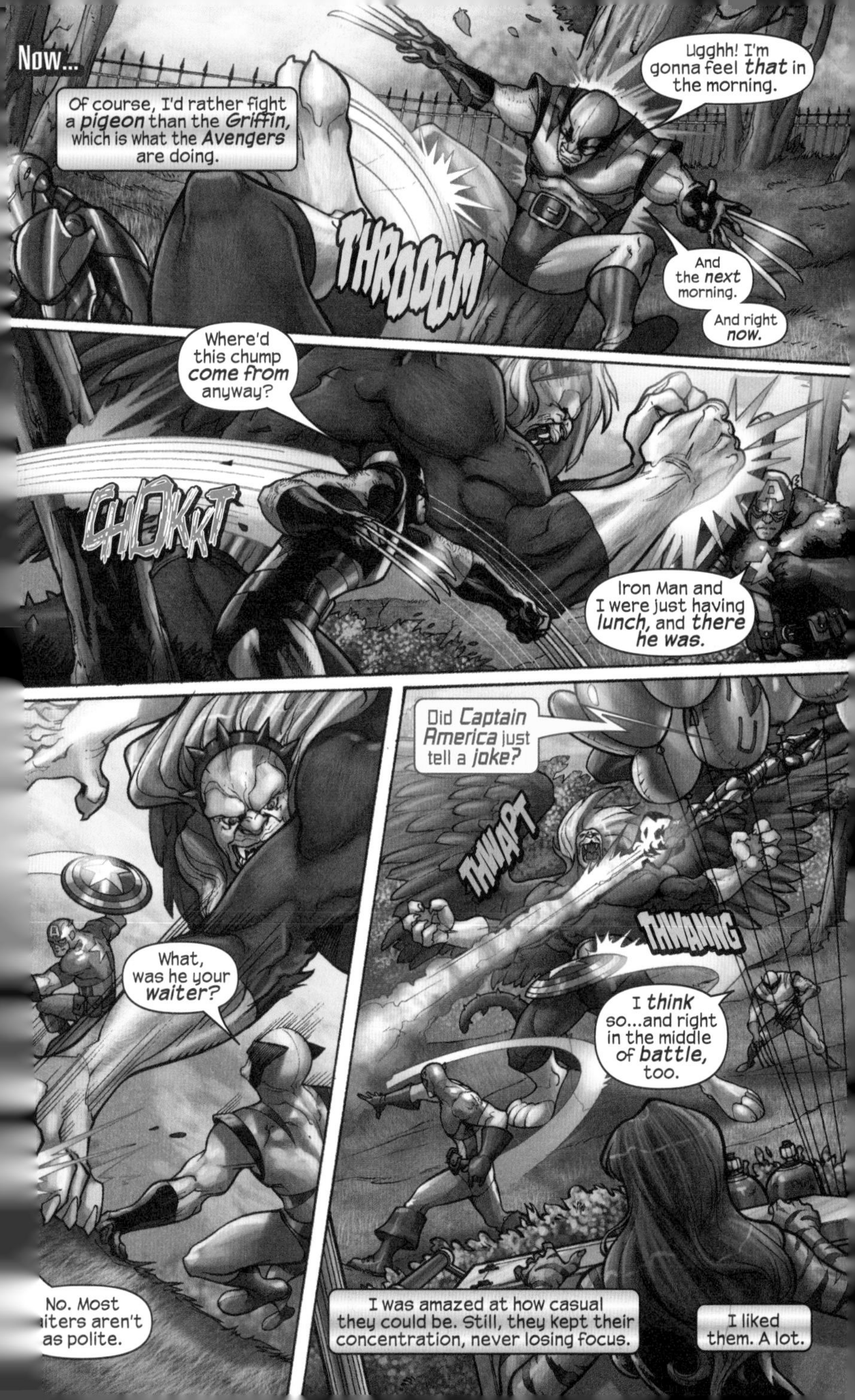
Now...
Of course, I'd rather fight a pigeon than the Griffin, which is what the Avengers are doing.
Ugghh! I'm gonna feel that in the morning.
THROOOM
And the next morning.
And right now.
Where'd this chump come from anyway?
CHOKKT
Iron Man and I were just having lunch, and there he was.
What, was he your waiter?
No. Most aiters aren't as polite.
Did Captain America just tell a joke?
THWAPT
THWANNG
I think so...and right in the middle of battle, too.
I was amazed at how casual they could be. Still, they kept their concentration, never losing focus.
I liked them. A lot.

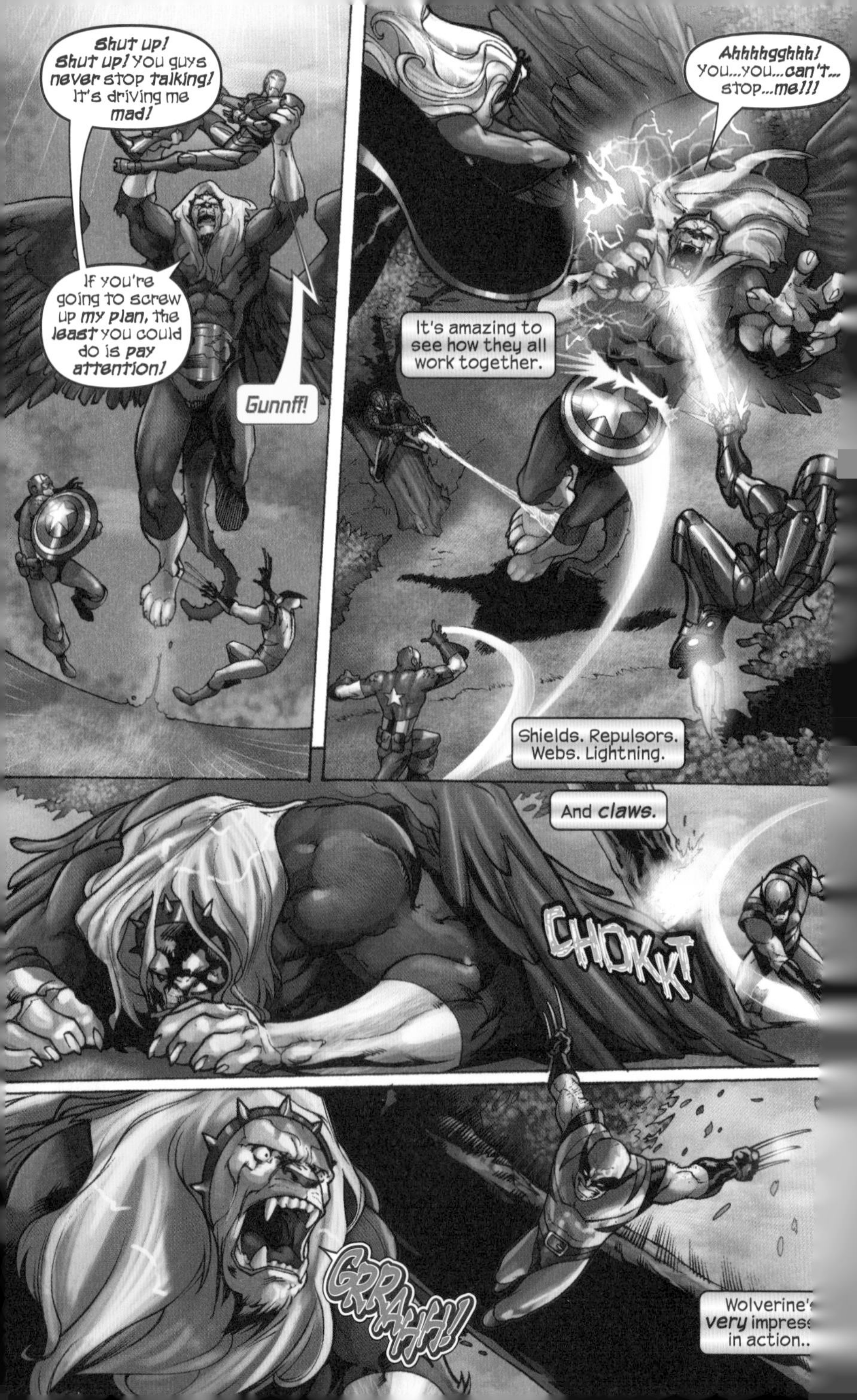
Shut up! Shut up! You guys never stop talking! It's driving me mad!
If you're going to screw up my plan, the least you could do is pay attention!
Gunnff!
Ahhhhgghhh! You...you...can't... stop...me!!!
It's amazing to see how they all work together.
Shields. Repulsors. Webs. Lightning.
And claws.
CHOKKT
GRRAHH!

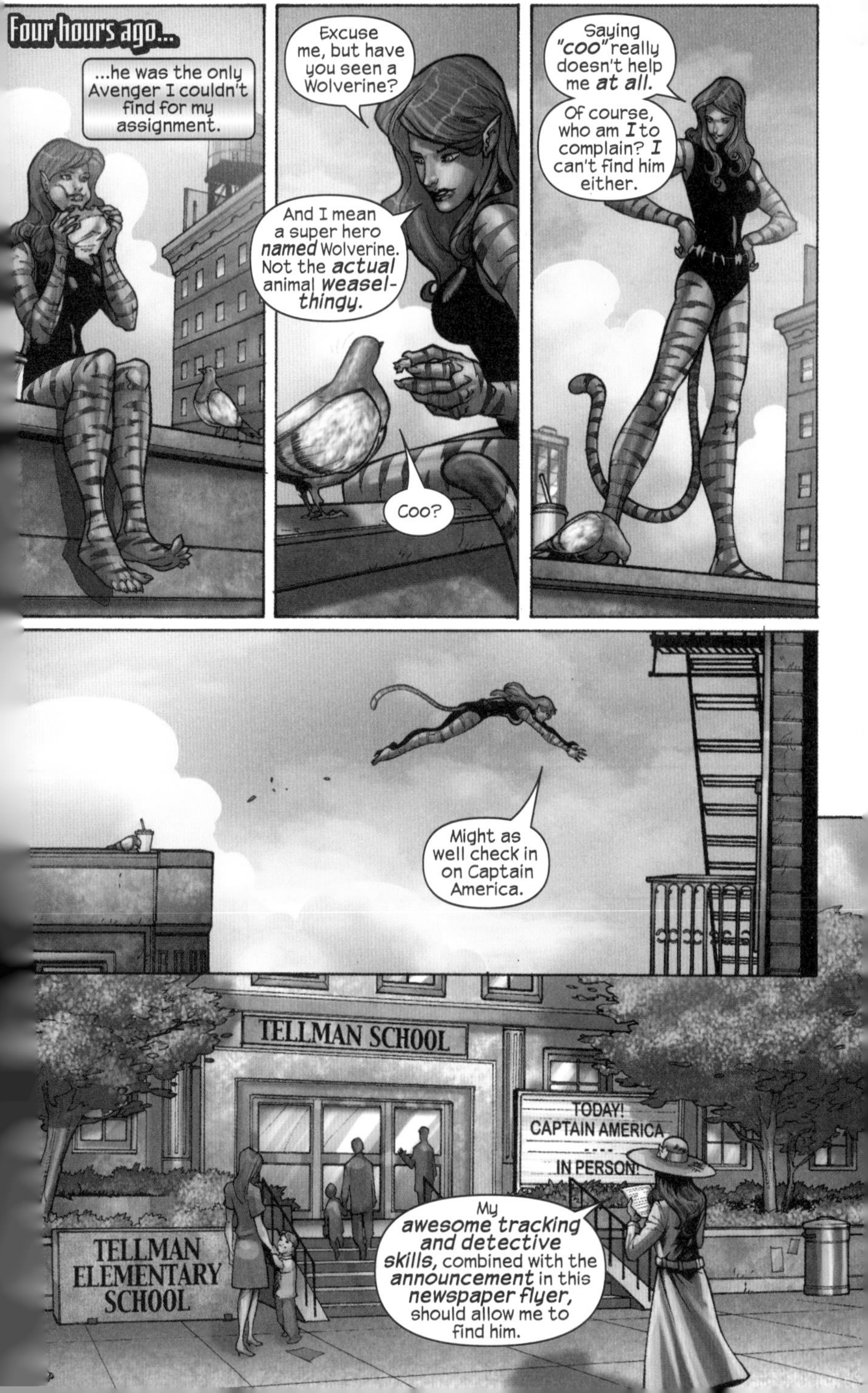
Four hours ago...
...he was the only Avenger I couldn't find for my assignment.
Excuse me, but have you seen a Wolverine?
And I mean a super hero named Wolverine. Not the actual animal weasel-thingy.
Coo?
Saying "coo" really doesn't help me at all.
Of course, who am I to complain? I can't find him either.
Might as well check in on Captain America.
TELLMAN SCHOOL
TODAY! CAPTAIN AMERICA IN PERSON!
TELLMAN ELEMENTARY SCHOOL
My awesome tracking and detective skills, combined with the announcement in this newspaper flyer, should allow me to find him.

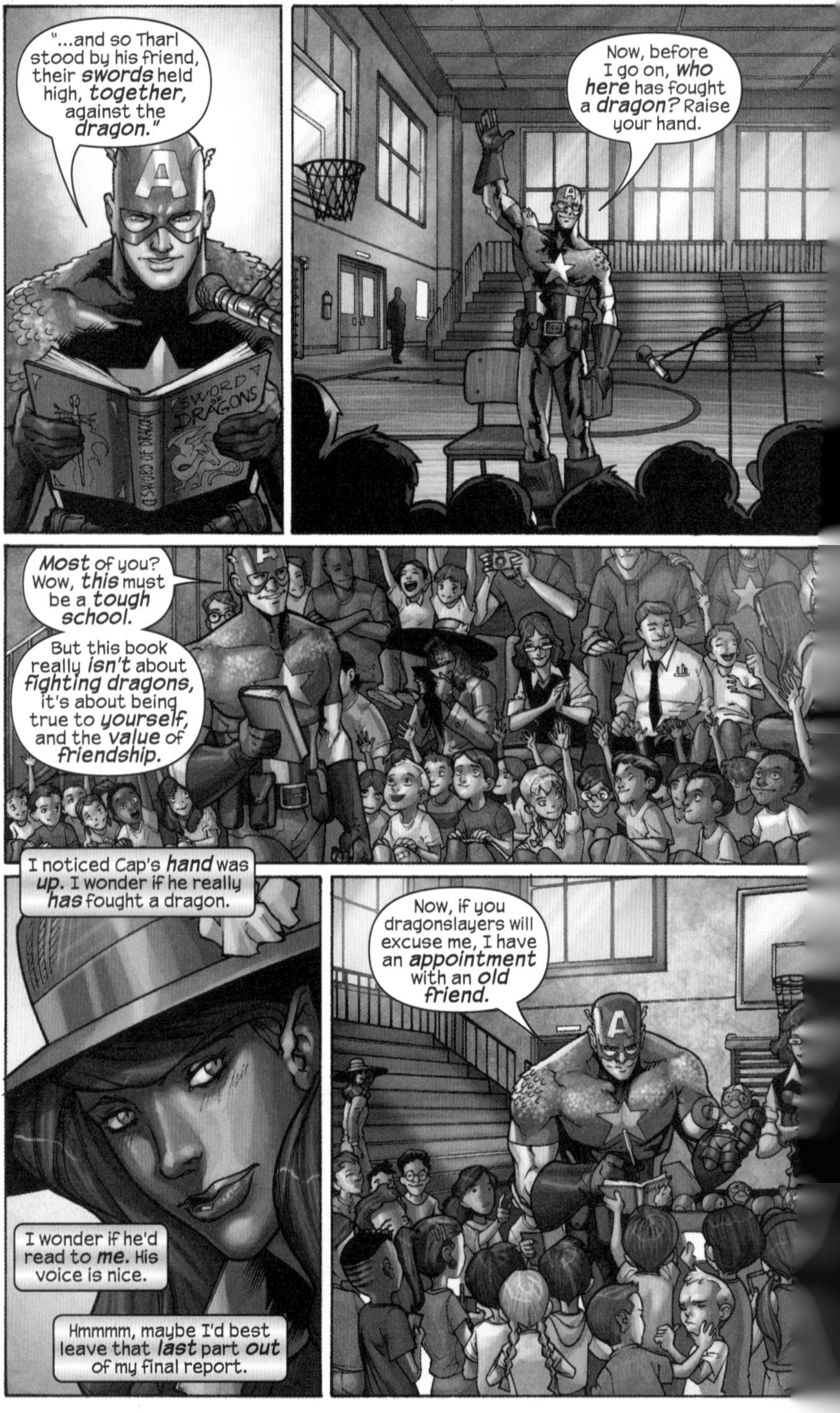
"...and so Tharl stood by his friend, their swords held high, together, against the dragon."
SWORD OF DRAGONS
Now, before I go on, who here has fought a dragon? Raise your hand.
Most of you? Wow, this must be a tough school.
But this book really isn't about fighting dragons, it's about being true to yourself, and the value of friendship.
I noticed Cap's hand was up. I wonder if he really has fought a dragon.
Now, if you dragonslayers will excuse me, I have an appointment with an old friend.
I wonder if he'd read to me. His voice is nice.
Hmmmm, maybe I'd best leave that last part out of my final report.

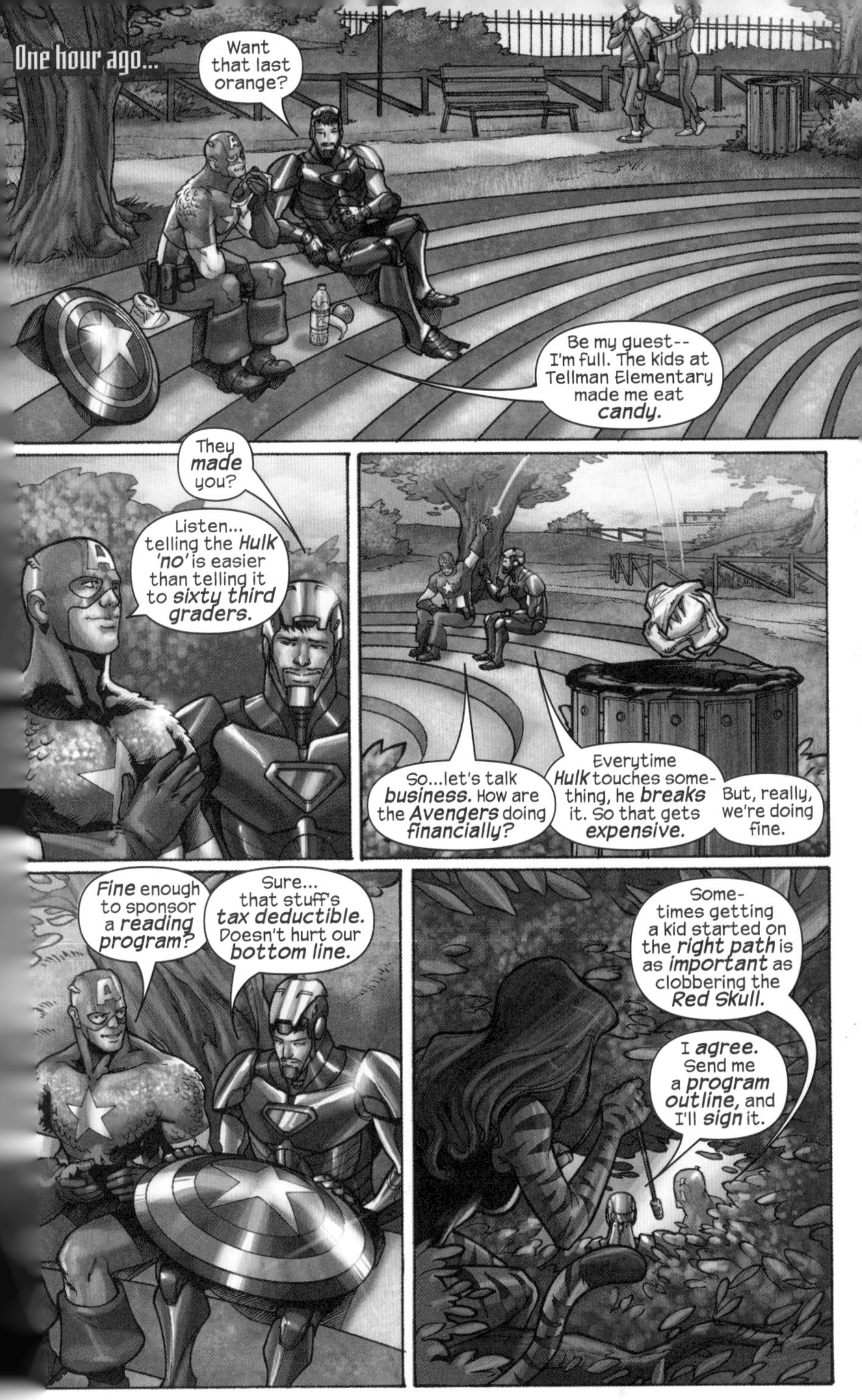
One hour ago...
Want that last orange?
Be my guest-- I'm full. The kids at Tellman Elementary made me eat candy.
They made you?
Listen... telling the Hulk 'no' is easier than telling it to sixty third graders.
So...let's talk business. How are the Avengers doing financially?
Everytime Hulk touches something, he breaks it. So that gets expensive.
But, really, we're doing fine.
Fine enough to sponsor a reading program?
Sure... that stuff's tax deductible. Doesn't hurt our bottom line.
Sometimes getting a kid started on the right path is as important as clobbering the Red Skull.
I agree. Send me a program outline, and I'll sign it.

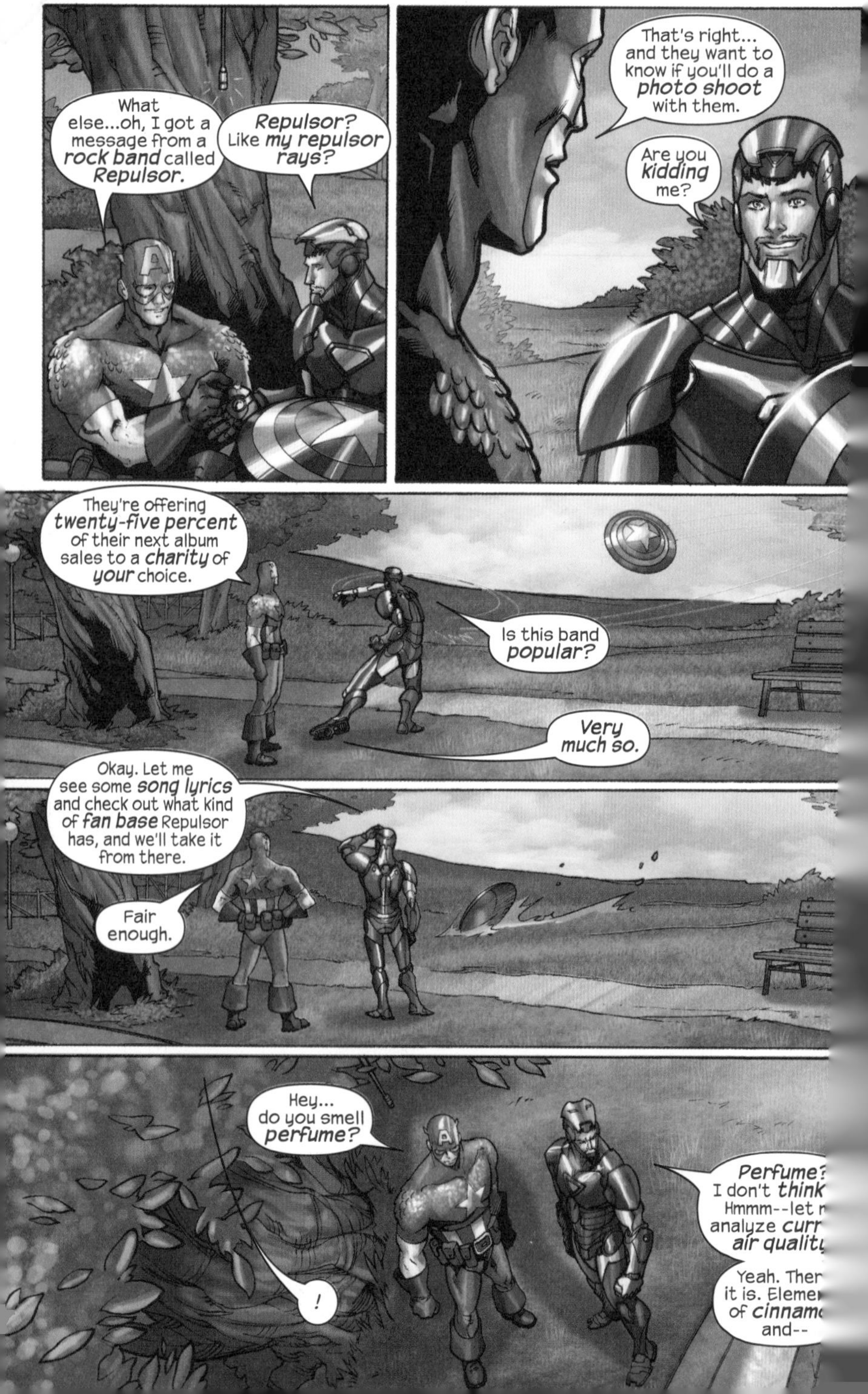
What else...oh, I got a message from a rock band called Repulsor.
Repulsor? Like my repulsor rays?
That's right... and they want to know if you'll do a photo shoot with them.
Are you kidding me?
They're offering twenty-five percent of their next album sales to a charity of your choice.
Is this band popular?
Very much so.
Okay. Let me see some song lyrics and check out what kind of fan base Repulsor has, and we'll take it from there.
Fair enough.
Hey... do you smell perfume?
Perfume? I don't think Hmmm--let analyze curr air qualit
Yeah. Ther it is. Eleme of cinnam and--
!

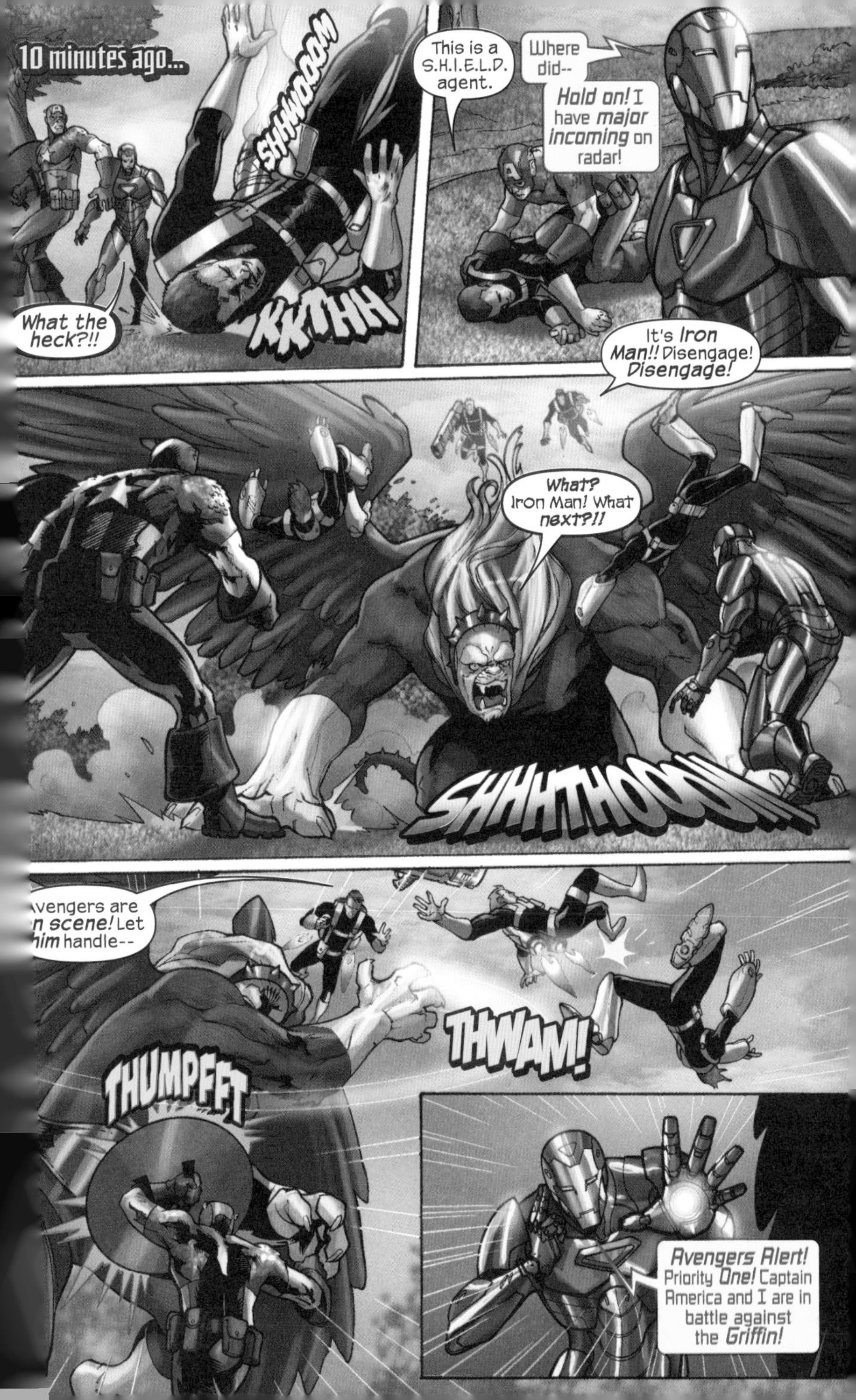

10 minutes ago...
SHHWOOOM
What the heck?!!
KKTHH
This is a S.H.I.E.L.D. agent.
Where did--
Hold on! I have major incoming on radar!
It's Iron Man!! Disengage! Disengage!
What? Iron Man! What next?!!
SHHHTHOOOM
vengers are n scene! Let him handle--
THWAM!
THUMPFFT
Avengers Alert! Priority One! Captain America and I are in battle against the Griffin!

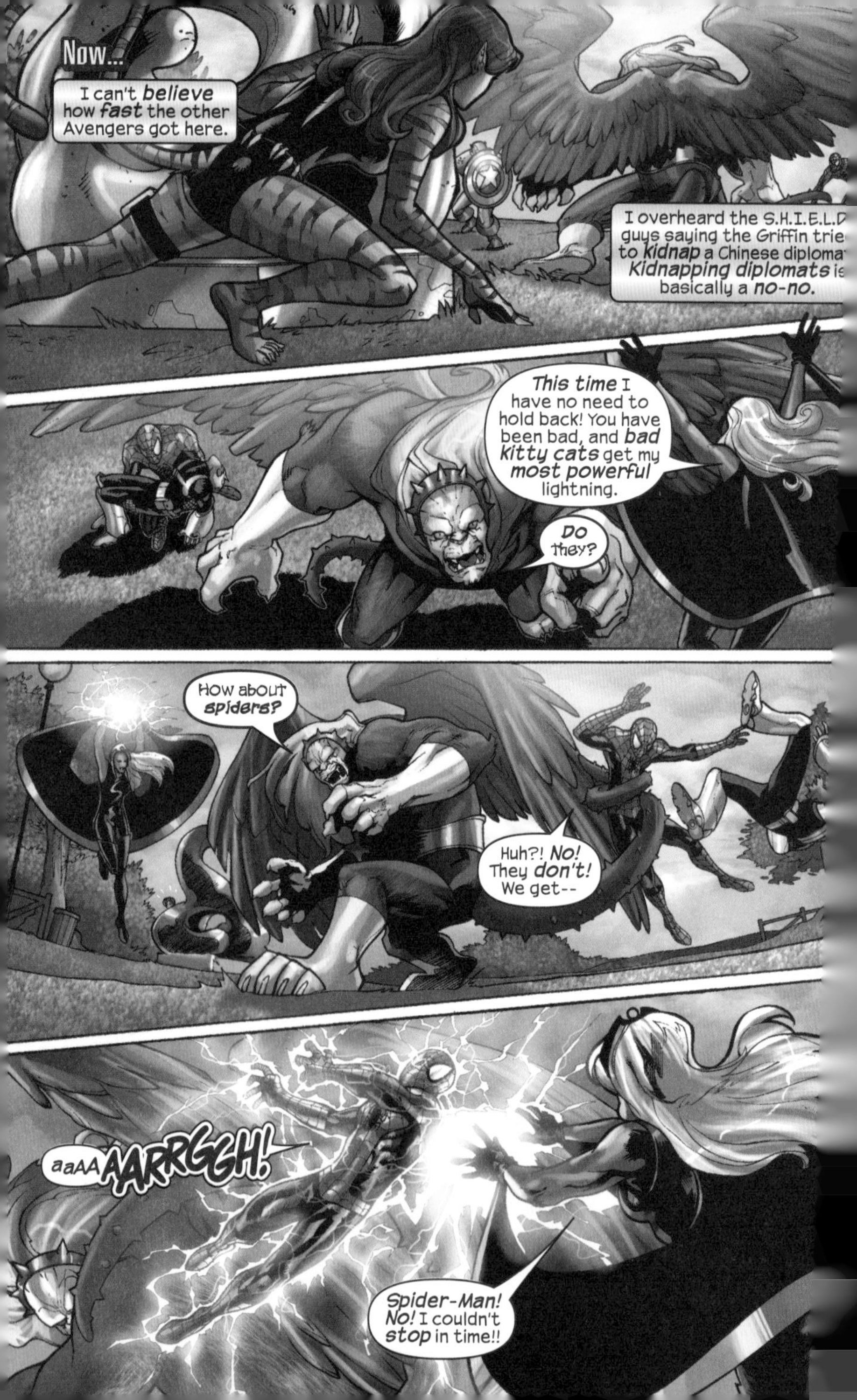
Now...
I can't believe how fast the other Avengers got here.
I overheard the S.H.I.E.L.D guys saying the Griffin trie to kidnap a Chinese diploma Kidnapping diplomats is basically a no-no.
This time I have no need to hold back! You have been bad, and bad kitty cats get my most powerful lightning.
Do they?
How about spiders?
Huh?! No! They don't! We get--
aaaAAARRGGH!
Spider-Man! No! I couldn't stop in time!!

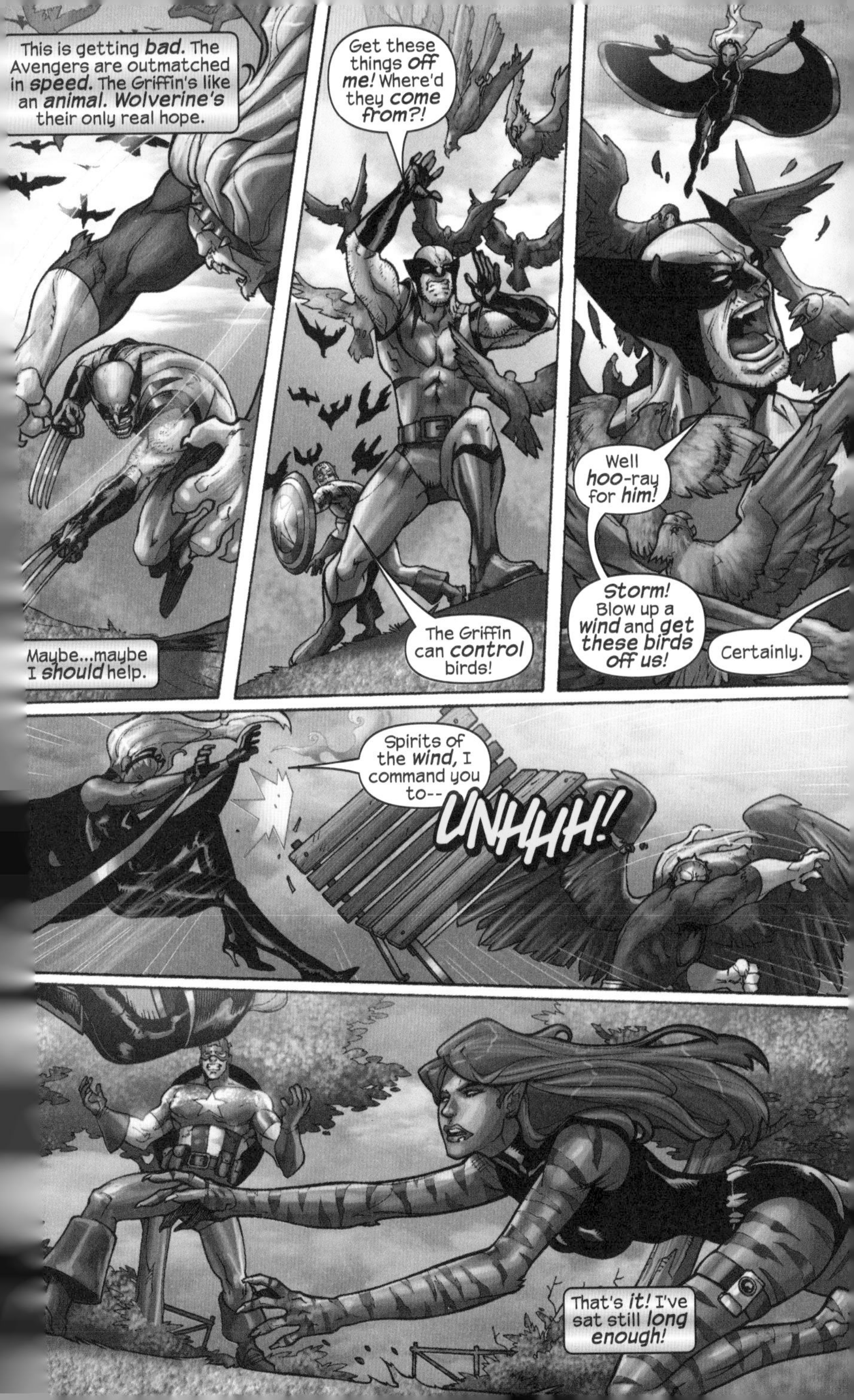

This is getting bad. The Avengers are outmatched in speed. The Griffin's like an animal. Wolverine's their only real hope.
Maybe...maybe I should help.
Get these things off me! Where'd they come from?!
The Griffin can control birds!
Well hoo-ray for him!
Storm! Blow up a wind and get these birds off us!
Certainly.
Spirits of the wind, I command you to--
UNHHH!
That's it! I've sat still long enough!

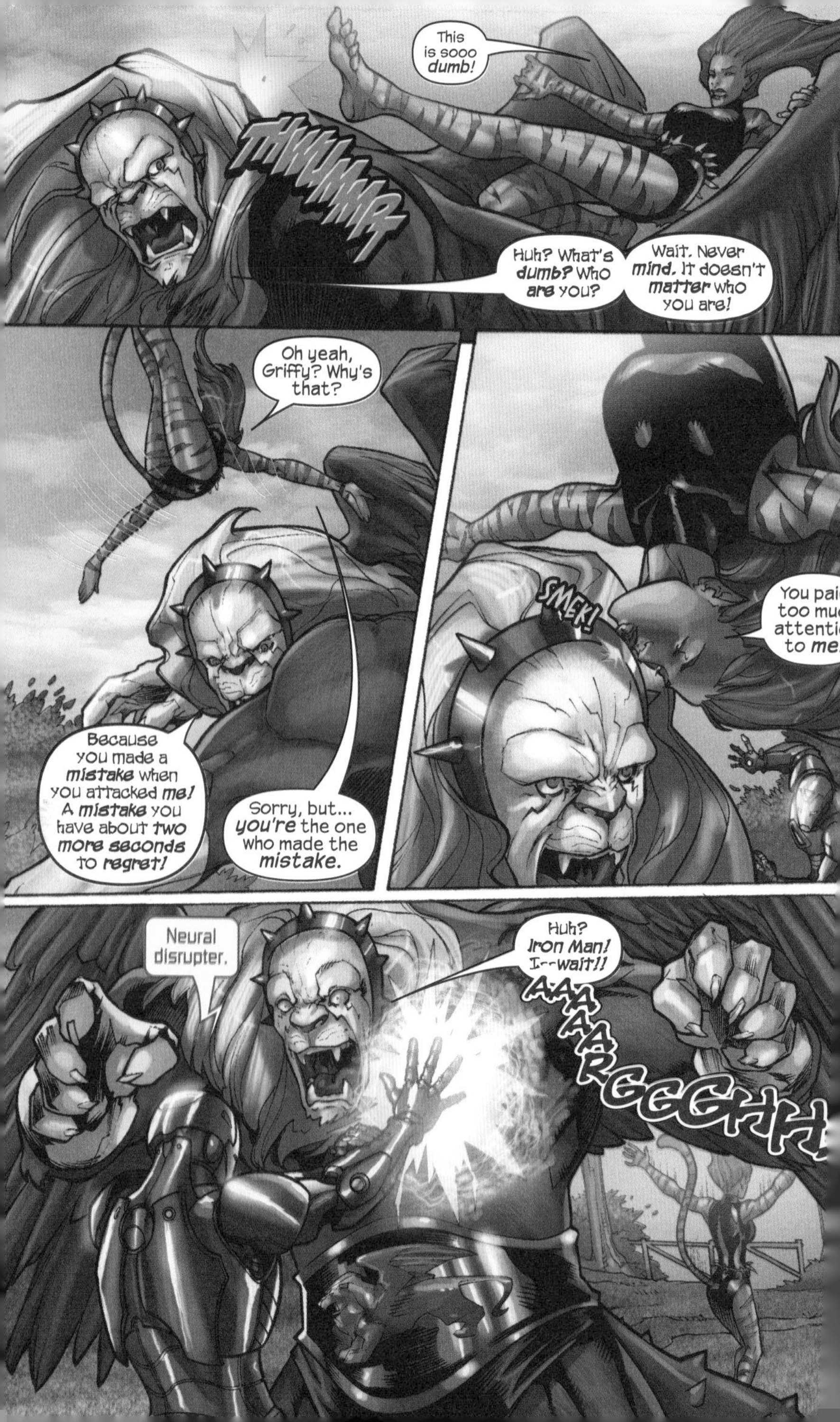
This is sooo dumb!
THWUMMR
Huh? What's dumb? Who are you?
Wait. Never mind. It doesn't matter who you are!
Oh yeah, Griffy? Why's that?
Because you made a mistake when you attacked me! A mistake you have about two more seconds to regret!
Sorry, but... you're the one who made the mistake.
SMEK!
You paid too muc attentic to me!
Neural disrupter.
Huh? Iron Man! I--wait!!
AAAAARGGGHH

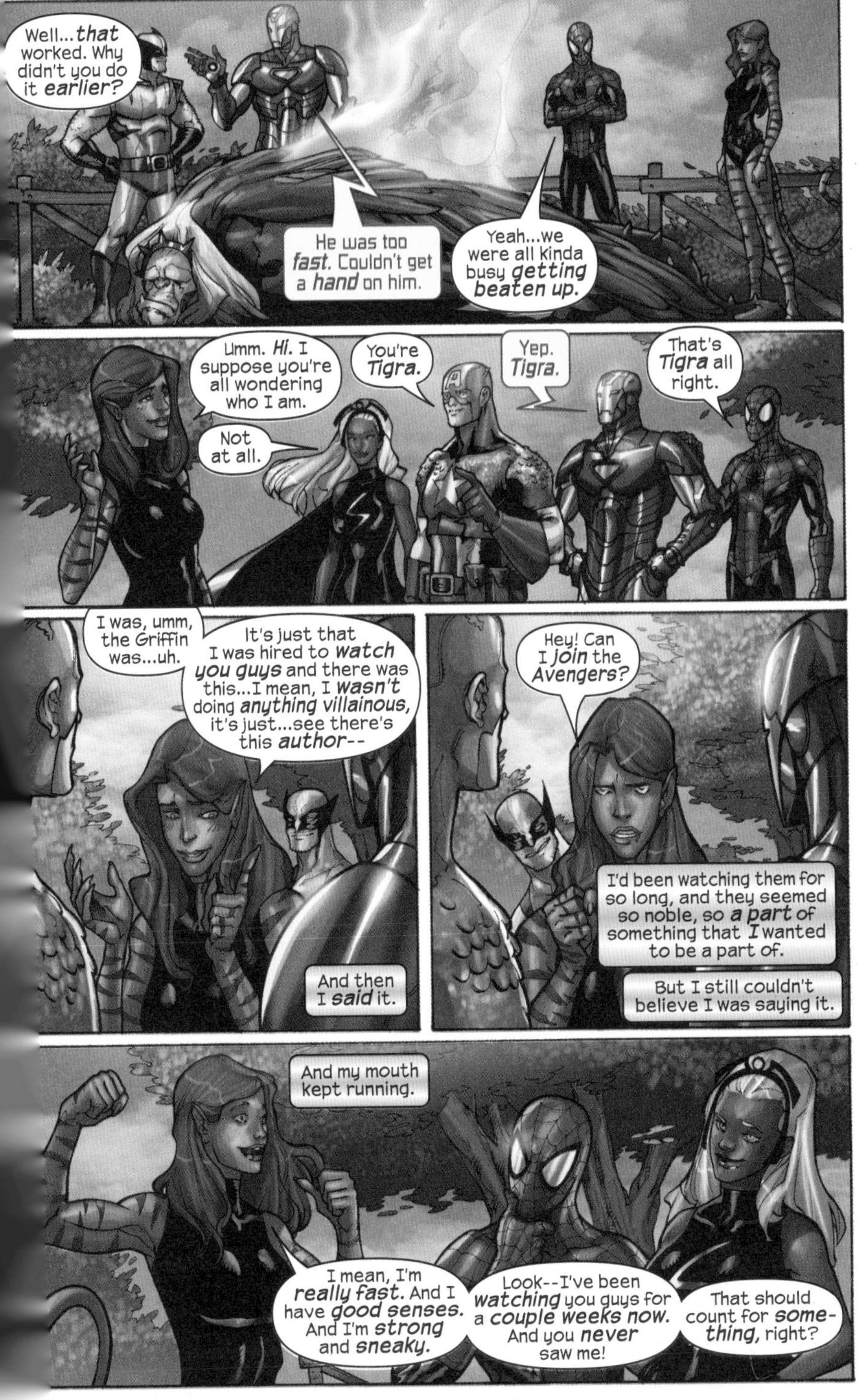

Well...that worked. Why didn't you do it earlier?
He was too fast. Couldn't get a hand on him.
Yeah...we were all kinda busy getting beaten up.
Umm. Hi. I suppose you're all wondering who I am.
Not at all.
You're Tigra.
Yep. Tigra.
That's Tigra all right.
I was, umm, the Griffin was...uh.
It's just that I was hired to watch you guys and there was this...I mean, I wasn't doing anything villainous, it's just...see there's this author--
And then I said it.
Hey! Can I join the Avengers?
I'd been watching them for so long, and they seemed so noble, so a part of something that I wanted to be a part of.
But I still couldn't believe I was saying it.
And my mouth kept running.
I mean, I'm really fast. And I have good senses. And I'm strong and sneaky.
Look--I've been watching you guys for a couple weeks now. And you never saw me!
That should count for something, right?

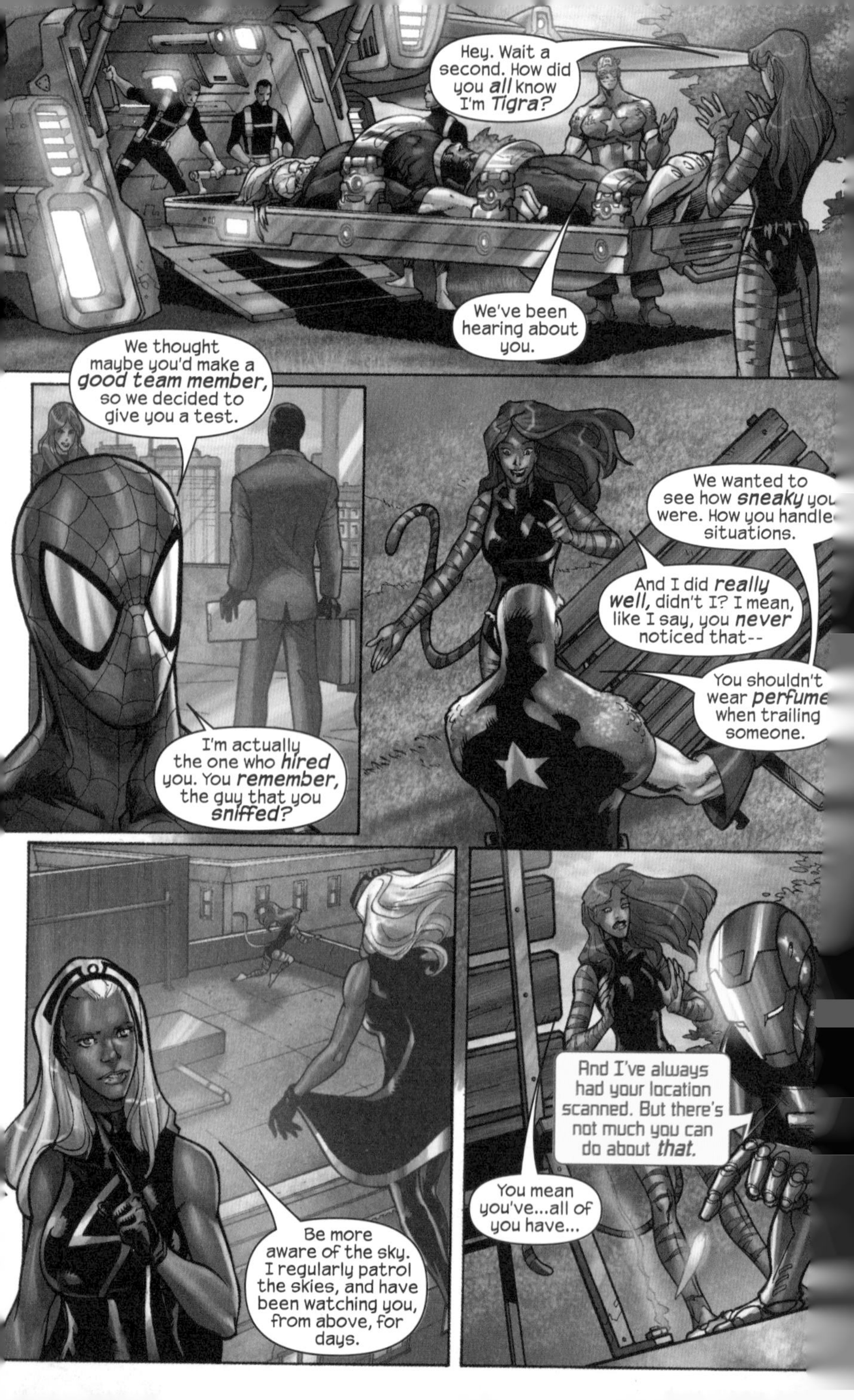
Hey. Wait a second. How did you all know I'm Tigra?
We've been hearing about you.
We thought maybe you'd make a good team member, so we decided to give you a test.
I'm actually the one who hired you. You remember, the guy that you sniffed?
We wanted to see how sneaky you were. How you handled situations.
And I did really well, didn't I? I mean, like I say, you never noticed that--
You shouldn't wear perfume when trailing someone.
Be more aware of the sky. I regularly patrol the skies, and have been watching you, from above, for days.
And I've always had your location scanned. But there's not much you can do about that.
You mean you've...all of you have...

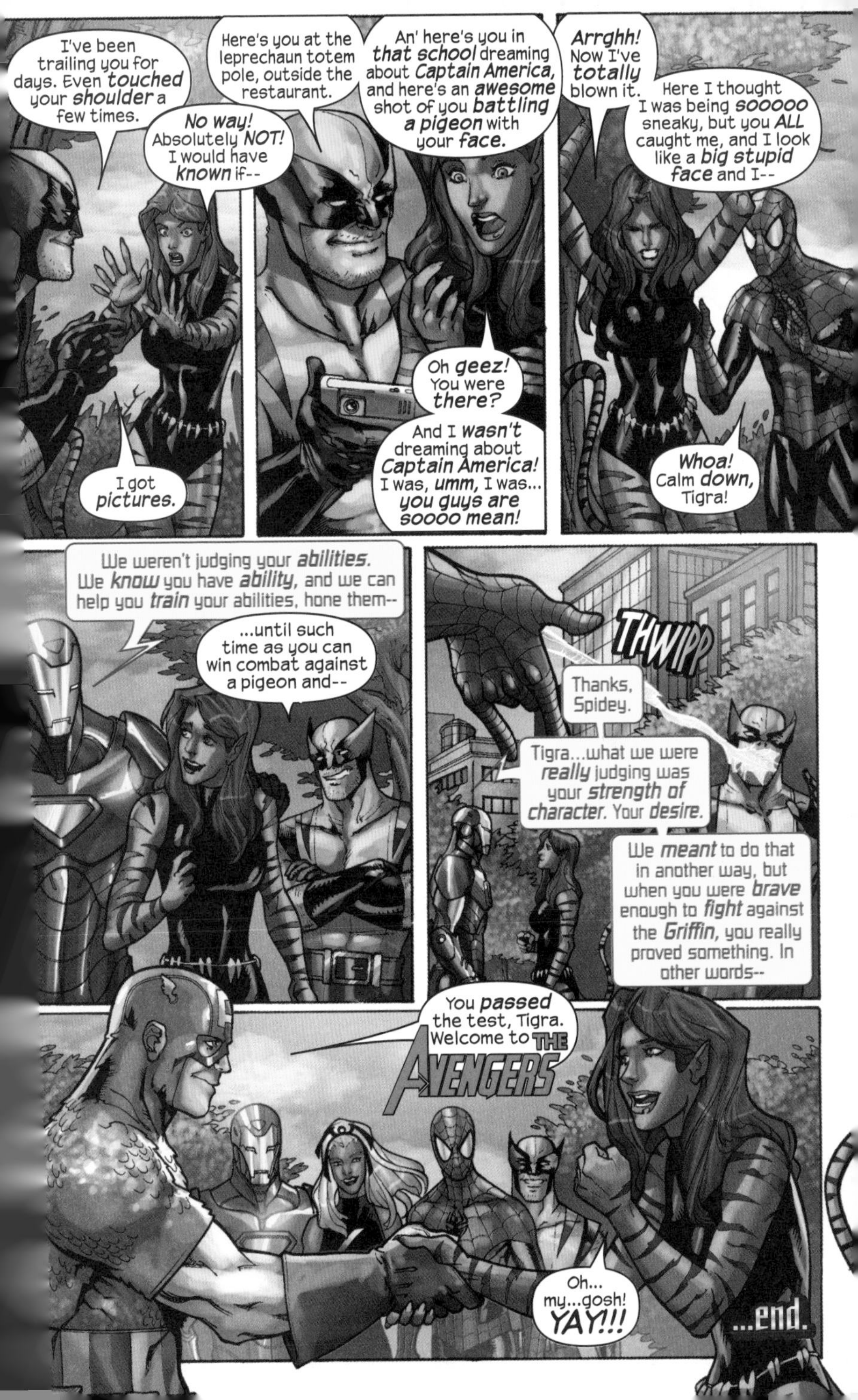

I've been trailing you for days. Even touched your shoulder a few times.
No way! Absolutely NOT! I would have known if--
I got pictures.
Here's you at the leprechaun totem pole, outside the restaurant.
An' here's you in that school dreaming about Captain America, and here's an awesome shot of you battling a pigeon with your face.
Oh geez! You were there?
And I wasn't dreaming about Captain America! I was, umm, I was... you guys are soooo mean!
Arrghh! Now I've totally blown it.
Here I thought I was being soooooo sneaky, but you ALL caught me, and I look like a big stupid face and I--
Whoa! Calm down, Tigra!
We weren't judging your abilities. We know you have ability, and we can help you train your abilities, hone them--
...until such time as you can win combat against a pigeon and--
THWIPP
Thanks, Spidey.
Tigra...what we were really judging was your strength of character. Your desire.
We meant to do that in another way, but when you were brave enough to fight against the Griffin, you really proved something. In other words--
You passed the test, Tigra. Welcome to THE AVENGERS
Oh... my...gosh! YAY!!!
...end.

#31

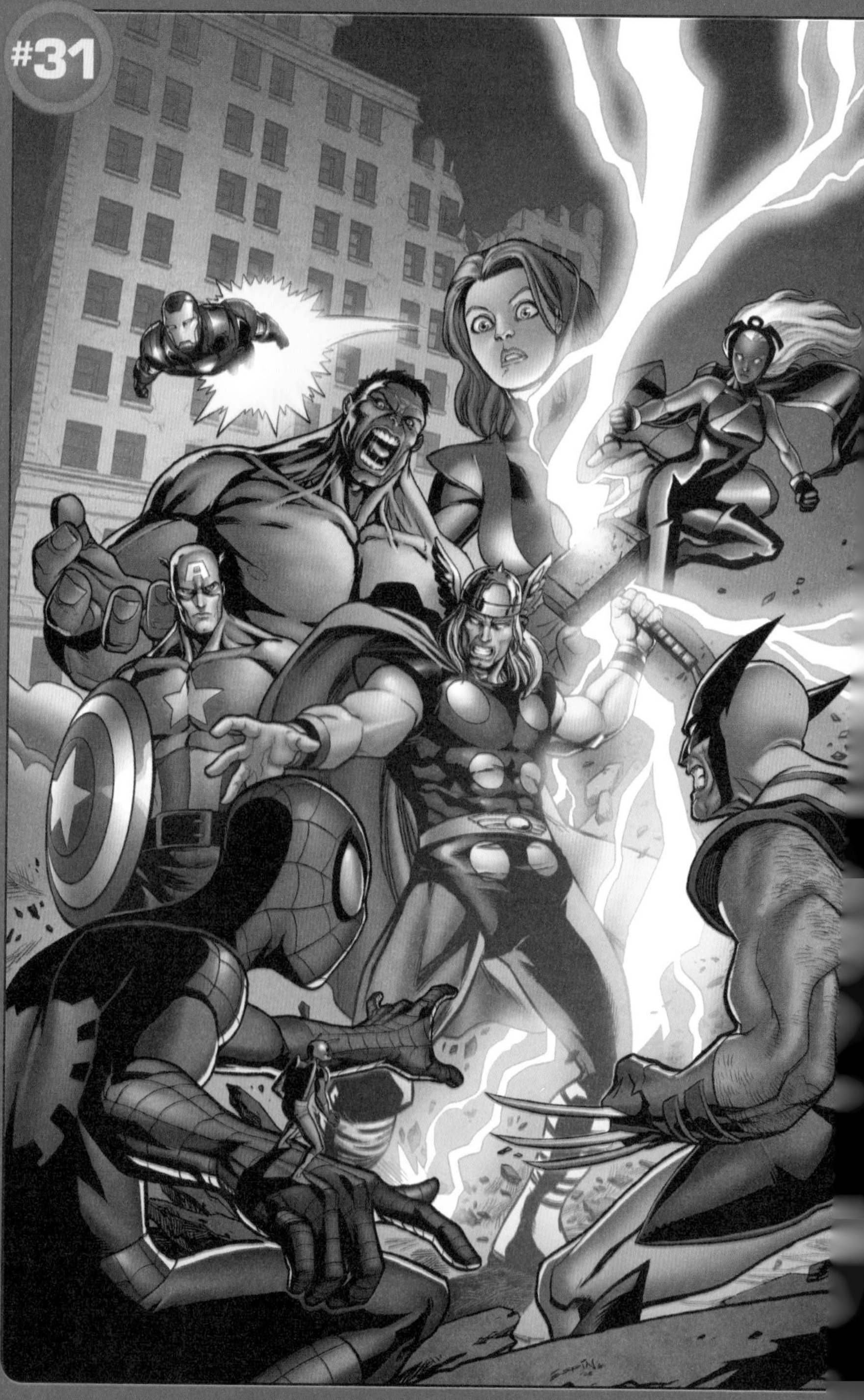

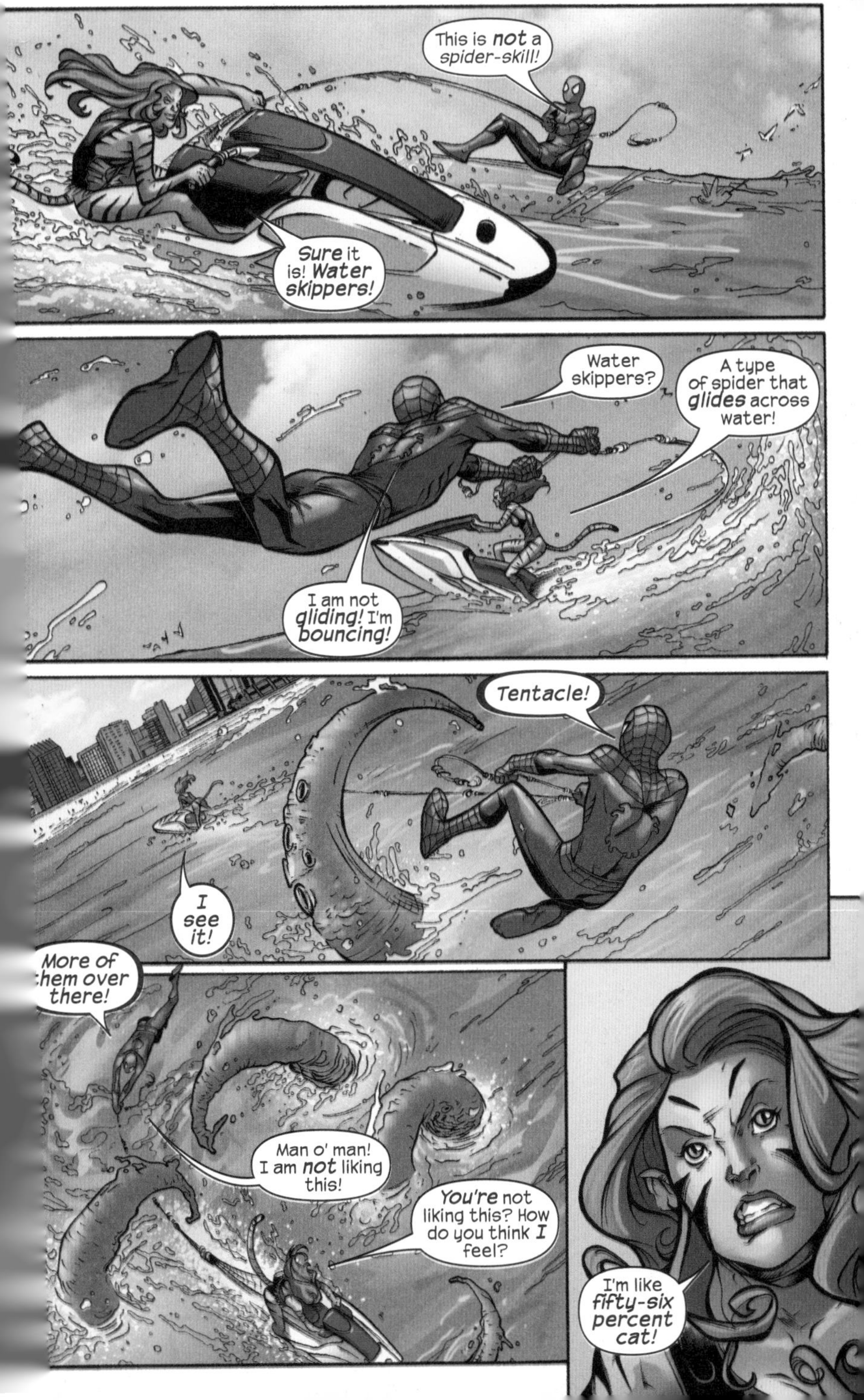
This is not a spider-skill!
Sure it is! Water skippers!
Water skippers?
A type of spider that glides across water!
I am not gliding! I'm bouncing!
Tentacle!
I see it!
More of them over there!
Man o' man! I am not liking this!
You're not liking this? How do you think I feel?
I'm like fifty-six percent cat!

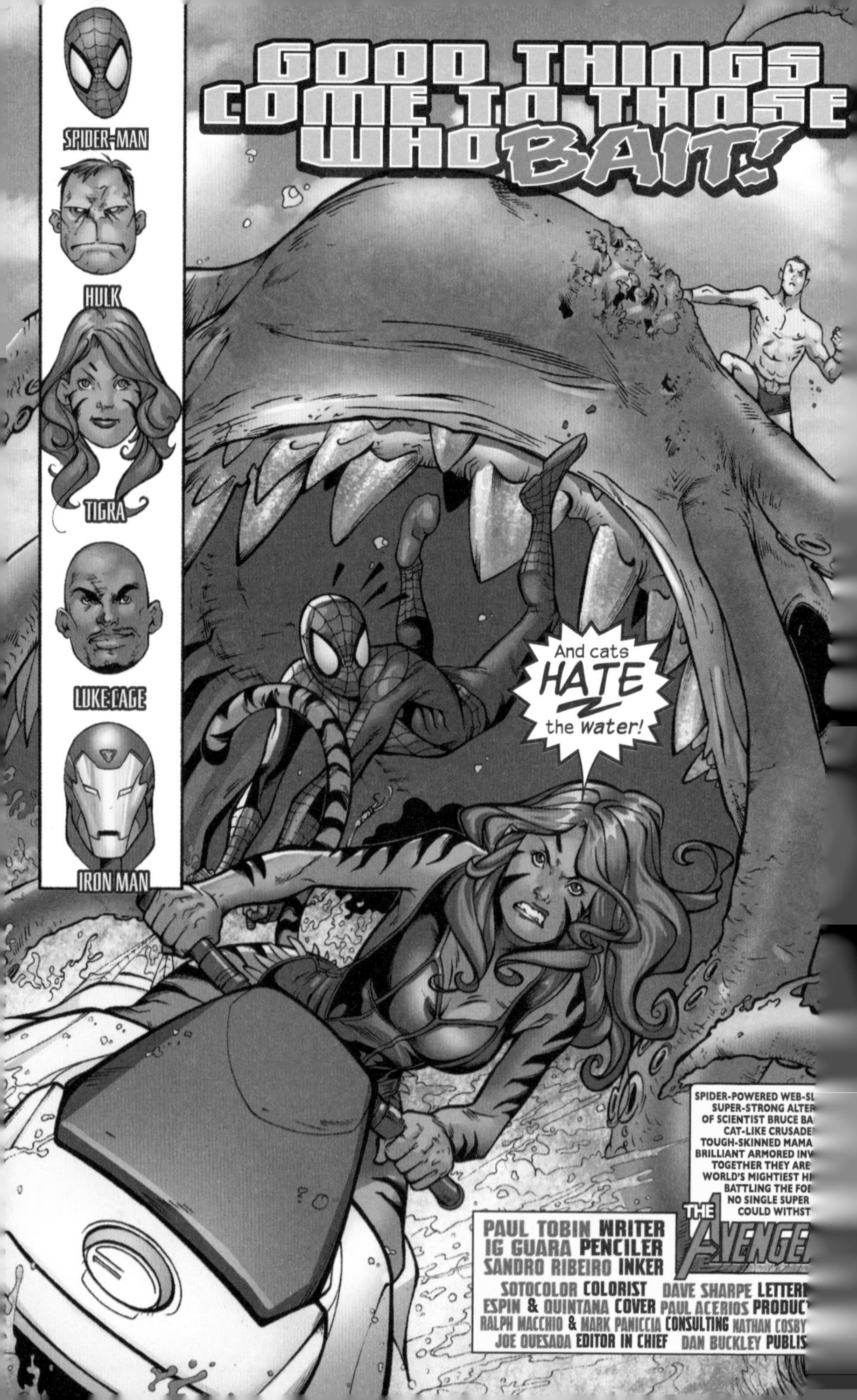
GOOD THINGS COME TO THOSE WHO BAIT!
SPIDER-MAN
HULK
TIGRA
LUKE CAGE
IRON MAN
And cats HATE the water!
SPIDER-POWERED WEB-SL
SUPER-STRONG ALTER
OF SCIENTIST BRUCE BA
CAT-LIKE CRUSADE
TOUGH-SKINNED MAMA
BRILLIANT ARMORED INV
TOGETHER THEY ARE
WORLD'S MIGHTIEST H
BATTLING THE FOE
NO SINGLE SUPER
COULD WITHST
PAUL TOBIN WRITER
IG GUARA PENCILER
SANDRO RIBEIRO INKER
SOTOCOLOR COLORIST DAVE SHARPE LETTERE
ESPIN & QUINTANA COVER PAUL ACERIOS PRODUC
RALPH MACCHIO & MARK PANICCIA CONSULTING NATHAN COSBY
JOE QUESADA EDITOR IN CHIEF DAN BUCKLEY PUBLIS

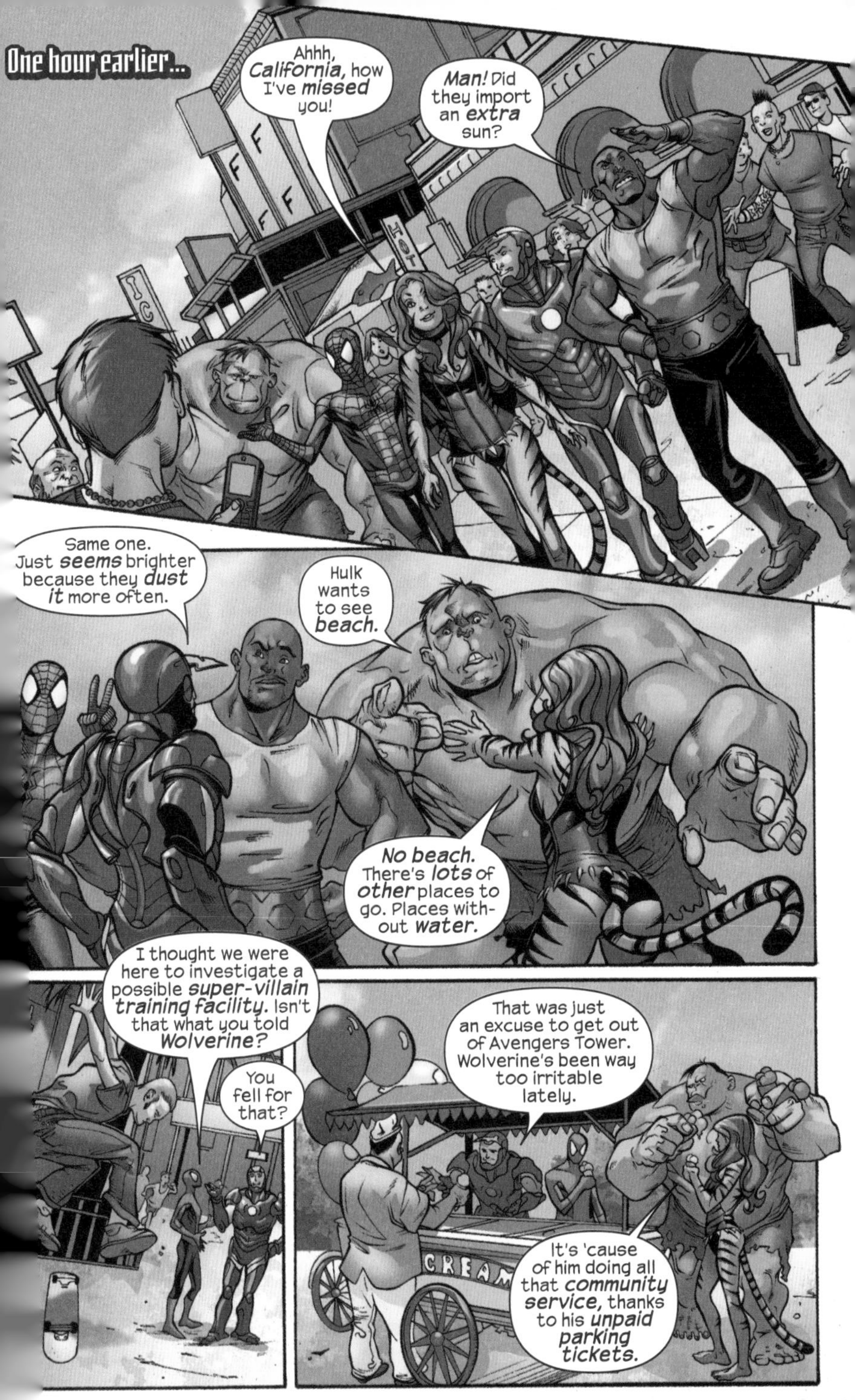

One hour earlier...
Ahhh, California, how I've missed you!
Man! Did they import an extra sun?
Same one. Just seems brighter because they dust it more often.
Hulk wants to see beach.
No beach. There's lots of other places to go. Places without water.
I thought we were here to investigate a possible super-villain training facility. Isn't that what you told Wolverine?
You fell for that?
That was just an excuse to get out of Avengers Tower. Wolverine's been way too irritable lately.
It's 'cause of him doing all that community service, thanks to his unpaid parking tickets.

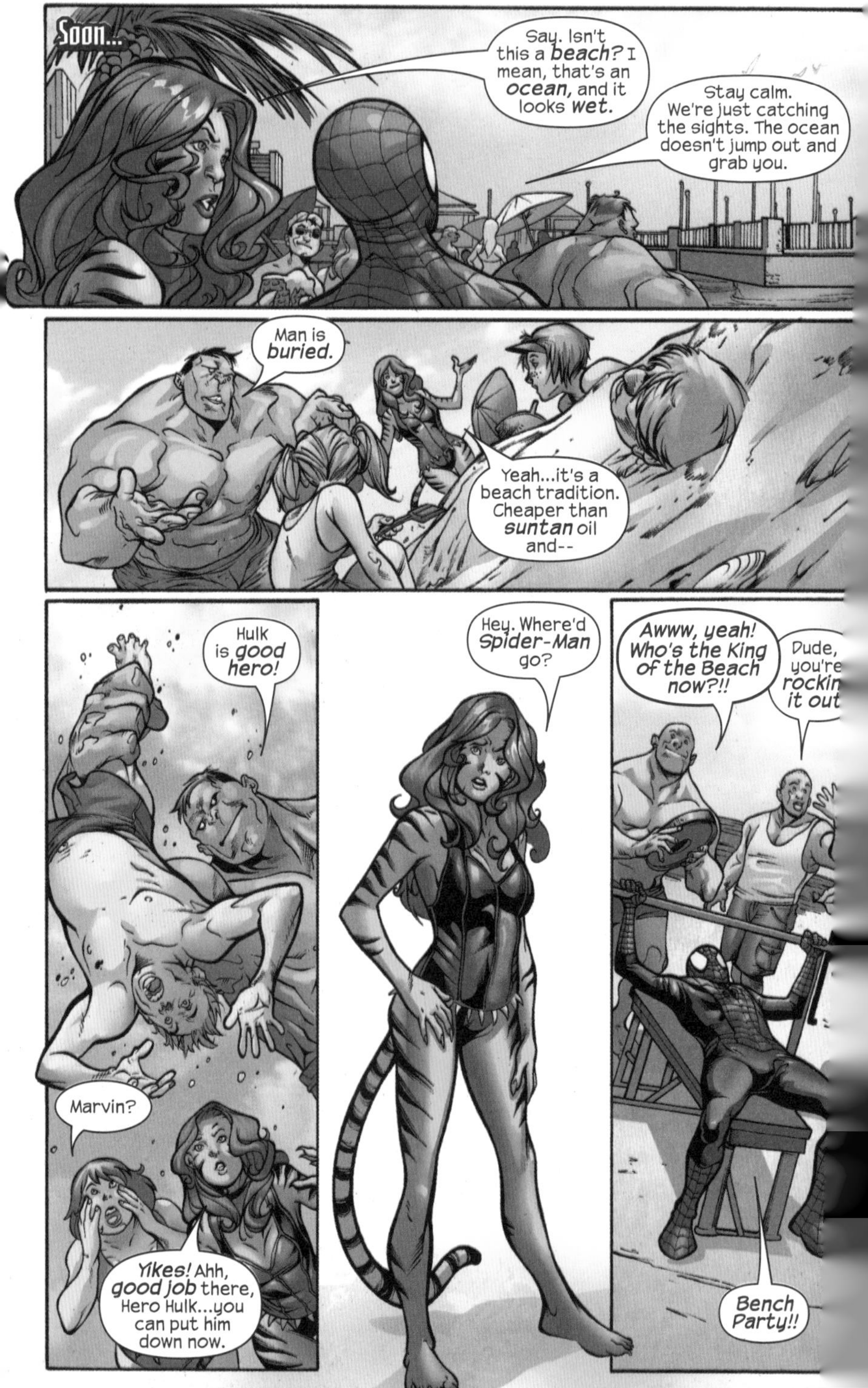
Soon...
Say. Isn't this a beach? I mean, that's an ocean, and it looks wet.
Stay calm. We're just catching the sights. The ocean doesn't jump out and grab you.
Man is buried.
Yeah...it's a beach tradition. Cheaper than suntan oil and--
Hulk is good hero!
Marvin?
Yikes! Ahh, good job there, Hero Hulk...you can put him down now.
Hey. Where'd Spider-Man go?
Awww, yeah! Who's the King of the Beach now?!!
Dude, you're rockin it out
Bench Party!!

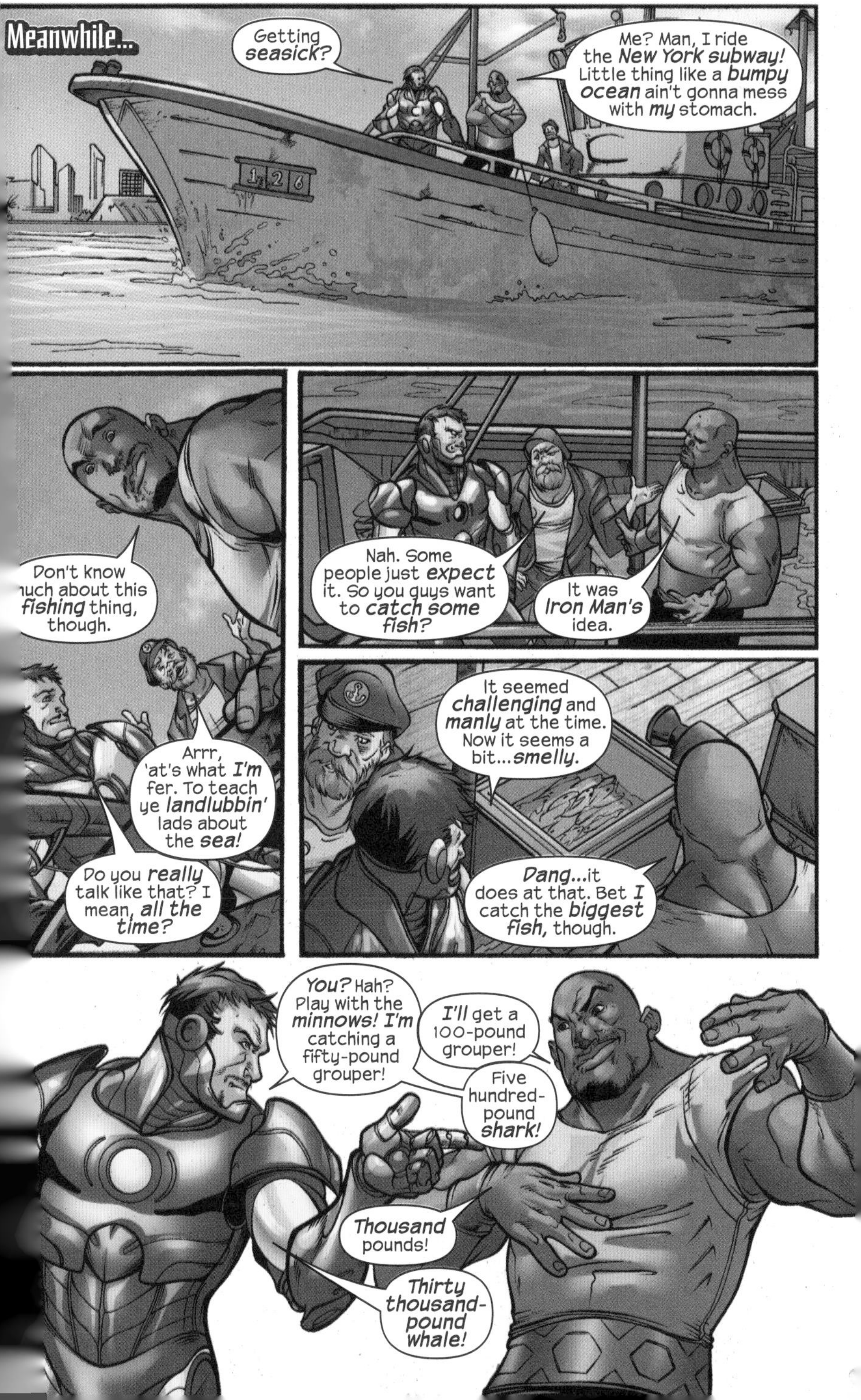
Meanwhile...
Getting seasick?
Me? Man, I ride the New York subway! Little thing like a bumpy ocean ain't gonna mess with my stomach.
Nah. Some people just expect it. So you guys want to catch some fish?
It was Iron Man's idea.
Don't know much about this fishing thing, though.
Arrr, 'at's what I'm fer. To teach ye landlubbin' lads about the sea!
Do you really talk like that? I mean, all the time?
It seemed challenging and manly at the time. Now it seems a bit...smelly.
Dang...it does at that. Bet I catch the biggest fish, though.
You? Hah? Play with the minnows! I'm catching a fifty-pound grouper!
I'll get a 100-pound grouper!
Five hundred-pound shark!
Thousand pounds!
Thirty thousand-pound whale!

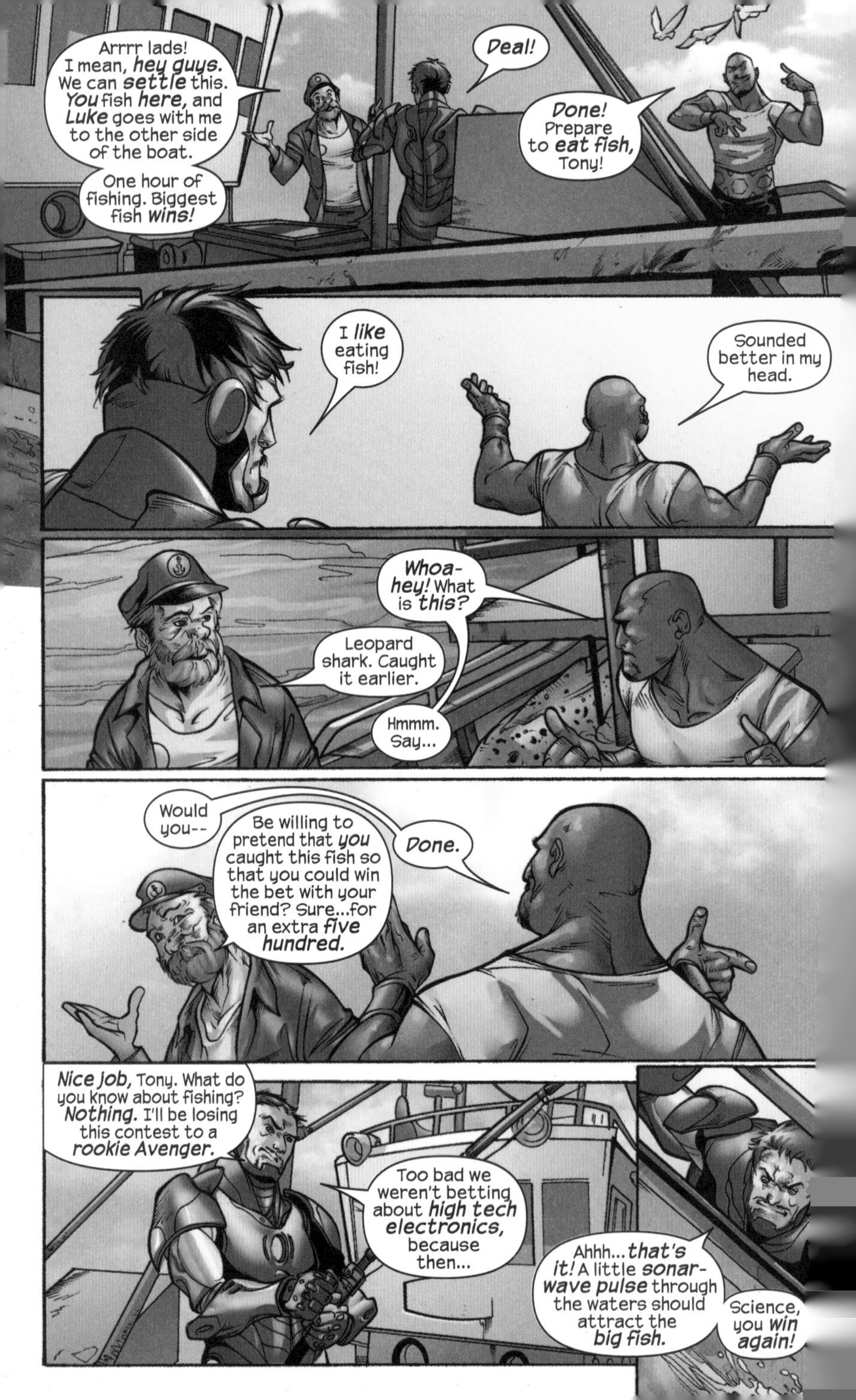
Arrrr lads! I mean, hey guys. We can settle this. You fish here, and Luke goes with me to the other side of the boat.
One hour of fishing. Biggest fish wins!
Deal!
Done! Prepare to eat fish, Tony!
I like eating fish!
Sounded better in my head.
Whoa-hey! What is this?
Leopard shark. Caught it earlier.
Hmmm. Say...
Would you--
Be willing to pretend that you caught this fish so that you could win the bet with your friend? Sure...for an extra five hundred.
Done.
Nice job, Tony. What do you know about fishing? Nothing. I'll be losing this contest to a rookie Avenger.
Too bad we weren't betting about high tech electronics, because then...
Ahhh...that's it! A little sonar-wave pulse through the waters should attract the big fish.
Science, you win again!

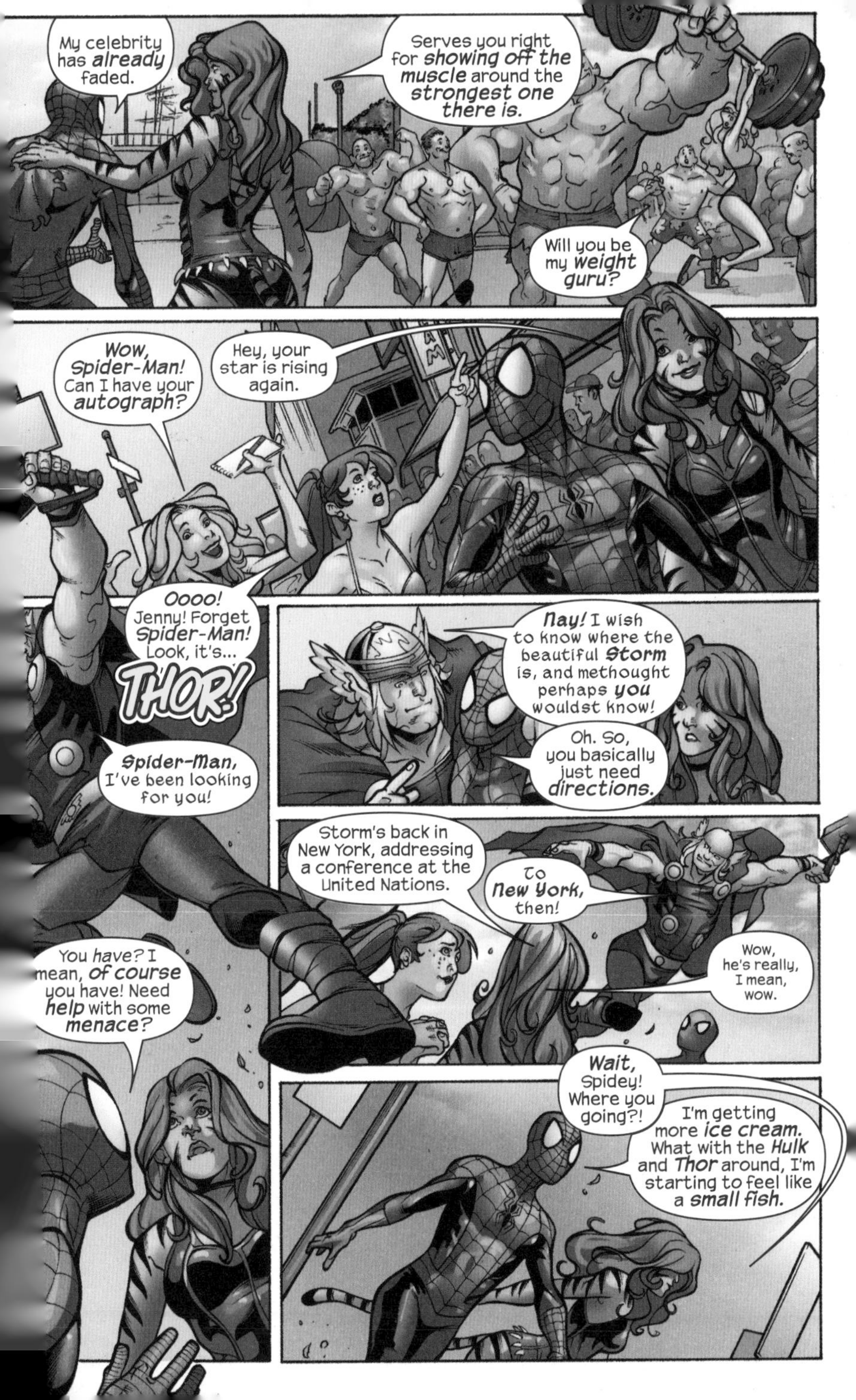

My celebrity has already faded.
Serves you right for showing off the muscle around the strongest one there is.
Will you be my weight guru?
Wow, Spider-Man! Can I have your autograph?
Hey, your star is rising again.
Oooo! Jenny! Forget Spider-Man! Look, it's... THOR!
Spider-Man, I've been looking for you!
You have? I mean, of course you have! Need help with some menace?
Nay! I wish to know where the beautiful Storm is, and methought perhaps you wouldst know!
Oh. So, you basically just need directions.
Storm's back in New York, addressing a conference at the United Nations.
To New York, then!
Wow, he's really, I mean, wow.
Wait, Spidey! Where you going?!
I'm getting more ice cream. What with the Hulk and Thor around, I'm starting to feel like a small fish.

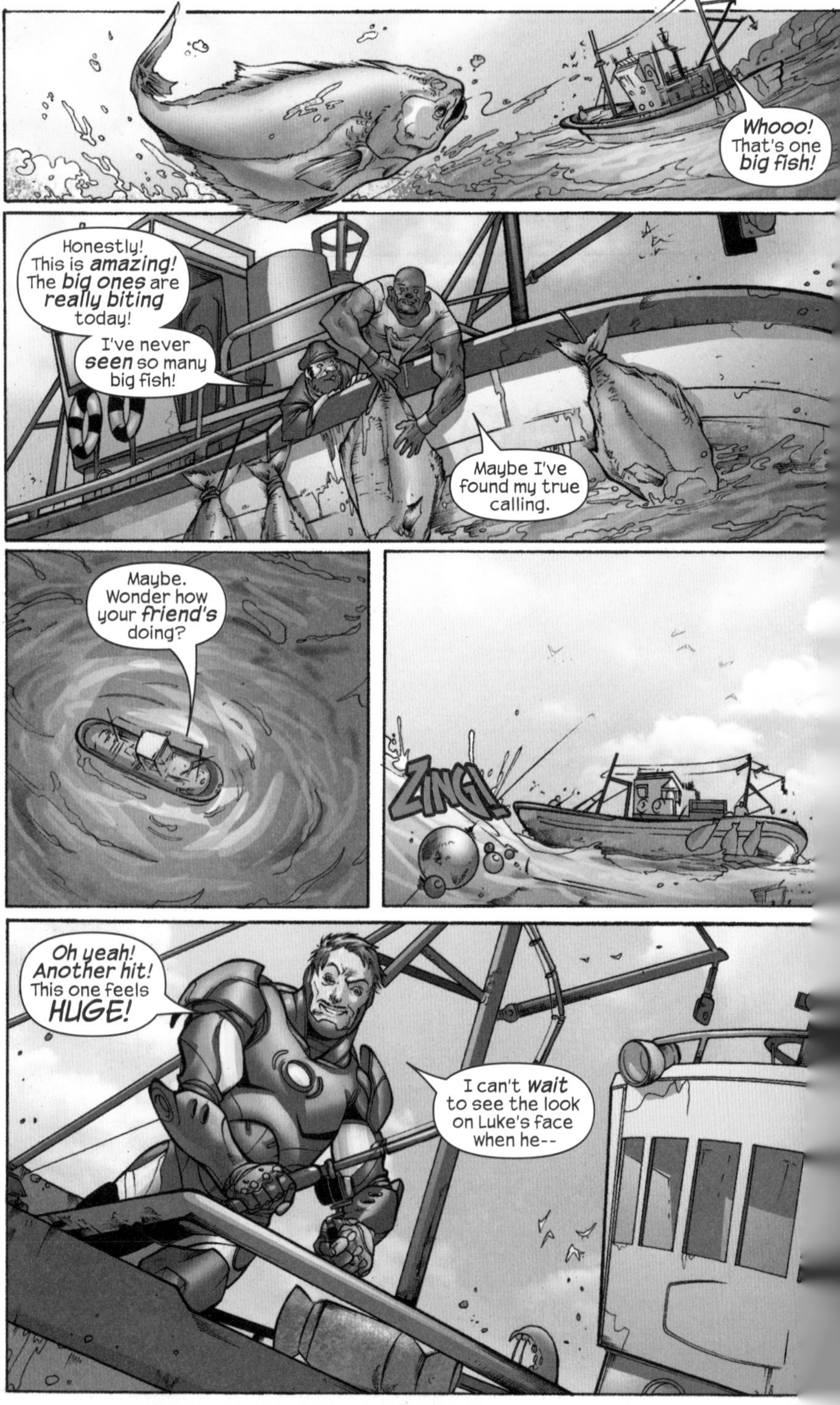
Whooo! That's one big fish!
Honestly! This is amazing! The big ones are really biting today!
I've never seen so many big fish!
Maybe I've found my true calling.
Maybe. Wonder how your friend's doing?
ZING!
Oh yeah! Another hit! This one feels HUGE!
I can't wait to see the look on Luke's face when he--

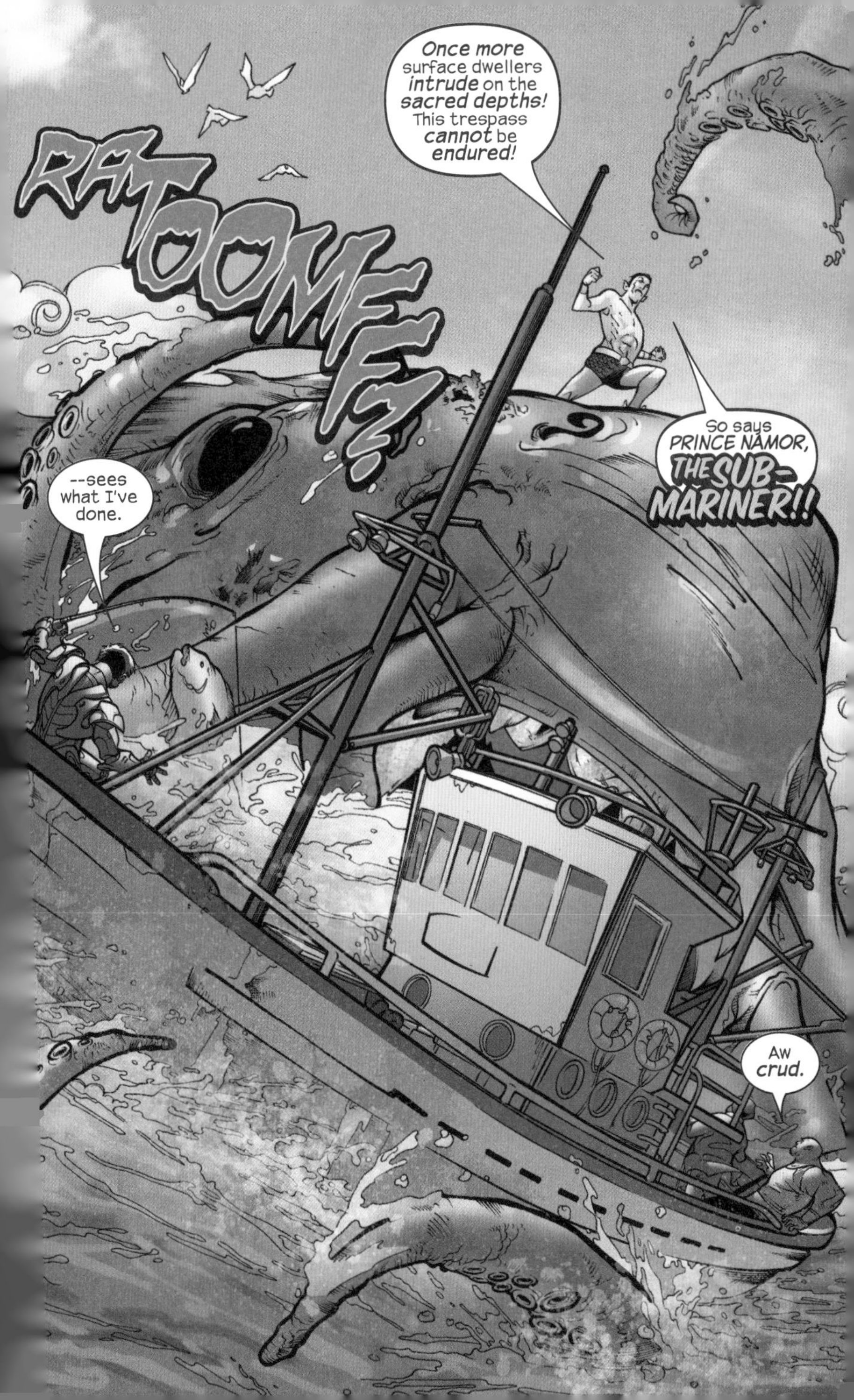
RATOOMF!
Once more surface dwellers intrude on the sacred depths! This trespass cannot be endured!
So says PRINCE NAMOR, THE SUB-MARINER!!
--sees what I've done.
Aw crud.

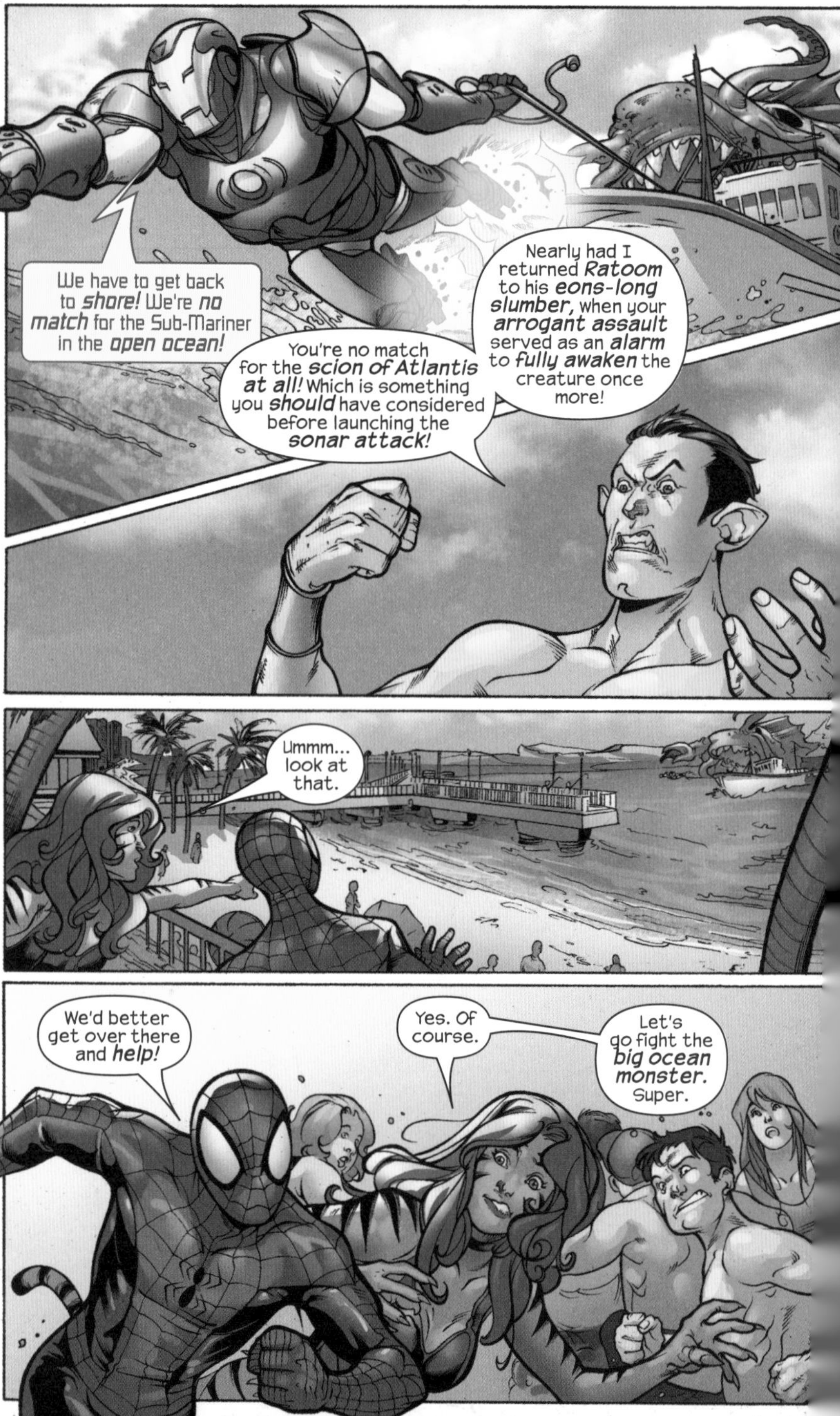
We have to get back to shore! We're no match for the Sub-Mariner in the open ocean!
Nearly had I returned Ratoom to his eons-long slumber, when your arrogant assault served as an alarm to fully awaken the creature once more!
You're no match for the scion of Atlantis at all! Which is something you should have considered before launching the sonar attack!
Ummm... look at that.
We'd better get over there and help!
Yes. Of course.
Let's go fight the big ocean monster. Super.

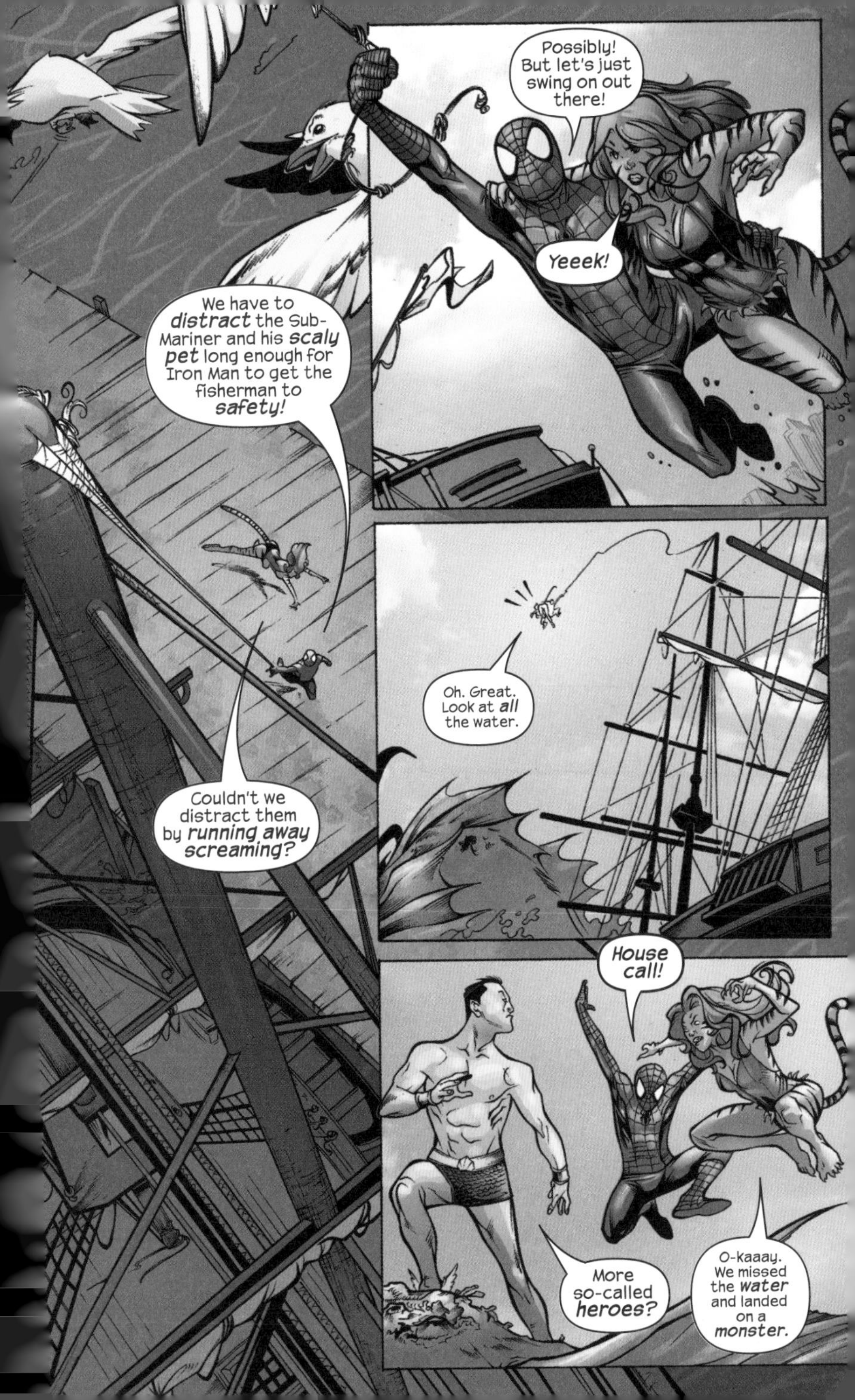
Possibly! But let's just swing on out there!
Yeeek!
We have to distract the Sub-Mariner and his scaly pet long enough for Iron Man to get the fisherman to safety!
Couldn't we distract them by running away screaming?
Oh. Great. Look at all the water.
House call!
More so-called heroes?
O-kaaay. We missed the water and landed on a monster.

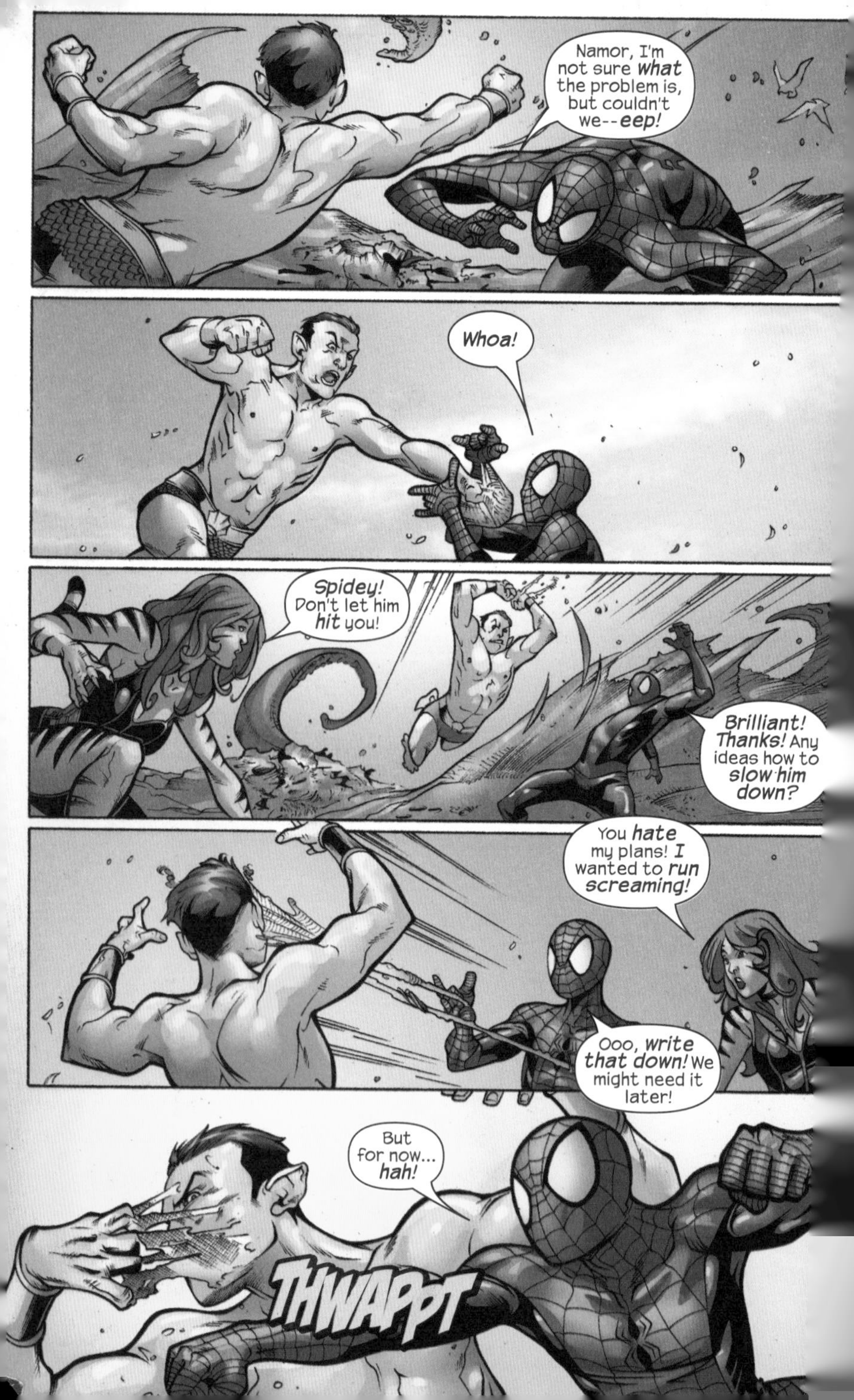
Namor, I'm not sure what the problem is, but couldn't we--eep!
Whoa!
Spidey! Don't let him hit you!
Brilliant! Thanks! Any ideas how to slow him down?
You hate my plans! I wanted to run screaming!
Ooo, write that down! We might need it later!
But for now... hah!
THWAPPT

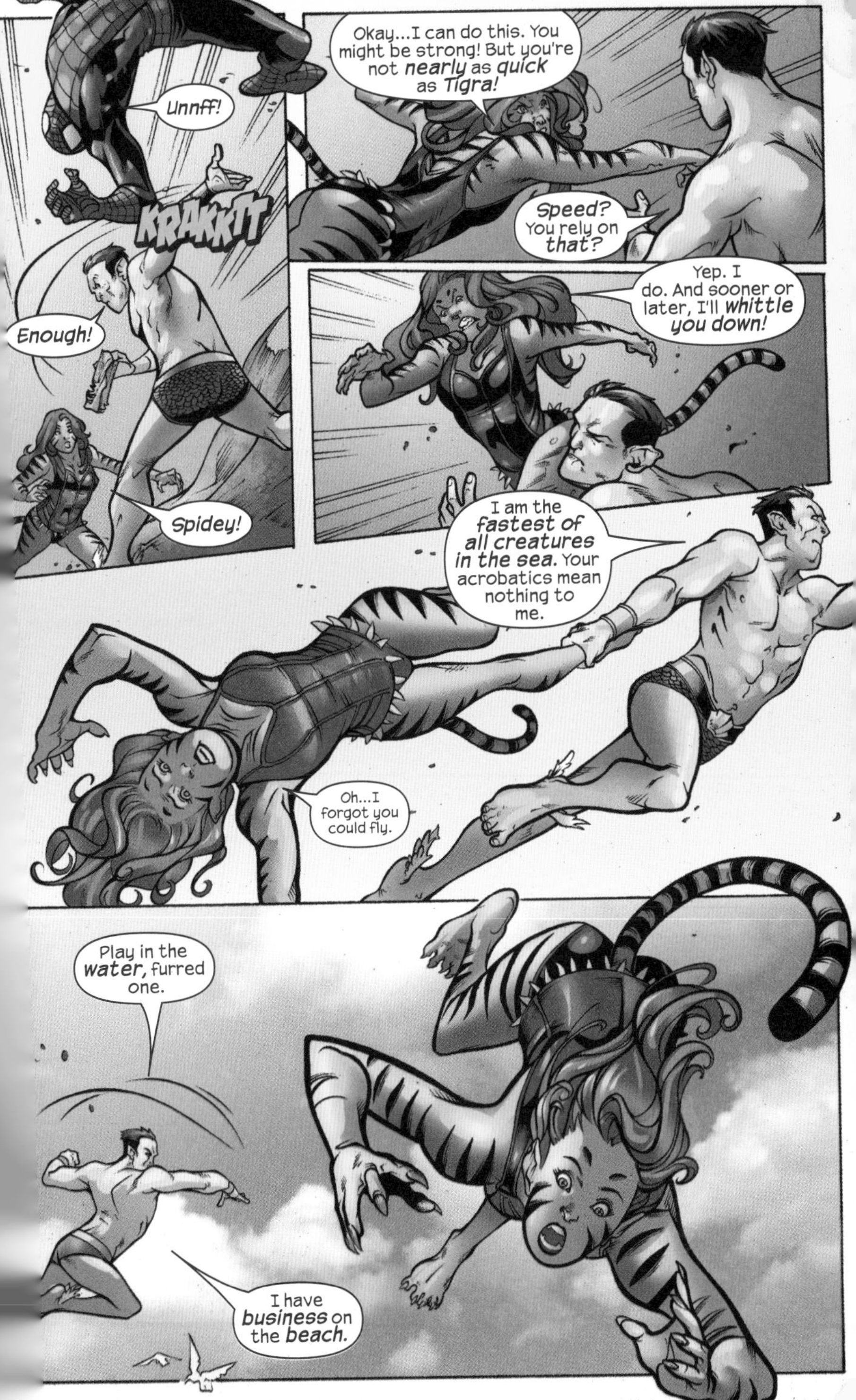
Unnff!
KRAKKTT
Enough!
Spidey!
Okay...I can do this. You might be strong! But you're not nearly as quick as Tigra!
Speed? You rely on that?
Yep. I do. And sooner or later, I'll whittle you down!
I am the fastest of all creatures in the sea. Your acrobatics mean nothing to me.
Oh...I forgot you could fly.
Play in the water, furred one.
I have business on the beach.

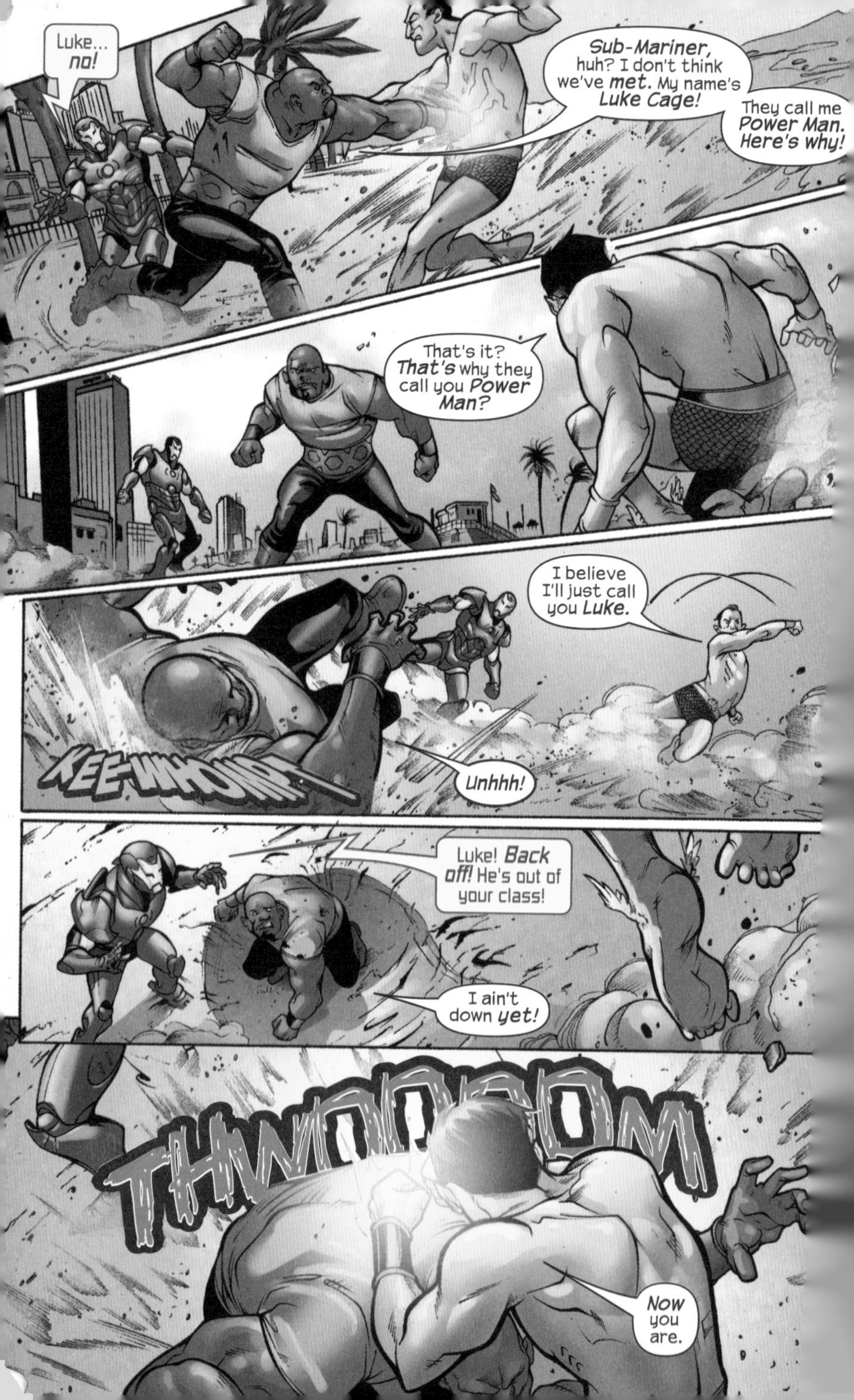
Luke... no!
Sub-Mariner, huh? I don't think we've met. My name's Luke Cage!
They call me Power Man. Here's why!
That's it? That's why they call you Power Man?
I believe I'll just call you Luke.
KEE-WHOMP!
Unhhh!
Luke! Back off! He's out of your class!
I ain't down yet!
THWOOOOOM
Now you are.

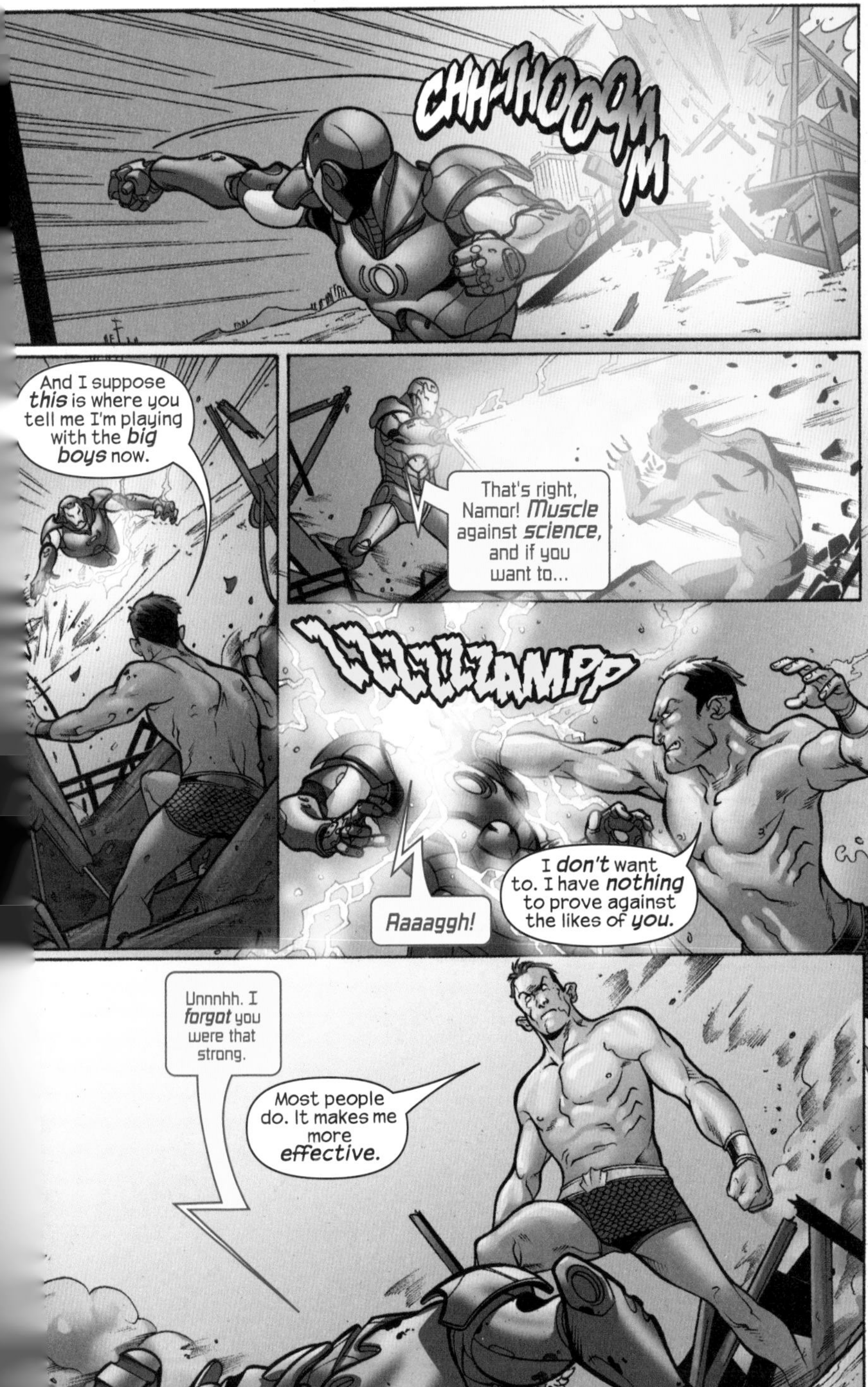
CHH-THOOOM
And I suppose this is where you tell me I'm playing with the big boys now.
That's right, Namor! Muscle against science, and if you want to...
ZZZZZZAMPP
Raaaggh!
I don't want to. I have nothing to prove against the likes of you.
Unnnhh. I forgot you were that strong.
Most people do. It makes me more effective.

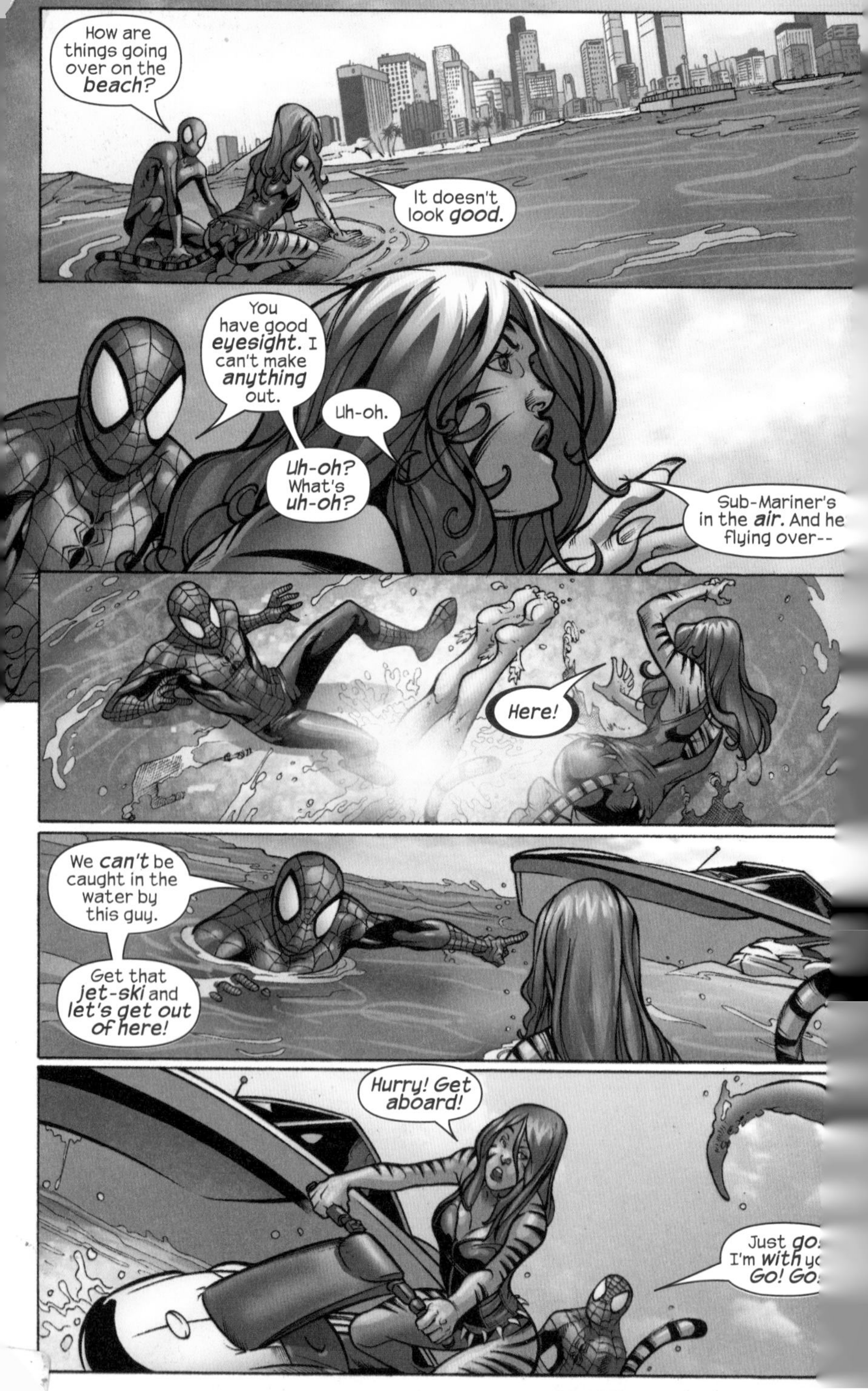
How are things going over on the beach?
It doesn't look good.
You have good eyesight. I can't make anything out.
Uh-oh.
Uh-oh? What's uh-oh?
Sub-Mariner's in the air. And he
flying over--
Here!
We can't be caught in the water by this guy.
Get that jet-ski and let's get out of here!
Hurry! Get aboard!
Just go
I'm with y
Go! Go

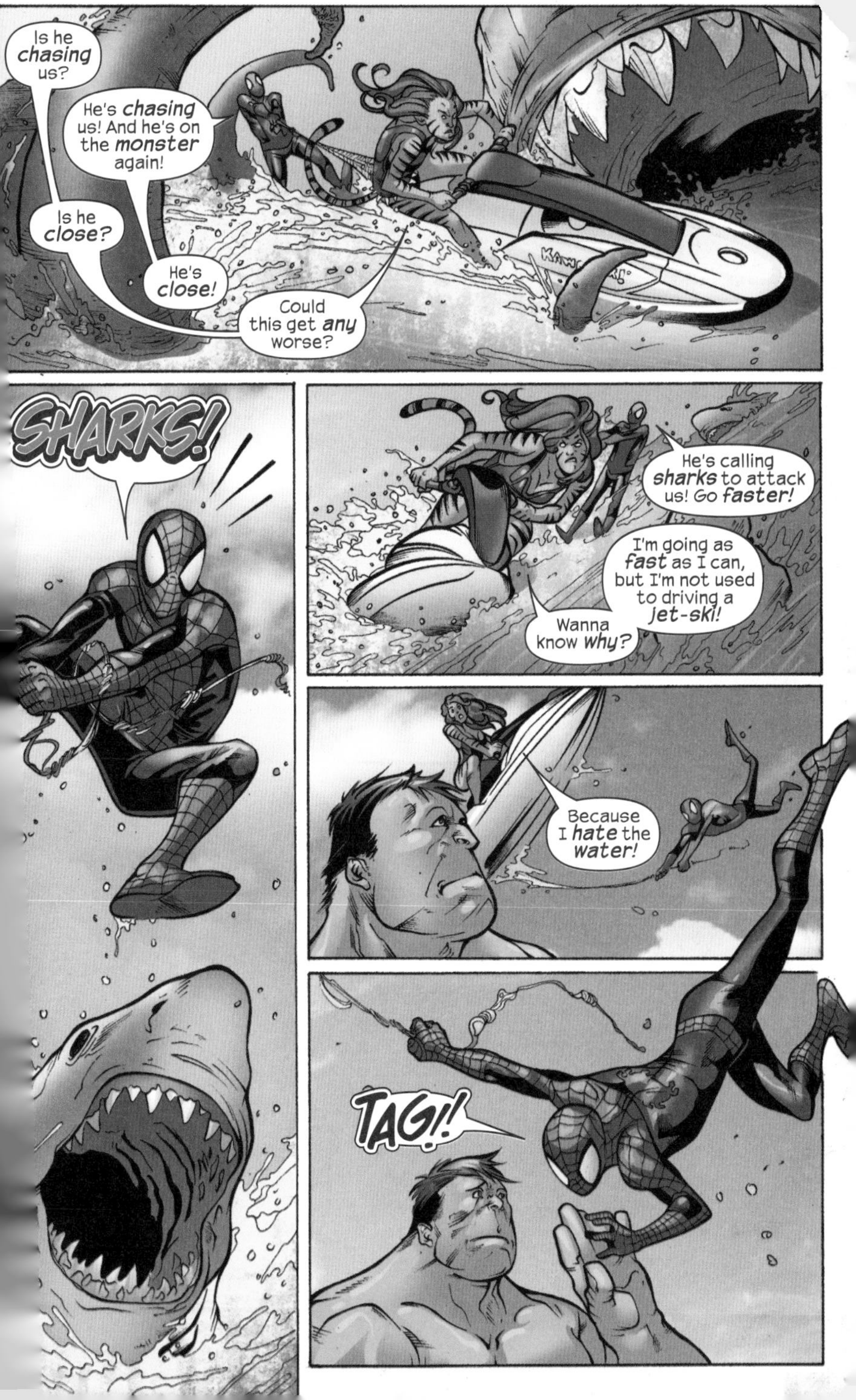
Is he chasing us?
He's chasing us! And he's on the monster again!
Is he close?
He's close!
Could this get any worse?
SHARKS!
He's calling sharks to attack us! Go faster!
I'm going as fast as I can, but I'm not used to driving a jet-ski!
Wanna know why?
Because I hate the water!
TAG!!

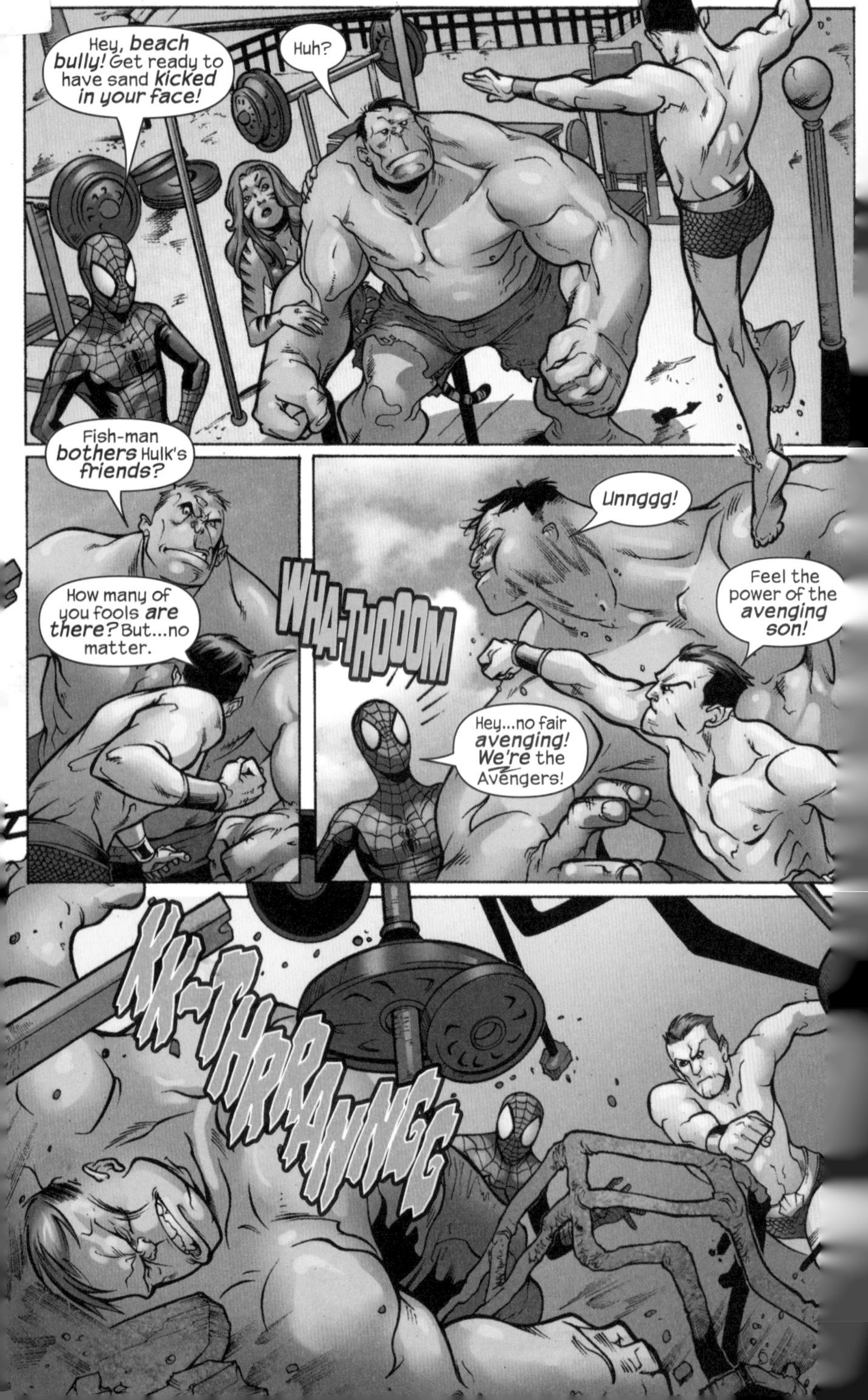
Hey, beach bully! Get ready to have sand kicked in your face!
Huh?
Fish-man bothers Hulk's friends?
How many of you fools are there? But...no matter.
WHA-THOOOM
Unnggg!
Feel the power of the avenging son!
Hey...no fair avenging! We're the Avengers!
KK-THRANNGG

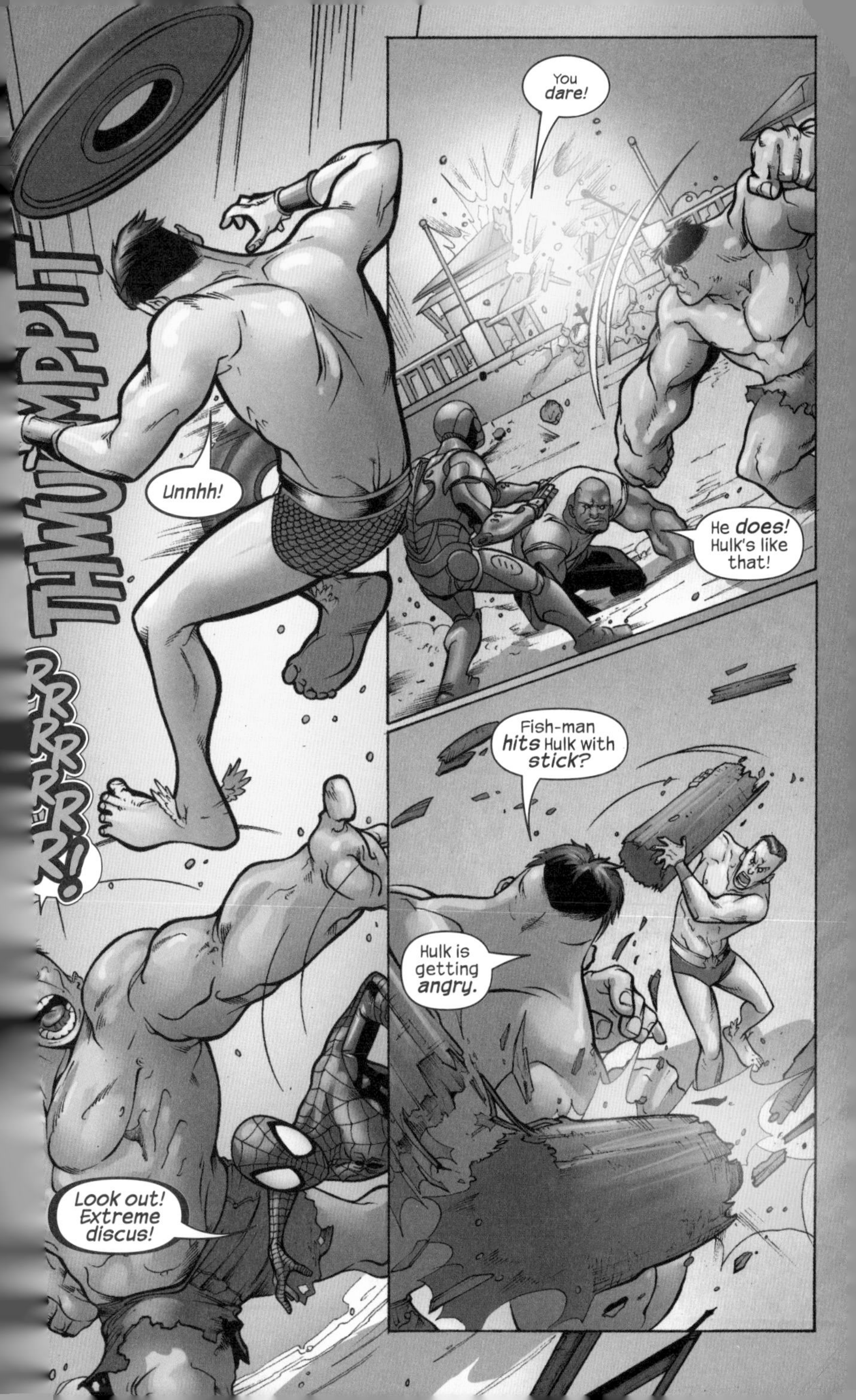
THWUMPPIT
RRRRRR!
Unnhh!
Look out! Extreme discus!
You dare!
He does! Hulk's like that!
Fish-man hits Hulk with stick?
Hulk is getting angry.

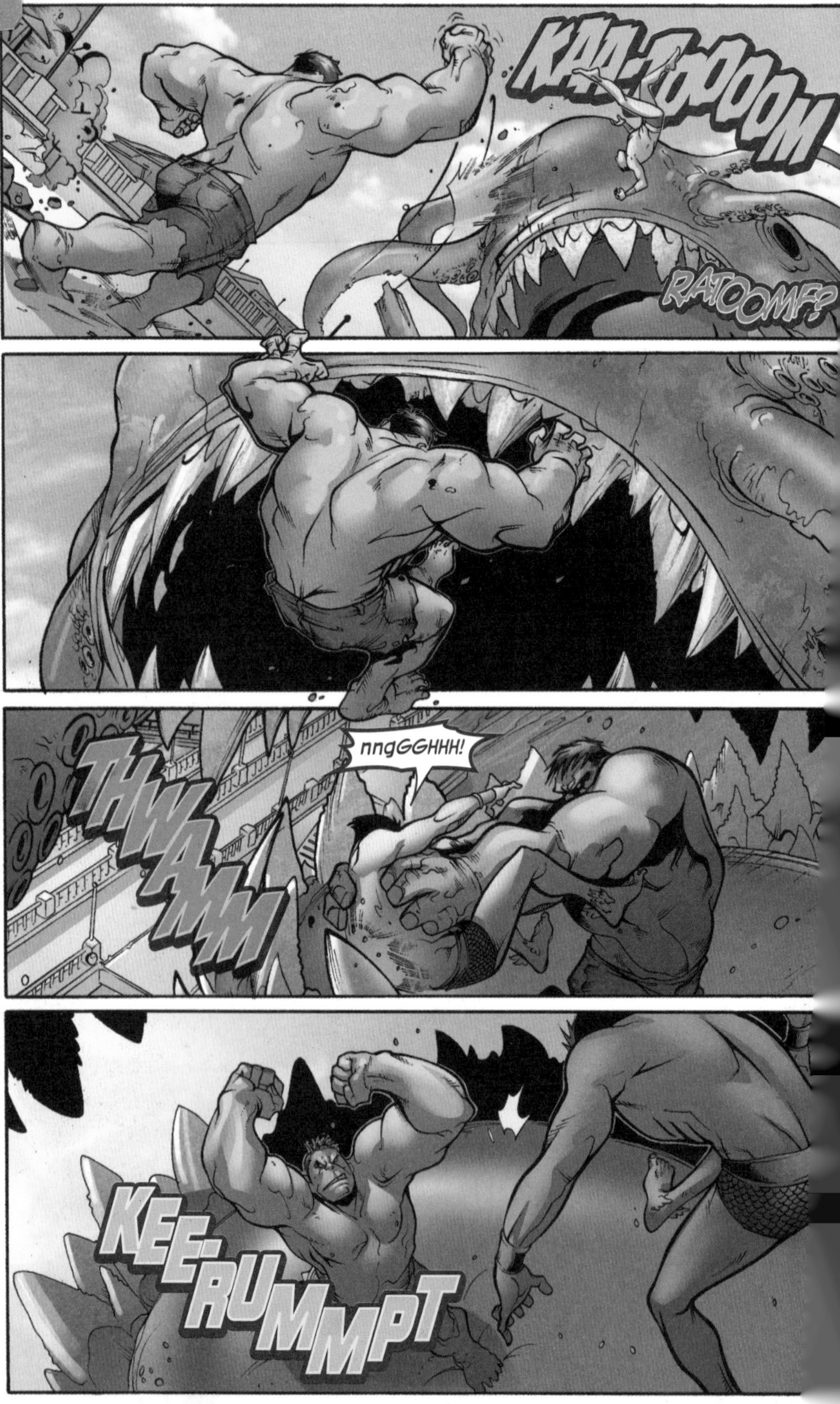
KAA-TOOOOM
RATOOMF?
THWAMM
nngGGHHH!
KEE-RUMMPT

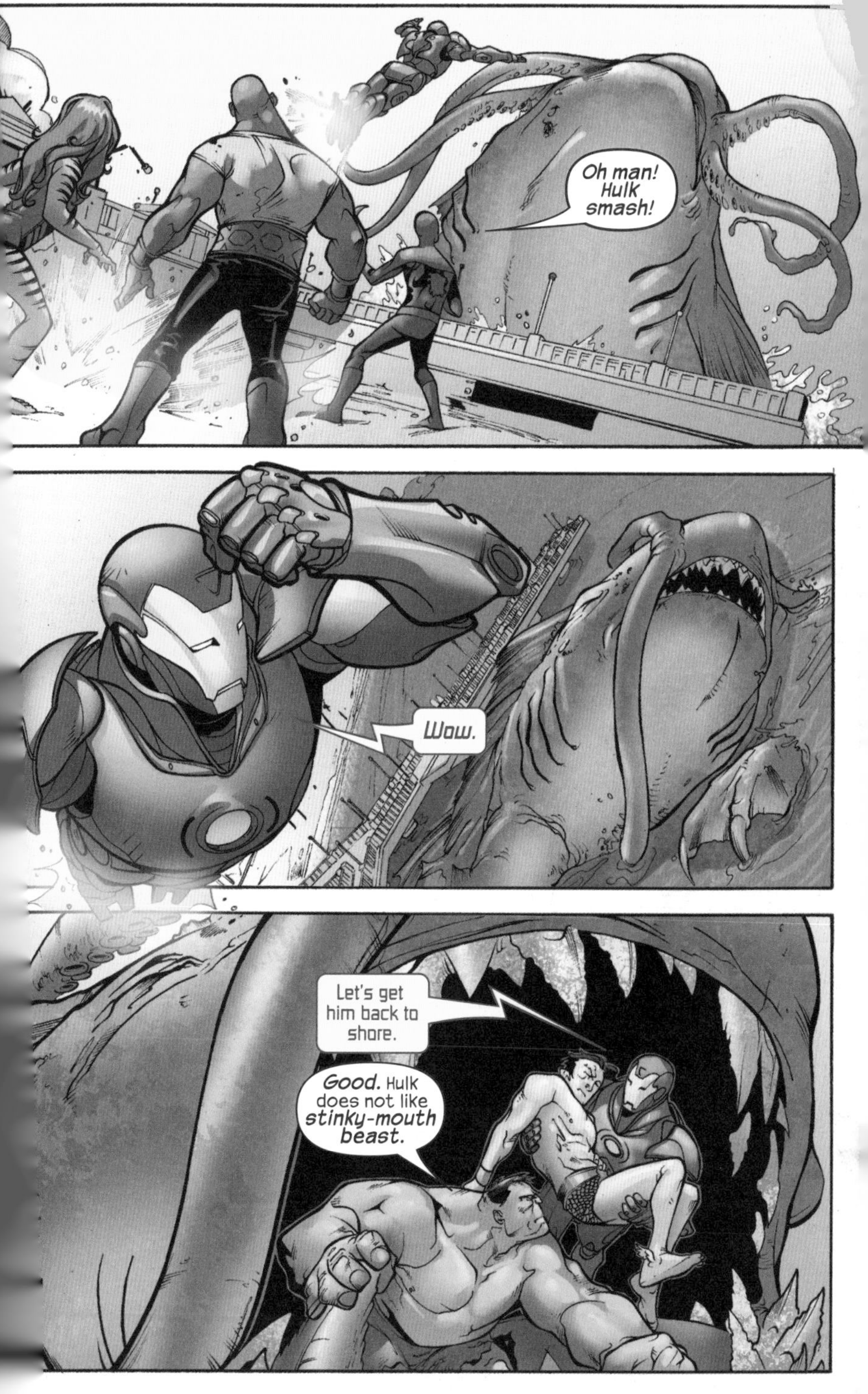
Oh man! Hulk smash!
Wow.
Let's get him back to shore.
Good. Hulk does not like stinky-mouth beast.

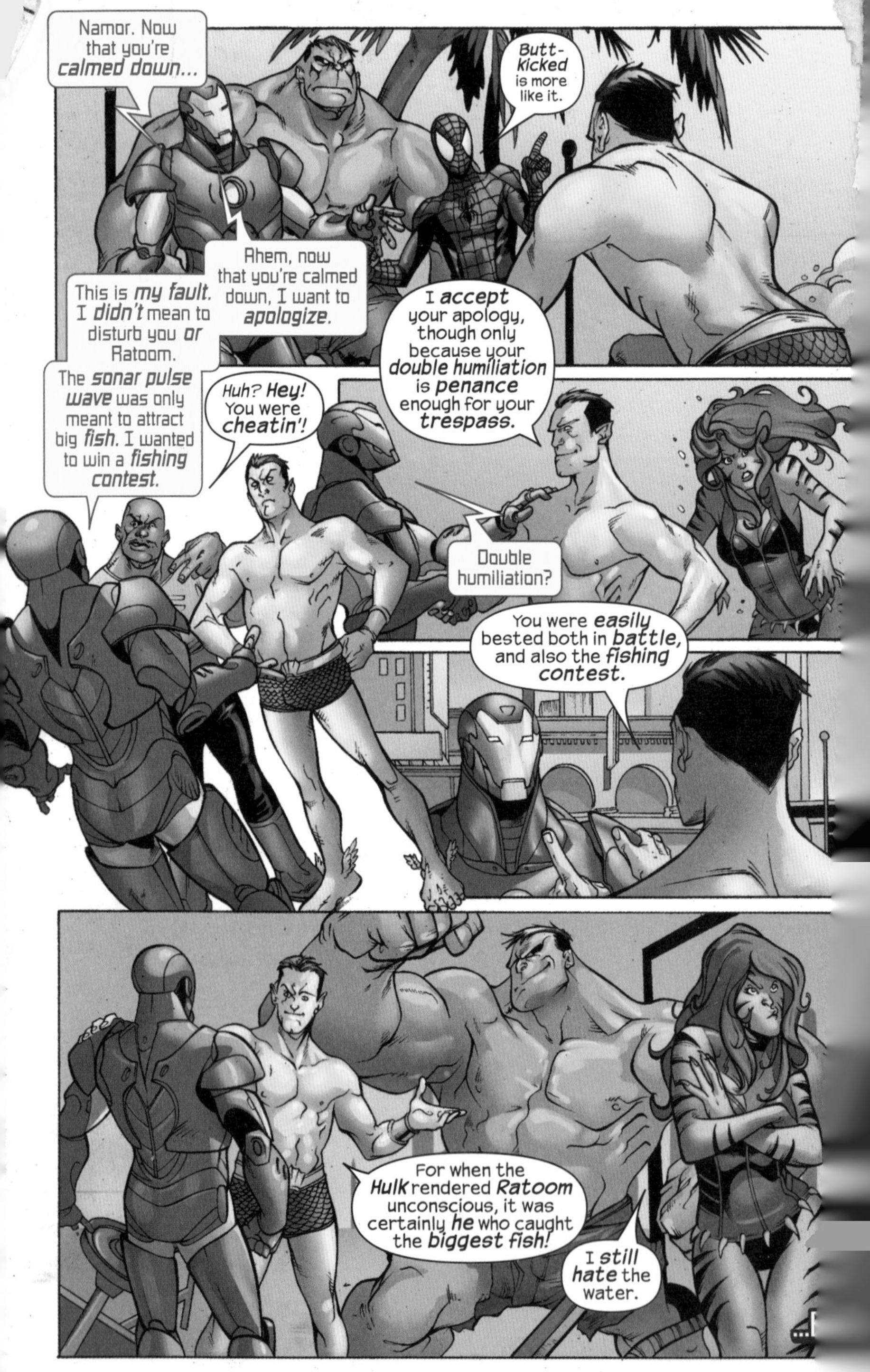

Namor. Now that you're calmed down...
Butt-kicked is more like it.
Ahem, now that you're calmed down, I want to apologize.
This is my fault. I didn't mean to disturb you or Ratoom.
The sonar pulse wave was only meant to attract big fish. I wanted to win a fishing contest.
Huh? Hey! You were cheatin'!
I accept your apology, though only because your double humiliation is penance enough for your trespass.
Double humiliation?
You were easily bested both in battle, and also the fishing contest.
For when the Hulk rendered Ratoom unconscious, it was certainly he who caught the biggest fish!
I still hate the water.